TEMPER

TERRAWAY
BOOK SIX

MARY E. TWOMEY

MARY E. TWOMEY, LLC

TEMPER

BOOK SIX IN THE TERRAWAY SERIES

By

Mary E. Twomey

COPYRIGHT

DEDICATION

For Craig McGlassion and Tom Gibson.

For never letting me fool myself
into thinking I know it all.
For listening, tolerating and leading in times where
I couldn't hear, was pretty much insufferable,
and felt utterly lost.

QUEEN OF THE DANCING FAIRIES

Two months was a long time to spend only working and going to sleep, but Ollie insisted I not be allowed back into Terraway in my current state: pregnant, father of the baby nowhere around, and newly orphaned. He worked with Finn to take the stone into Dagat, dropping it uneventfully into their main well. Just like that, Ollie brought calm waves, *buhay* and vitality back to the Merpeople, who were already so happy that their evil King Banak was dead, the whole land practically rolled out the red carpet for Ollie.

My brother had a good many dreamy-eyed stories about Mermaids after that. He trailed off when I knew they hit the PG-13 realm I didn't need the details of. Ollie was good at talking. I was not.

I went reaping with Mason during the day. We teamed up with Danny and Mariang, who were so in love, I couldn't help but watch them with fascination as they bloomed for each other. Mariang was simply glowing, and Danny? Well, Danny smiled at least once a day since he'd popped the question, which had to be some kind of record. I knew from the shared bedroom wall that they were going at it like rabbits at night, making up for lost time when Mariang had been too sick and weak to do much of anything other than psychic lovemaking.

Speaking of psychic relationships, Von was still nowhere to be found. I saw him in my dreams at night, which hurt even more than not seeing him at all. He put a vast prairie between us, stretching our perfect park to a distance I couldn't reach him at if I ran all night long, which I had no intention of doing. I'd taken to napping as soon as we got home midday from reaping, sleeping until Von showed up in my dream at night, at which point, I woke myself up.

No, Von still didn't know that I'd kept the baby, that the baby was his, or that I was miserable without him. He wanted to be gone, and that was the thing that mattered. He'd found out that I was knocked up, and he ran. The only person I was more upset with than him was myself for still being in love with the guy. He hadn't just ditched me, he'd ducked out on Terraway. There were still Omen duties to be done, and Von dumped all the responsibility on Mason, assuming he would pick up the slack.

Ollie tried to be a good distraction, but I didn't have much to say. We'd had Bev cremated. The whole thing happened without ceremony, without debate, and without Allie. My sister remained gone, and while Ollie assumed her dead, I was certain she was very much alive and simply wanted nothing to do with us. The truth is, I couldn't really blame her, either. We were damaged. Some days it seemed the damage was beyond repair.

Ezra mourned in the traditional sense, wearing black and crying in private. He hovered around Ollie, Mariang and me more than usual as he dealt with losing his fiancée to the Ekeks and Manas she was trying to save.

Kabayo had explained it all to us in as clinical detail as possible. The group had been on the mission to take the sagrado stone to Lumipad, but in the wake of the political upheaval of their queen Sylvia getting shanked, the country shifted violently, making it a dangerous place for travelers passing through. The group moved through Lumipad with Bev fully affected by the stone, devolving back into the woman who'd thrown me away time after time. I understood that the stone poisoned her, but it didn't make her blatant hatred of me any easier to bear.

They'd made it almost to the well when a swarm of Manas swooped in, tearing Bev apart because they assumed she was me. It should've been me. Bev had stolen the stone and went in secret to save me from the danger when she'd been able to think clearly.

Somewhere buried underneath all the poison, my mama loved me, and gave her life up for mine.

I wasn't sure what to do with that, so I sat by the

window in my bedroom at Ezra's mansion most nights, afraid to go to sleep and face that stupid prairie across the way from Von, who was there but not. When I was alone in my slumber because Von was awake doing whatever he did to avoid life, I had nightmares replaying the attack from the gang of Siyokoys. The wicked Mermen dragged me under the water, molesting me and trying to take me so Finn would have one more loss under his belt.

I stared out the window for hours on end, not sure how my life in the mansion made any sense at all. Every now and then Ezra would sit in a chair next to me, saying nothing, but staying with me through my silent pain. In those quiet moments that knit together over the weeks, I started to trust Ezra with my grief, occasionally answering hard to face questions when he asked. Did I miss Bev? Was I starting to feel anything for the baby growing inside me? Was I sleeping enough?

I wanted the answers to all his questions to be an easy yes, but Ezra stayed with me even when I wasn't sure. It's a good man, the one who waits for you to puzzle things out. Ezra never pushed; he simply sat by my side in his spare moments of free time. It's a good dad, the one who stays with you, even when you know deep down, you're utterly leave-able.

I was just beginning my second trimester. My stomach started to stick out a modest amount, no longer giving me the space for a healthy dose of denial. I wore baggy sweaters and felt like death warmed over. All the books

Danny obsessively quoted at me said morning sickness was supposed to end in the first trimester. All I can tell you is that the books are a lie. A vicious, stupid lie to give pregnant women false hope that maybe tomorrow you won't barf until it hurts because someone mentioned the word "cracker".

I did my best to compose myself when Kabayo came to visit that evening. He played it off like it was a work call, but his purpose was only half for business. He requested I be brought in on the meeting he'd scheduled with Ezra, but Ezra excused himself to go see to getting us some tea before the meeting formally started. Kabayo sat across from me at the polished wooden oval table in the conference room. He waited until we were alone before he leaned his elbow on the surface and lowered his voice to speak to me. "I can feel this, you know."

My shoulders were hunched in and my arms banded around my baggy sweater. "Feel what?"

He displayed his forearm, showing me the same two Xs branded on his arm that matched the scarring on mine. It was our limited psychic link, letting him feel if I was in danger, or any significant shifts in me. He motioned to my closed expression. "This isn't you. You were funny and willful, if not annoying. You're sad all day now, and it's time you started pulling yourself out of it. I can feel it, you know. Even when things are going alright in my kingdom, there's always that depression that weighs it all down. It's starting to get irritating."

My eyebrows crinkled as I lifted my chin to stare at him in surprise. "First off, I didn't realize you could feel that. Second, I don't want to hear that my grief is inconvenient for you. My mama just died, my sister's MIA, I'm nine kinds of knocked up, I'm barfing all the time, I'm down a Reaper, and the father of the baby's nowhere in sight. I think I've earned the right to a little piece of sadness pot pie."

Oo, pie.

Kabayo jabbed his stubby human finger at me. "If you'd heard the things your mother was saying about you toward the end, you wouldn't be so sad to see her go. You're better off. I barely know you, and I can say that for sure."

"That's a cracked-out thing to say to me. I know who Bev was both on and off the stone. It warped her. She died to keep me from risking my life, taking the stone to Lumipad." I tucked a stray auburn curl behind my ear, my shoulders lowering as I exhaled. "I get that she's hard to love, but I'm pregnant, and I don't have a mama around to show me what's what. It's sad, Kabayo. Just let it all be sad."

He sighed heavily. "I really hate that you don't use my title when you address me. Ezra's my equal, and even he uses our proper titles."

"Fine. I'll call you King Kabayo, but you have to call me October, Queen of the Dancing Fairies."

"There's no such thing as fairies."

I quirked my eyebrow at him. "I think you mean there's no such thing as Tikbalangs, you giant reverse centaur. I'd actually heard of fairies before Terraway. I'd never heard of anything like you before." I motioned to his black horse head, smirking as he snorted derisively. "You gave up on that awful quick. I think you like that I'm not afraid of you."

"Kings don't bargain with children."

"Whatever you say, Kabayo."

He grumbled under his breath as Ezra came in with the tea tray, giving me a cup that warmed my hands. "To what do I owe the pleasure?" Ezra asked Kabayo. He sat at the head of the table, his hands folded politely over his stomach.

"Something's off with my people. The rain's been enough to start to heal our land, which is great. There've been almost no deaths, and the suns are finally regulated."

"This all sounds like wonderful news." Ezra and I waited for the other shoe to drop. It always did.

Kabayo rubbed the back of his neck, gearing up for the big reveal. "When our land was on the brink of collapse, there was a steady trickle of bodies that died of dehydration or starvation mostly. If the bodies weren't buried properly, they'd reanimate and head east for Sombi, just like every other country's unburied dead." He stared into his tea, not drinking. "My people have stopped dying so often, but the pilgrimages to Sombi haven't stopped. In fact, I've found people who are still very much alive traveling there."

Ezra frowned. "Well, that's not too strange. Some go to

Sombi to see if their loved ones are still roaming. Mason used to reside there to bury the dead. Now that he's working Topside, perhaps your people wish to take up his mantle. It's a noble cause."

Kabayo shook his head. "That's what I thought at first, but the Tikbalangs who are going to Sombi are nearly catatonic. They're unresponsive and focused only on getting to Sombi. My men have tried reasoning with them, but they're on a mission. They don't know why, and they can't converse much. It's like they're all touched in the head, but this should be the time we're getting back on our feet."

Ezra did not look as confused as I thought he should. "I was afraid you'd come to me with something like this. Prince Langgam's reported the same problem in his country. It's not all over, mind you, but in the western territory of Sakuna, the people seem to have a singular focus. They finally have the elements they need to rebuild their land, but they've given up in that sector. They're unable to do anything that isn't related to the pilgrimage to Sombi. I didn't know what to make of it, but now that it's happening in two countries, it's a definite problem."

"I'll make a point to talk with Prince Langgam, then. See what all lines up."

I spoke up, which neither man expected me to do. "You might get farther with Geon. He's still locked up in your dungeon awaiting execution, right?"

Kabayo leaned his elbow on his armrest, sitting back in

his chair as he eyed me. "But Geon's been in my prison for months, long before this started happening. What light could he shed on it?"

I tapped my fingertips on the table, aiming my response into my teacup rather than across the table. "Maybe none. But if I had to put my money on it, I'd bet it had something to do with Sama."

Kabayo's eyes narrowed as his temper flared. "Sama's spirit and his army were chased out of our land. I would know if he was there, luring my people away."

"I remember the battle, dude. I fought it right alongside you. What I mean is that in Lang's country – you said it's the western territory that's migrating, right?"

Ezra's head bobbed up and down slowly. "That's correct. What's the significance of that?"

"They're the territory that was hit hardest by the famine in Sakuna. They're the only territory in Sakuna who took Sama's rations. What about your country? Where did they start taking rations first? And are they still taking them?"

"The fourth district, and of course. *Buhay* crops don't grow in full overnight. We've still got a long road ahead of us. The rations are supplementing the growing crops, seeing us through. We have a large store of them that'll last us until well after our *buhay* shoots grow back, and we're on our feet again."

I tried to cross my legs, but couldn't do it without my mid-sized belly getting in the way. I sat straighter, uncomfortable in the chair. "Don't you find that strange? I mean, I get why Sama tried to take the rock from me. It would make his rations unnecessary, right? Supply and demand."

"Well, yes. But it was never our plan to live off of rations forever."

"But then why doesn't he go after your stockpile of rations? Hit you where it hurts? It's like after that big battle on your land, Sama went completely off the radar. Not a peep. Don't you think that's weird?"

Kabayo postured. "We defeated his army. We took his muscle, so he has no way to fight us."

I cocked my head to the side, and I could see Kabayo's conviction failing him as the reality of my words sunk in. "Really? Are we just going to believe that Sama couldn't raise a whole other army of undead in a heartbeat? There's a ton of dead Terraway citizens who haven't been buried correctly. Mason's been up here. There's no one to stop Sama's spirit from coming into Sombi and raising up what he needs to take back all the rations without a blink."

"If it's as easy as you say, then why isn't Sama doing exactly that?" Ezra asked, not so much challenging me as he was wondering.

"It's like he wants you to have the rations. Like it plays in his favor for you to keep giving them out. Now you've got live zombies making their way to Sombi? Bodies without decay that have no will? Sounds like a fantastic recipe for a new and improved soldier to me. I'd be careful, guys. If it was me, I'd stop the rations first thing."

"That wouldn't go over well. We don't have enough food to sustain us yet."

"You will soon, if your people keep deserting your country for Sombi. You'll have plenty of food and no citizens. I don't know what Sama needs live people for, but it looks like he's got them in spades now. And anything that Sama needs? My guess is we shouldn't give it to him, no matter how little we understand about how it all works."

Kabayo gave a half-hearted snort, as if he wanted to scoff at me, but couldn't fully dismiss my warning. Ezra's mouth was hanging open until he put all the pieces in order, snapping to attention. "I'll make some calls and warn the other heads of state."

Kabayo stood and rested his fist on the table, shaking out his mane as he stared down at me, hesitant. "If I didn't think we were equals before, I have no choice now." He bowed his head to me. "I'll have the rations boarded up until we get to the bottom of this."

"That might be a good idea for now. See if it puts a stop to the migrations." I shot him a sympathetic look, worried about the fallout of cutting off their steady food supply. "For what it's worth, I hope I'm wrong."

Kabayo moved around the table to stand next to my chair, extending his hand to me. Our scarred Xs brushed together as he gripped my forearm, forcing me to do the same to him. "Thank you, Queen of the Dancing Fairies."

2

BUTTHOLE

The next morning, I awoke to the sound of the door to my bedroom in the mansion creaking open. A sliver of light shined on Mason, who was snoring softly next to me. I was expecting Ezra to poke his head in to see if I was sleeping, just as he'd been doing once or twice a week since I'd decided to stay in the mansion. Only this time he caught my eye and whispered my name. "October Grace, are you awake?"

"Yeah. What's up?"

"Get dressed and come on out, please."

I pried Mason's covetous hand off my belly, smiling softly when his hand searched the bed for me in his sleep after I gingerly climbed out.

If you've never seen a pregnant girl climb out of a bed stealthily, I highly recommend the replay button. I felt like a cow trying to tiptoe. Totally entertaining and YouTube worthy – unless you're the pregnant woman. Then it's all just irritating.

Mason was the only person I allowed myself the luxury of wearing clothes that weren't two sizes too big around. We slept in the same bed, so he knew the shape of my body – no use hiding it from him and making myself sweaty all night under too many layers. I pulled on a red hoodie to cover over my tank top, and exchanged my pajama pants for maternity jeans that Mariang swore up and down were at the peak of fashion trends these days. I moved into the light of the hallway, my toes bunching in the carpet as I stuffed my socks into my pocket.

"What do you need?" I asked in a whisper, pulling my auburn tangles into a messy bun atop my head.

"I thought you might like to go for a drive. I figured you were most likely awake."

I raised my eyebrow at him. "Um, sure. That's fine. Where to?"

He offered me his elbow, treating me like a lady, as he always did. "The joy is in the journey, and the surprise of the destination."

"That's nice. Is it a famous quote or something?"

"Only if you consider me famous. Come, now. Let's you and I have ourselves a little adventure. I'm bored of the inside of the house. Aren't you?"

I shrugged as I clumsily toed on my socks when we reached the foyer, hopping as I tried to balance on one foot. Yet another missed opportunity for the blooper reel. I leaned my butt on the wall as I fumbled with my shoes. Though my belly was sticking out only just enough to make me uncomfortable, pregnancy had made me a total klutz. I was always bumping myself in doorways, tripping over my own two feet, dropping things... I'd even fallen quite a few times. Mason had gone from zombie slayer, to losing his hulking muscles because of me, then getting them partially back in the healing waters, only to have to use his bulk to pick up a pregnant woman who couldn't walk like a normal person. Though he never complained, it felt like a demotion to me.

Ezra smiled as he watched me try to tie my shoe standing up, my heel resting on my knee as I wobbled. He knelt down before me, taking my foot and placing it on his knee, where he patiently tied my shoe for me. It was maybe the sweetest thing a father figure had ever done for me, or maybe I was just mood-swingy. It was hard to tell anymore. I'd cried in bed last night because Mason told me he was grateful we were getting to be good friends, and had gotten past our uncomfortable romantic stuff. That was what started the tears. Then when he told me he'd help me raise the baby, I sobbed in his arms for a solid twenty minutes. I blinked down at Ezra, determined not to cry. "Thanks, Dad. You didn't have to do that."

"But you let me do it. Good for you. You're getting better at having a dad." He placed my foot on the floor and double-knotted my other shoe, standing and offering his elbow again. Ezra had been insistent that even though he'd never married Bev, he was very much our father still. Ollie and I had no objection to that, lost as we were.

Somehow Ezra kept me on his arm while still opening the door for me, making me feel like a princess instead of a single mom.

Ezra drove us onto the freeway, his classical station featuring a violinist who could only play sad songs that made me tear up. *Again.* "Another package came for you. The sender seemed quite put out that you wouldn't let him deliver it in person."

My spirits lifted a moderate amount before the guilt crashed down on me. "It's best for Finn if I'm not in his life. I told him as much."

"Some of us are just thick in the head, I guess." Ezra steered with one hand and reached into the backseat of his sleek, black top-of-the-line sedan to hand me a package wrapped in brown vellum and tied with red twine.

I slowly undid the knot, an unbidden smile creeping across my lips as I pulled out a book, the cover old and the pages stiff and waterproof. The title was written in Mer, which was the written language of Dagat. I'd been working hard to figure out how to read it when I lived in Dagat for a short while – me teaching myself the bulk while Finn was at work, and then him coming home at night and reading to me the most beautiful stories. This particular series of books were about a Mermaid who fell in love with a dude who had legs, and the forbidden love between Ricardo and Lissima that forever changed the ocean. I'd read the first book in the series while staying at his house, and over the past two months, Finn had been sending me the next book every few weeks. Each book had a note with it that tugged at my heart. He would either remind me of a fun time we'd had together, or he would tell me he'd wait for me to get over Von so I could see him clearly.

If only it was that simple.

The logical side of me knew that I couldn't be with a man who'd enslaved hundreds of his own people for the sexual torment of his boss. I could overlook it to some extent when he'd been controlled by Banak, but the harem wasn't disbanded until long after Finn's curse was lifted.

There was also the matter that being an Omen was a lifetime commitment. I couldn't ask him to give up his job no more than he could ask me to give up mine. A whole country depended on him remaining at his post of power, and a whole world depended on me continuing with my reaping responsibilities.

My eyes flitted over the note, translating as best I could without a guide.

"May I be so bold as to inquire what the letter says?" Ezra asked, changing his approach from polite interest to out and out prying.

I read slowly as the words started to make sense, taking a chance and letting Ezra in an inch, since he'd planned an after-hours adventure for us. "I think it says, 'My Dear *Sinta*, This is where the story gets sad. But don't worry, I only believe in happy endings for you. Have Ezra call me if you need a translator.'" I scanned the next few sentences, picking out the words "love", "forever", "come home to me" and "kiss". I cleared my throat. "Then there's a bunch of personal stuff, but that's the gist."

"Ah, I see. And would that personal stuff be the reason you won't see him when he comes to drop off the packages he brings you?"

I nodded, staring out the window at the scenery rushing by as we traveled on the freeway to... wherever. I hadn't even thought to ask where we were headed. "I let it get too complicated in Dagat. He's a good guy. I think he's only just realizing that about himself. Figuring out he can be good, I mean."

"I've known Captain Finn for many years now. I admit, I never imagined him capable of such humility and restraint. But when I sent him away, he didn't fight it. He just looked sad, almost resigned. Like he knows you're unattainable, but he's still trying, even if the closest he can be is on our front porch." He shot me a sideways smile. "It seems he's quite smitten."

"He's part fish, and I can't swim." I tucked the letter into the book. "And there you have it. Everyone around me seems to be dying off. Finn's safer in his world. He'll find someone nice, someone who can be what he needs. I know myself, and I'm not that girl."

"You're firm on that, yeah?"

I shrugged, fingering the book I was itching to dive into. "I'm pregnant with another dude's baby, Ezra. I'm in love with Von. Fat lot of good that's doing me. When there's a pill that lets you control who you love, let me know. I'll buy that sucker by the bucket."

Ezra gripped the steering wheel. "Von will come home. He always does. He has a habit of running away when he gets scared."

"What a nice luxury, to be able to run away from your life. If only millions of people wouldn't die if I ditched my responsibilities, I might do the same thing. Good thing I've got a spare Duwende. You know, the one who'll eventually want to eat me and my baby." I pursed my lips, having had too much time to think about this. "Von doesn't give a crap about me, to leave me pregnant with a Matruculan to pull the corroding souls from me. I get that it's hard to wrap your mind around, but he split without making sure Mason could handle the temptation. Von doesn't care if I die."

Ezra hissed. "You and I both know that's not true. He doesn't know the baby's his. For all he knows, you're pregnant with some other man's child."

"Yup. Ran that through the ol' logic filter, too. It's cool. I'm fine." I fingered the letter. "Stuff like this, though? It's like a stab through the heart, knowing there's someone out there who'd be with me even though I'm having another man's baby, while the father of the baby's MIA. Penny isn't Von's biological child, and he still stuck around to help raise her. Just hurts, is all." I worked up a convincing smile. "Poetic, isn't it? I feel like I could play the princess in any number of fairytales right now. Knocked up Cinderella, Morning Sickness Merida..."

"You'll always be a princess to us. And I've been keeping a close watch on myself and on Mason. I know the whole thing is troublesome," Ezra said, steering me away from my dismal parade I seemed to be stuck in. The books from Finn were one of the few highlights I allowed myself to enjoy.

"Thanks, Dad."

Ezra's chest always swelled when Ollie and I claimed him as our father. "Are you hungry, dear?"

"I'm alright. Hey, where are we going?"

Ezra chuckled that it had taken this long for me to ask. "To the airport. We're picking up an old friend."

"Oh yeah? Someone who knew you back before you were King Ezra the Mighty?"

Ezra laughed. "I rather like the sound of that. Maybe I'll change all my letterhead to that title. We're picking up Boston. He's going to come stay with us for a little while."

"Huh." I swallowed hard, wishing it was anyone but Boston. He was Bishop's identical twin, and I'd been the last one to see Bishop Vandershot alive. I'd held him in my arms while he died when we'd been captured and tortured by the vindictive Manas. Bishop had been a wonderful person right up to his last breath. Boston, on the other hand, was a pervy tool who'd had more conversations with my breasts than my face. "He bored of Europe?"

"No, but it seems Europe's tired of him. He stopped

showing up for work at the steel mill, lost his job and has been more or less floundering since Bishop passed. He's normally a hard worker though, so I thought perhaps a change of scenery might help. Lavinia, his mother, is worried about him. I try to help her out whenever I can. She's my oldest friend, so we've always tried to look out for each other through the years, both of us being single parents and all."

"That's right nice of you. Is he staying at the mansion?"

"I suppose that'll be up to you." Ezra paused, and I knew that whatever came out of his mouth next wouldn't be all that great. "Mason's going to have to take a leave of absence soon. Your third trimester's just around the corner, and he's not as practiced at abstaining as I am."

"Abstaining?" My nose crinkled in confusion, but then it dawned on me his meaning.

"We're Matruculan, darling. It's difficult for us to be around a pregnant woman without getting hungry." He said the last word with a note of guilt in his voice. "Apologies for the frightful topic, but you need to be made aware of the changes coming. Mason will take a leave of absence from the start of your third trimester until probably a month or so after the baby's born, just to be safe. I myself had a sabbatical when Mariang's mother gave birth. Dreadful time to desert my wife, but it was the only option, and she understood completely."

My voice was small, but I had to get everything out on

the table. "So you won't be with me when the baby comes?"

Ezra closed his eyes for a brief moment of pain before looking at me with such sadness, I could barely stand it. "I want to, my dear. More than anything in the world, but it's not safe for you or the baby. I can control myself until the due date, but Mason's not as practiced as I am. Then I'll be gone for a short few weeks to make sure you and my grandchild are safe."

I fought down the depression that was always so close to the surface. "That's cool."

"No, it's not, but it's unavoidable, I'm afraid. I would do anything to change it, but there's nothing to be done. It's my genetics, which I'm sad to say cannot be altered."

I cleared my throat, reaching for a change of topic. "So Boston's coming to hang out for a while?"

"He's coming to see if he can manage taking over for Mason while he's gone. You won't do any reaping while Mason's gone, of course, but for day-to-day pulling, you need someone. Really, you need two someones, especially now with the baby."

"But Von's being a butthole."

Ezra managed a wan smile. "Yes, I suppose he is."

"I dare you to say it. Say 'butthole' for me. Give me a good laugh, Ezra." My mischievous smile migrated to him, painting his face with a boyish guilty charm.

"Very well. Von is being a... a butthole."

I laughed loudly, clapping my hands at the entertainment as Ezra blushed through his shame at being so crass. "Woo! That was incredible. I wish I'd gotten it on video."

His hand migrated from his steadfast ten-and-two on the steering wheel to straighten his shirt, as if that would undo the awesomeness. "I suppose I'll never live that one down."

"Oh, Dad. That was priceless. Thanks for that. I needed a good laugh."

Ezra was my good medicine, and we drove the rest of the way with matching smiles.

3

BOSTON 2.0

I wasn't sure what to make of Boston when he met us at baggage claim. I expected the brash smile and cocky smirk, but what greeted us were slumped shoulders and a hard look that had no small talk hidden in it. He shook my hand like a colleague and endured Ezra's hug without smiling or participating in the gesture.

Ezra filled in the gaps on the way home with details of Danny's proposal, the oceanic parade Dagat had thrown Ollie for delivering the stone without incident, and other happier things that didn't inspire much from Boston, other than the occasional grunt. Ezra finally gave up, sighing. "Do you have any questions, son?"

Boston leaned forward from his place in the backseat. "I've never done pulling full-time. When do I start?"

"You can discuss that with October. She's got an aversion to being touched, so best she knows when it's coming."

I cleared my throat when the conversation was thrown to me. "Um, yeah. The touching thing, especially since we don't really know each other. In the beginning, Von and Mason would rub my arms every now and then. They never snuck up on me. That way I knew it was coming."

"I can do that. How often?"

I shrugged, unsure what alien had taken over Boston, replacing his brash behavior with a coachable professional. "You'll have to ask Mason. I don't really know what I need as far as that goes."

Ezra chimed in with, "She needs light layers of pulling often. Mason hasn't been able to get her to zero since she was returned to us. Perhaps it's the pulling for two issue, and the fact that he's used to sharing a job with another Duwende."

"Pulling for two?" Boston inquired. "Like pulling for October and Mariang?"

Ezra's head snapped in my direction. "You haven't told Von's family?"

I pulled my sweater down, giving Ezra a sideways look. "Why would I? I barely know them. You only just sprung this on me now. Why didn't *you* tell him? You're the one who's hiring him. Seems like basic job description stuff to me."

"Yes, well, I told Von's mother. I just assumed she'd spread it to her sons."

"I haven't been home in a while," Boston admitted. "Missed a few phone calls, I guess. I pretty much jumped at the job offer when you called, and hopped on the first plane out. I didn't think to ask for details."

"Well, here we are, then." Ezra put on a lighter tone as he addressed Boston. "You should know that your charge is pregnant, just starting in on her second trimester, by our best guess."

This brought about a flicker of life in Boston's eyes. "Pregnant? That's... Well, congratulations. Who's the lucky bloke you passed on Von for?"

I kept my mouth shut and chickened out, leaving Ezra to do the dirty work, spilling my secrets and cluing Boston in on a bit of magic we didn't even know was possible until now.

Boston's mouth was practically on the floor. "So Von doesn't even know he knocked you up? You've never actually had sex?"

Ezra hated the term "knocked up", and cringed whenever any of us threw it around. "Yes. My daughter is pregnant, and we're all very happy about it."

"Wicked." Boston came to life in bits and pieces as he thought through all the things we'd already covered. "But Mason's Matruculan. Ezra, so are you!"

"Yes, which is why we brought you on. It's not just to replace Von while he's off on holiday. It's to cover for Mason throughout the whole third trimester, and the first month or so of the baby's life. You'll also be watching the grounds with Danny while I take my leave when the baby comes."

Boston covered his mouth as the information crashed over him. "Oh, wow. I mean, this is…"

"Are you rethinking the job offer? I can always call in Alton or Graham. We're trying to keep it in the family, since we've had trouble with spies before."

"No, no. I'll take the job. It's just more of a job than I realized. I thought I'd be shadowing Mason until Von comes back, but this is a whole big thing."

"Indeed. And I expect you to treat it as such. My daughters are national treasures. Their safety is of the utmost concern to me. If you can handle the job, I want to give it to you."

"I can handle it, no problem. I might need to watch Mason the first day, though."

"You should have a few months still before Mason has to take his leave of absence. Ask questions. Do what you need to be able to take over when he goes. You won't be doing any reaping, of course, but daily pulling will keep you plenty busy."

"Has no one told Von the baby's his? I can't imagine he'd stay away if he knew."

I finally opened my mouth, but immediately wished I hadn't when my attitude flared, exposing my vulnerable underbelly. "Yes, it's every girl's dream. Your special guy who wouldn't commit to you before, ditches you with no warning, no conversation, but comes back out of duty to your unborn baby. So romantic. If there isn't a ballad written about it, there should be."

"Ah. I see." Boston looked out the window, though it was too dark to see anything outside just yet. "He should still know."

"If he wanted anything to do with me, he would. I'm not purposefully not telling him. I called him that first day and asked him to come home. He didn't, and he won't, so there we go."

Ezra reached over and held my hand, taking my flinch in stride. I let him hold my hand because he needed to, and because I was trying with everything in me not to let my issues play such a prominent role. The healing waters had done something; I could feel the desire to claw at my skin and wash my hands too many times diminished significantly after I came out of the waters. But just like the bat-shaped scar across my back, the waters could only do so much. Some wounds were too deep to heal without scarring.

NO SPACE BETWEEN US

Danny was so happy to have Boston in the mansion, he started smiling at least three times a day, which honestly looked like it might hurt his facial muscles that were so prone to grumpy old mannish scowling. Boston spent a good chunk of time firing questions at Mason and Danny. They were mostly concerning me and the details of the job.

I made myself scarce for that one, hiding in the bedroom so I could read my book. I wished I could see Finn, to lounge around with him and let him read the more complicated passages to me, but I knew that wouldn't be fair to him. Despite not being in love with him, I did possess a great deal of love for him. It just wasn't enough, and certainly not the right kind of love needed to sustain things. Also, I knew I was pretty well beyond salvageable by this point. Finn deserved a woman who had a shot at a normal life. That ship had sailed for me long ago.

I read to the baby aloud in the bedroom I shared with Mason, praying the baby wouldn't care that I read slow and choppy, stumbling over words and butchering pronunciations while I translated on the fly. Occasionally my hand would migrate down to rub my belly. In the quiet of the bedroom, I let myself feel a connection to the baby – however weak and unsteady that bond might be. It was something, and after months of trying to mute any and all emotions so I didn't break down sobbing every day, the small something was actually a very big thing.

When Ollie came back from his uneventful jaunt with Lang and Kabayo to deliver a chunk of the remaining sagrado stone to Hayop, I could tell something was on his mind. He loosened the collar of his dress shirt and took his time removing his shoes. He sat on the edge of the bed next to where I sat propped against the headboard in a mass of pillows, steeling himself to say his piece. "October, I think it's time you moved on. This, what you're doing? It's not healthy. It's been months. If Von was coming back, he would've done it already. I don't mind staying here, but it's not our house. Maybe something familiar would help you feel better – a little more yourself."

I rested my book on my chest. "Whatever you want is fine," I sighed, not caring one way or the other. Either way, I'd still be up a creek. "Clear it with Ezra and the guys, and I'll start packing."

"That's it? No fight? Now I really know something's wrong. I want you to start up with your shrink again."

I rolled my eyes. "Seriously? Everything that's wrong has the flavor of centaurs and monsters about it. I can't actually talk about anything to outsiders."

Ollie let out a dejected sigh that I'd raised a valid point. "Fair enough. I guess I didn't think that one through. What about me? You've always been able to talk to me."

I blinked at Ollie, wondering when it was that I stopped wanting to tell my big brother every little detail. "You've got enough on your plate. You just lost your mama."

Ollie gave me a hard look. "So did you."

I waited a few beats, but guessed it was time for therapy to be in session. "It's kind of too sad, right? I mean, she was just starting to be a person. And she stole the stone to save me from having to go there. I don't remember her doing anything for me that wasn't selfish. Then she does, and she dies? She doesn't even die as the person she was deep inside. She died all poisoned up by the stone." I shook my head. "It's too sad or something."

Ollie nodded slowly, fiddling with a thread on his khakis. His hair was the same color as mine, only he'd recently washed his. I hadn't showered in two days. Bathing was the one time I couldn't hide my belly from myself, so I avoided it until the last moment. Given my usual proclivity for cleanliness, that was a sure sign that I wasn't myself.

Ollie cleared his throat. "She definitely was the Bev you know toward the end. Slapped me across the face when I told her to let me take the stone so she could have a break. She told me I was always ruining things, taking her stuff away. Then a swarm of Manas attacked. We split up: me, Alton and Graham with the stone, and Bev and Kabayo heading in the opposite direction. We made it to the well and dropped the part of the stone in, but when we got back?" Ollie shook his head. "Last thing my mama ever said to me was that I always ruin things." He postured and looked at me, his resolve plain on his face. "I won't let that be true. You're not ruined, but you're acting like you are. It's selfish, carrying on with this permanent sadness like you are. It's time to get in the shower, get dressed in real clothes and face your life."

My upper lip curled. "Are you friggin' kidding me with this, Reese? Selfish? I've given everything up for everyone else's plans. What about my plans? What about what I want? Now I've got a baby I didn't even help make. You get that, right? This isn't just a bump in the road, this is a twenty-year commitment, at minimum. Then you have the nerve to come into my room and call me selfish? Tell me, how long is acceptable to mourn the loss of the woman who hated me? How long is it okay to feel scared that I'm pregnant with no plan? How long can I be sad while I'm still working, still performing, still interacting? What's acceptable to you, Sergeant?"

"I didn't mean it like that. Chill out."

"How did you mean it? Where do you get off, calling me selfish? Are you the king of dealing with things? I haven't heard you talking to Gabby lately. Are you set on still keeping her on hold for all of eternity? How's that working out for you?"

Ollie stood. "You're in a mood. I shouldn't've tried."

"Wow, that was the quickest therapy session I've ever been to. Hope you don't charge by the minute, Doctor."

"For the record, you're talking to *me* like this. I didn't do anything to deserve this from you. It's Von you're mad at, not me."

"Being mad at you works just fine."

Ollie gave me a look that tugged at my conscience, reminding me that he'd just lost his mama, too. He was going through the crap of it, but was more worried about me. Or more likely, he was occupying his mind with *my* demons so he didn't have to deal with his own. My mouth opened to apologize, to invite him back so he could pretend to fix me, but he was already out the door. If it would give him a reprieve from his pain, I'd play shrink with him. Though everything else felt upside down, Ollie was my constant, and I was treating him like he could be thrown away.

My heart sank, and just as my feet hit the carpet to go get him, he burst back in through the door, his scowl in place and temper flaring. "You don't get to push me away," he commanded. "Do that to everyone else, but I've earned the right to be intrusive." He motioned to the air between us. "There doesn't get to be space between us. We hold our chins up and lie to everyone else, but not each other."

Our hug was a crash of emotions, making me feel the sting of life anew. "I know. I'm sorry, Ollie. I'm all turned around."

He went from lion to puppy in my arms, melting into the hug he needed to get, every bit as much as he needed to give it. "Then we'll fix it, okay? But we'll fix it together. No more of this shutting the door on everyone. I know it sucks, but I'm right here."

"Please don't leave me," I gusted out in a desperate prayer, clinging to my brother like he was my life raft. "Don't give up on me. It's just taking longer than usual to process."

Ollie held me tight. "Oh, kid. You're going to have to work a lot harder to get rid of me. I'm permanent. It's you and me till the end, got it?"

I nodded, but couldn't let him go just yet. I didn't want to be so lost. Ollie grounded me to the earth, keeping me from drifting. After several months of drifting, I decided it was about time to stand up again. "What's first on the agenda, Doc?" I asked in a playful tone. The levity sounded off on my lips, but I went with it, as it was a hair better than total despondency.

"I think we should go pick out a crib."

My spirits deflated. "I don't want to do baby stuff. I thought you meant normal fun stuff."

"I'm the doctor, and I think it's time you came to terms

with the baby in your belly. We're all excited about it, but we're afraid to even smile at you. You wouldn't believe the nutso stuff Mariang's been planning for you and the baby." He kissed the top of my head. "Hop in the shower, and I'll make you some lunch. We don't have to get a crib today, but it's coming, kiddo. Deal with it."

I held him tight when he tried to let go. Though I knew I was being childish, Ollie was the perfect person to let my guard down around. He melted, his whole body softening when I silently admitted that no matter how old I got, I still needed my big brother to put my puzzles back together when they got all wrecked.

5

HISTORY REPEATING ITSELF

After about a week of getting out of the house and owning up to the fact that I was pregnant – which as it turns out, wasn't the end of anyone's world – I started to feel a little better. Add that to the fact that I now had two Pullers, my morning sickness seemed to have passed, and I was feeling a little more myself. Mariang talked me into a day of shopping for the baby after I categorically refused to have a baby shower.

"Who would even come? You're my closest girlfriend. Probably my only girlfriend at this point. I haven't seen the regular crew in months."

Mariang frowned back at me from her place in the passenger's seat. "You have a whole group of friends. Gabby and all of them? Don't you think they'd like to get you presents? Celebrate the baby a bit?"

Ezra's SUV was the only car that could carry all of us,

but when the confession eked out of my mouth, I wished there was a bit more space. Like, a whole planet or something that kept the conversation concealed from the entire household. "I sort of haven't told anyone yet."

Mariang gaped at me, Danny shook his head, Mason frowned at me and Boston hissed his disapproval. Ezra spoke up from the backseat. "You're running out of time, darling. We're on our way to find out the sex of the baby. Don't you think they'd like to know?"

"Oh, probably. But Von was sleeping with my friend Katrina, who doesn't know we got together. She doesn't take kindly to people playing with her old toys, even after she's tired of them. Plus, I don't really know how to explain my life to them. What?" I said of the accusatory looks. "Ollie said I could tell them when I was ready."

"And when would that be? When the baby starts Kindergarten?" Mason took my phone out of my messenger bag and handed it to me. "Start dialing."

"So I can get the pity looks from everyone? So they can know I've got no job, a baby and no father of the baby?"

Danny, of all people, took it upon himself to school me. "You have to start acknowledging this baby. Your mum treated you like she never wanted you, and now you're about to go do the same thing? Be smarter than this."

Ezra and I both glowered at Danny, who was unapologetic. "Be sensitive, Danny," Ezra warned.

"What? Someone had to say it. Von's a waste. Big deal. It's nothing I didn't tell you from the start. But I won't sit back and have this one turn out with issues like yours. Not on my watch."

Boston snarled at his brother. "Jeez, Danny. Ease up. You'll stop running Von down in front of me. This is how you've been talking about him since you moved out here? It stops today. Sure, about the leaving October thing, Von's a wanker. But everything else? Von doesn't care how you talk about him, but I do. And running him down in front of the baby? That's not happening anymore." Boston laced his moderately stubby fingers through mine. No matter how many times he did that, it never got less confusing. Boston had been such a pervy tool before Bishop died. Now he was humble, somber. He was nice, if not a little spaced out. Invasion of the d-bag snatchers, for sure. His kindness was unnerving, though his loyalty to Von was good to see.

Danny grumbled, "What do you want me to do? It's nothing you're not all thinking, but you're too chicken to say to her. You all treat her like she's ill or something. I've got news for you, kid: Von's not coming back. This torch you're carrying for him? Get over it. Believe it or not, the world still spins without Von as the center."

I didn't mean to snap back, but it just sort of came out like a punch. "I haven't dreamwalked in a week, you jag. I'm not naïve, and I'm not carrying a torch for him. I'm making peace with signing over my life to this baby. Forgive me for not being jolly about the whole thing just yet."

With the absence of dreamwalking came the return of Philip, who was oddly protective of me and the baby. I guess that's what my subconscious wanted – a great guy who loved me and the baby, no matter what. Philip brought me presents and held me while I cried out my fears. When he'd brought me a black leather container the size of a shoe box with a green weed inside of it for me to eat, I knew my imagination had gone weird. I'd choked it down to be polite, but after that I asked that he bring me flowers instead.

Maybe that's high maintenance, but you know, he's fake, so I figure I'm alright asking for what I want.

Danny's voice lowered. "We don't need you to be jolly. We just need history not to repeat itself."

Mason put his arm around me, clutching me while Boston leaned forward and punched his brother in the arm. "She's been doing better. Don't push it, you lousy tosser."

I hated that I needed to hear what Danny said. He was a jackweed, but he was right. This was exactly what happened to Bev. She fell for a man who left her a pregnant single mother. I wrecked my mama's life, and I carried that weight around with me in an emotional knapsack to hit men with when they got too close.

I wouldn't do that to my kid. My kid wouldn't be better off without me, like how I'd been with Bev. My kid wouldn't have to leave just to be safe. I would make sure the baby had everything he or she needed. "Maybe I should get a crib?" I suggested, uncertain. "Babies need cribs, right?"

Mariang turned to me with an excited grin. "A crib is a great start. How about a bassinet too, so the baby can sleep next to you for the first few months, but still be in its own space?"

"Is that a thing? Don't they just sleep in a crib once they come home from the hospital?" It began to dawn on me that a baby was coming, and I had no idea what to do with it.

Mariang was too excited at the prospect of shopping for baby stuff to care about the details. "Now I'm really excited. Once we find out the sex of the baby, we can pick out colors. Pink for a girl, blue for a boy. Or green. You like green, yeah? It would certainly match your bedroom. What do you think?"

I was reticent to voice any opinion, lest it be the wrong one and reveal that I had no idea what I was doing. "Um, that's fine."

Mason cuddled me into his nook, knowing me better than most. "You can pick whatever color you want." He'd been extra gentle with me, growing sweeter the more pregnant I looked. Today I was wearing a form-fitting black stretchy dress shirt with maternity jeans. For some reason this made his hand migrate to my stomach whenever he got the chance, rubbing it like a crystal ball. The only time his hand left me was when Boston took a tentative turn. It was sweet, but a little claustrophobic at times. I was getting better at letting people touch me, though it felt more like baptism by fire at this point.

"I kind of like green and purple. Can the baby have that?"

Mariang nodded so enthusiastically, her eyes seemed to rattle around in her head. "Yes, of course! We'll go shopping right after your appointment. It's done. It's decided."

"That's fine." I squeezed Boston's hand reassuringly as he let slip a labored sigh. He'd been subjected to no end of baby nonsense and hadn't complained once. He seemed to like the baby itself, but none of the additional frills. We were actually on the same page about that.

Danny pulled into the hospital's parking lot, honking once when he saw Ollie. My hopeful look to find my brother died in a low curse when I saw him waiting at the door with Gabby. She stood next to him, a mix of emotions on her face. I frowned at Mariang. "You knew about this, didn't you."

Mariang shrugged guiltily. "Maybe a little. Ollie told me this morning."

"Yet another thing that wasn't my choice," I muttered under my breath.

6

ULTRA-SHOCK

Ollie was squeezing one hand while Ezra held the other. Mariang pointed at the screen with so much glee, I didn't know how my confusion would ever catch up. "Show me again?" I asked the ultrasound technician.

"Right here," she pointed to a spot on the screen using her mouse.

"One more time?"

She explained the body parts adequately, but I asked over and over until Ollie's grin started to fade. "Here, let me print it out for you," the tech in scrubs offered.

I didn't know what to feel or how to react. I don't even know that I was fully processing any of it. I mean, just a baby existing in my uterus was a big enough blast to my sanity. "You're sure? You're sure it's a girl? Show me again, please."

The tech was patient, which was to her credit, as I knew I was being annoying. I couldn't help it. The second she opened her mouth to announce the baby's sex, I couldn't hear anything else. It was like cotton and white noise filled my ears, clouding out common sense and ordinary words.

It was then it started to hit me afresh that I was having a baby, and this was all real. "Ollie? Ollie?" I squeezed my brother's hand, terrified and confused. My breath came in too shallow for comfort, making me give in to the early stages of a panic attack. "Ollie?"

He rubbed my arm after the medical professional wiped the clear jelly off my stomach so I could pull my shirt back down over the bump. The swell of my belly had been impossible to hide for a while now. "You're having a girl! That's exciting," my brother said, informing me of the emotion I was supposed to be feeling, trying to bring me up to speed. Ollie and Ezra sat me up, and while Ezra was overjoyed, Ollie understood me better than anyone. He knew I was silently freaking out. He sat at the foot of the hospital bed and stared me down. "This is a good thing, kid. You can do this. Remember: keep your chin up, take it slow."

I shook my head, feeling like I was twelve years old. "I can't do this!" I whispered, the muscles in my fingers going numb from gripping the edge of the bed. "It's getting real now. A baby girl? Me? I'm... I don't know how to be a mama. I've never changed a diaper before! What do I do if the baby never learns to crawl? What if she takes one look at me and never stops screaming? What happens if I..." I tried to catch my breath, but it came to me in syncopated pants that did me no good at all. "I can't do this!"

Ollie cupped my face in his hands to focus me. "Look at me. You can do anything! Allie and I didn't know what the heck we were doing raising you, but we figured it out. For a long time, there wasn't even room for you to puzzle out how to crawl, but somehow you learned. Somehow you turned out perfect. I'm telling you, if Allie and I could take care of a baby before we hit our teens, you can do it now. I've seen you take on a challenge. There's nothing you can't figure out. All this takes is a little research." He kissed my forehead and wrapped his arm around me. He turned us so our legs were dangling off the side of the bed. "I'm here. I'll be right by your side for the whole thing."

A tear dripped down my cheek. I'd been crying so often; I didn't even have the decency to be embarrassed about it anymore. "I don't even have a crib, Ollie. A good mama would already have a crib. She'd already have a plan. I don't have a plan. I've been too selfish, thinking about me in all this. My life, my plans." I looked up at my brother, eyes wide. "Ollie, there's going to be a baby soon! We need to get organized. I need a car seat and diapers and clothes for her." I touched my belly, feeling suddenly protective of what was inside. "A little girl."

Ollie rested his cheek atop my head. "My little girl's having a little girl. Man, I'm old."

I snorted through a laugh that I desperately needed. "Will you help me figure this out?"

"You're about to be real sorry you asked me that. You thought I was bossy before? Don't unleash me. Don't tell me you need help making plans. That's only like, my favorite thing in the world. Give me a legal pad. Set me loose, kid."

Mariang sat down on my other side, holding my hand and grinning at Ollie. "It's not too late to revisit the idea of a baby shower."

7

JUDGED

'd never been to a baby shower before, but I guessed by the looks on my friends' faces that this wasn't what they'd been expecting. Mariang had picked out my silver silk dress that fell like a waterfall over my belly and hung to my knees, hugging my breasts in a way that actually made me feel like a woman instead of a giant anamorphous blob. I mean, at least now I was a dead sexy anamorphous blob, for sure.

Mariang had rented a room in a banquet hall. There were long silver tapestries, an overlarge lavender bow on the backs of each chair, and long pearl-colored taper candles that made the afternoon luncheon feel like a cozy evening affair. Mariang had thought of everything, including playing "The Way You Look Tonight", which I'd once told Mariang Von had sung to me while we danced together. It was the sweetest and most horrible thing, and I loved her for the effort. I loved her for a lot of reasons, and this shower was just one of them. I'd resisted for too long the idea of even being pregnant, but she'd been patient, helping me pick out all the things I needed to prepare myself for a life with two.

Though my friends were more the beer and poker type, they dressed up for the occasion, and in the midst of the hugs and kisses and shocked well-wishes, I realized that this baby was the occasion. I was having a baby, and that was a happy thing, no matter how it came to be.

Darius showed up, which I couldn't believe. He came in with two nicely wrapped gifts in his hands and a self-protective vibe to his stiff shoulders. He'd been one of us, once upon a time. When he'd fallen into his older brother's business, the distance had been inevitable, since none of us approved of Judge's illegal and often deadly antics.

I watched the tension build as Darius stood awkwardly in the doorway. The flight or muscle through it debate was plain on his face. I decided I had enough factions of my life that were separate. Setting the tone for my friends, I walked up to Darius and wrapped my arms around him, smiling softly as he melted in my embrace. "Thanks, Bait. Congratulations, kid. Judge sends his love."

I kissed Darius' freshly shaved ebony cheek, still holding onto him. "Thank you for coming. I know we're not your favorite people in the world. It means a lot."

"It's time, I think." Darius jerked his head toward the door he'd just come in through. "Judge is out front. He doesn't want to come inside, but he asked me to send you out to see him for a minute."

"Sure. Come on in. Say hi to everyone." I raised my voice to my friends, who weren't quite sure what to do with the unexpected guest they had all once loved. "Guys, Darius needs a beer. Jordan, will you get him something good?"

"Sure thing, Bait. Hey, Nefarious," Jordan jabbed with an edge to the lighthearted smile on his face.

I kept my arm around Darius and ushered him into the room. "Now, now. In here he's just good old Darius."

Ollie moved forward and gave Darius a one-armed dude hug, enforcing my rule that we would all be cool on my baby's special day. "Good to see you, man." With Ollie on my side, the others quickly fell in line. In the next second, Darius had a smile on his face, a beer in his hand, and too many hugs to choose from. It was the old crew back together, minus Allie.

I moved toward the entrance, wondering what Judge could possibly want to see me for. Boston moved to open the door for me, watching but maintaining his distance, waiting while I walked out into the sunshine. I strolled down the entryway toward Judge's silver BMW, bracing myself against the winter chill. Big Mike was his driver, and he regarded me with a curt nod to his head. The back door opened, revealing Judge in pressed gray pants, a light lavender dress shirt and a blue tie. He had always been a sharp dresser, having an eye for details. He stepped out of the car when I refused to climb in; I knew Boston would throw a fit if I disappeared in the backseat of Judge's vehicle. "Congratulations are in order, I hear." His words were kind, but his dark eyes and clenched jaw were holding back a storm.

"Thank you. You're welcome to come in. You can even bring Big Mike, if you like." I leaned down to speak into the car. "You feeling hungry, Michael? There's plenty of food inside."

Judge answered for Big Mike, as he always did. "No, thank you. We're fine out here."

"Okay." I rested my hands on my belly awkwardly. The silk of my dress felt like frozen water, transformed by the iciness of the moderate breeze that chilled me. My coat was somewhere in the building, so I hoped Judge would come out with whatever he wanted to say quick.

I stood facing Judge, unwilling to shrink beneath his scrutiny. It's like he showed up just to make a point that he wasn't going to come to my baby shower. I hadn't been in charge of the invitations, so I could only guess Judge's presence was Ollie's doing, trying to get us to put the past behind us. "So, how's business? Help any old ladies across the street lately?"

Judge pointed a mocha-colored finger at my belly in dismay. "Who did this to you?"

My smile tightened. "No one you know."

"Don't play games. What's his name?"

"What do you care?"

"Just tell me Ollie's broken his legs so I can sleep better at night."

I blinked up at him in confusion. "You showed up just to tell me you're mad?"

"I showed up because I had to see for myself. This," he said with disdain, jabbing his finger at my belly again, "wasn't supposed to happen to you. You're the one who was supposed to make something of herself."

My head started to swivel with attitude, and I began talking animatedly with my hands, riled up after the first few verbal punches. "I'm sorry, am I dead? No. There's still plenty of time for me to make something of myself."

"This isn't what I wanted for you. Who did this?"

"Why do you care?" I repeated, confused.

"Because you're my sister! Or you were before I..." He shook his head, his midnight eyes filled with palpable heaviness. "I'm so disappointed in you."

Anger rose up in me like a kraken just waiting for the right trigger to set its tentacles of torment loose. In an act of indignant rage, my hand flew out and smacked Judge across the face. Big Mike got out of the car, but otherwise didn't intervene. Judge's nostrils flared dangerously, and I knew I'd traipsed over deadly ground. To be fair, so had he.

My voice was low and lethal as I fumed at the man I'd regarded as a secondary older brother, back when I'd been young and foolish enough to trust his kindness. "How dare you. I don't care about meeting your expectations. You lost every good thing in my eyes when you turned us away all those years ago. You think you're disappointed in me? Get used to that feeling, Judge. I've been disappointed in you for sixteen years." I stabbed my finger to his chest, which was letting him off easy from the right hook I wanted to clock him with. "You don't get to care about me or my baby. You don't get to put standards on me that you don't even hold yourself to."

"I made something of myself!" he roared, finally letting the cracks in his armor show. "You don't get to look down your nose at me just because you don't like how I got here."

I didn't shiver from the cold weather, no; it was the arctic chill between us that had finally built to an avalanche we were both ready to bury each other under. When Judge opened his mouth to defend himself further, I threw my shaking hands up between us, trembling at the showdown that had been years in the making. "I can't do this right now. I'm having a baby, Judge. A baby. You get that, right? You took yourself out of my life years ago. You don't get to make demands on my choices now."

Judge's defiance was firmly in place, his clenched jaw making his whole face taut with barely controlled fury. "Who did this to you?"

"I did," I answered with sad eyes. I tried to anchor us so we didn't destroy what was left of the diminishing goodness I knew we both had buried deep. "I did this to me. I thought I had a handle on my life, but I let things get out of control. I'm dealing, though, so you should either support me or get out."

His fist tightened. "That's nothing like you. You never let things get out of control. Control is your touchstone. You're like me."

I blinked up at him, confused at the declaration. "I am?"

Judge's eyes softened infinitesimally. Had I not known him for ages, I might not have noticed. "Always have been. Why do you think neither of us ever wins when we go head to head?"

I pursed my lips, weighing his words and wondering at the truth of them. "Well, I don't want to be that way, always fighting for the upper hand. Some things can't be controlled, no matter how hard you try. I want to get my life in order. I have to do right by this baby, Judge. Disappointment that I am to you, I can't afford to let my daughter down. She's the one who matters now. Not me, and not you."

"See that you don't disappoint her, then. Shouldering the shame of letting a little girl down? It's a slow death." He shook his head, saying so many things with his eyes, his body and his voice that confused me. "That hard look in your eyes has been killing me for years. I know it's me who put that there."

Ollie trotted out to us, a friendly expression forcing itself to overshadow the volatile one lurking beneath. He extended his hand to Judge, who shook it with that same firm look to him that told me he wasn't dropping this anytime soon. "Hey, Judge. You coming in?"

"Judge was just stopping by to tell me what a disappointment I am for throwing my life away, getting knocked up. He's not allowed in. In fact, he was just leaving."

Ollie's jaw tightened, and the two men exchanged nods of understanding that, though they respected each other, distance was the best thing for all involved. "Come on in, kiddo. We were just about to get started when we realized we'd lost the guest of honor." Ollie held onto my shaking hand and glanced up with a warning at Judge. "Look, October's been through enough. You'll do well not to put unnecessary stress on my sister. What's done is done, and you won't look down your nose at her about it."

Judge stepped back, gripping the handle on his car door. "Expect a gift when the baby comes. You won't be hearing from me before then."

My anger came back unfettered. "You can expect your gift sent back to you in ashes! I won't have your pity gifts. I don't need your disapproval, and my daughter doesn't need your charity."

Judge shut himself in his car and left with a respectful nod to Ollie before Big Mike drove off.

BABY, BOWS AND BEER

I had given Mason the day off, sticking Boston with the duty of guarding the door, which he seemed ever vigilantly determined to do. Either he was very concerned about keeping me safe, or he was trying to distance himself from the abundance of bows and ruffles that seemed to explode out of every package. He remained distant and quiet, and I completely understood. Kinda wished we could switch places.

Ollie never left my side, helping me cut the ribbons and speaking when I didn't have the guts to answer the harder questions. He was the buffer between the Brits and our people, his professional manners reminding our friends to be cool.

When the formalities ended, Ezra introduced himself to each of our friends, letting me answer when Beto asked how we knew him. "Ezra's my new stepdad. He was Bev's fiancé. And Mariang's my new sister."

That was all it took for Ezra's grin to brighten his face, close the gap between us and kiss both my cheeks. "I'm honored to be your father."

Ezra, Danny, Mariang and Lynna said their goodbyes after the ceremony of the baby shower was over, leaving us to our devices. Darius took that as his easy exit, leaving while things were still smooth, and before anyone could get in a jab too glib to be ignored. I hadn't seen our friends in several months, and when it was just the regular crew sitting around the tables we pushed together, the questions didn't stop coming.

"Who's the baby-daddy?" Jordan asked, as usual, unaware of the layers of discomfort laced throughout that question. After the presents were opened and dinner was eaten, the ties came off and the company manners were tossed under the table. Jordan sat back in his chair, sizing me up like I had suddenly grown a dinosaur head. "I mean, the last we saw you, you were normal. Now you're our little Bait, with child."

"It's Von," Ollie answered when I clammed up. "You met him a couple times. He's overseas visiting his family before the baby comes. He wishes he could be here, though." It was a sweet lie, and I knew in that simple explanation that Ollie was hoping for Von to return. It was nice to know that after everything, some part of Ollie existed that was an unjaded romantic.

Katrina's head snapped in my direction, the queen bee inside of her coming out swinging. "Von? British hottie, leaves before sunrise, got a joke for everything, Von? *My* Von?"

My elbows rested on the round table we'd pulled chairs around so we could all sit together. I blew my breath out through pursed lips. "Yup. Just like how Jessica's with *my* Beto, and none of you said a thing to me while it was going on behind my back. Von and I got together months after you two had your thing." I cast Beto an apologetic look for throwing him under the bus, but really, he was getting off pretty easy.

Katrina was livid, which wasn't a good color on her when it was aimed at me. I'd always stayed off her vindictive girl wrath radar because I never drew the eyes of her conquests, but somehow I found myself in the crosshairs now. "You're seven months pregnant, Bait. Von was in my bed two months ago. Don't tell me there wasn't any overlap. I mean, we weren't exclusive, but still."

My mouth dropped open, my skin cold and clammy. When I finally spoke, my voice was meek, and barely above a whisper. "You saw Von two months ago? You had sex with Von?"

Jordan, Beto and Nick scooted their chairs back in unison, eyes wide and hands up to make sure everyone knew they were not getting involved in the ensuing catfight.

Katrina nodded, clearly angry. "He was pissy and

barely looked at me the whole time. We tried to do our usual thing, but he couldn't get it up. Then he was gone. I knew something was going on, but I didn't think a baby was the something." She touched her forehead. "He seriously got you pregnant?"

I nodded. "It's complicated. We're not together. Obviously. I mean, he's sleeping with other people. It's fine."

Ollie draped his arm around the back of my chair and stared Katrina down. "Now that you know, I'd appreciate it if you didn't sleep with Von anymore. It's very complicated, and October will never tell you how hard this all is for her. And no offense, but baby trumps your burning loins, so if he comes back for more, send him home to his responsibilities."

I wasn't the love of Von's life. I was Von's responsibility.

Katrina didn't start anything, but I could tell she was still miffed at being told point blank to put the lid on her cookie jar. *Whatever.* "I guess that's fine. Happy for you, Bait. Wow, though. I didn't think he was the raise a child type. Didn't think you were, either."

"They both are." Ollie jumped in before I could admit that Von wasn't the type, and he wouldn't be raising the girl with me. "Von's been great with the whole pregnancy." He held my hand under the table, and I squeezed it, wishing his lies were true.

I could feel Boston's eyes on me from the doorway across the room. He was starting to pay attention to our conversation, and my notice of him drew a few of my girlfriends' eyes to where he stood. "Who's the brooding hottie?" Rachel asked. I could already see a plan for takedown formulating in her mind, raring to get to the fresh meat before Katrina sunk her hooks into the new guy.

"That's Boston, Von's brother."

Rachel put her drink down and winked at us. "Watch and learn, ladies." She made her way over to him, her hips exaggerating her walk as her smile turned coy. Rachel wasn't coy, so that look always came out forced on her. She was a tiger, taking what she wanted so Katrina didn't snatch it away. It didn't leave a whole lot of room for shyness.

Boston rolled his eyes at me, as if I'd sent her over to annoy him. I shrugged in innocence, watching her touch his arm, laugh at the joke I know he didn't make and do her best to break him out of his stoic demeanor. I felt bad for her; had this been a few months ago, she wouldn't have to work so hard, or at all. Boston had been such a perv. Now his spirit was broken. I guess that wasn't a bad thing in terms of annoying the women of the world, but there was a tragic glass-shattering sadness about seeing a brash eagle's wings get clipped all the same.

"I'm on duty," he explained without really explaining. He removed Rachel's hand from his chest like it was an annoying bug.

Her nose crinkled. "On duty? Do you work for the banquet hall?"

"No, for October. I'm her guard."

I sank in my chair, knowing there would be less intrigue if he'd called himself a male stripper. All eyes turned to me for confirmation. "Boston, come sit down. Yeah, guys. He's sort of my guard. Ezra's the overprotective type. No big deal."

Katrina balked. "No big deal? You locked down Von, and this handsome hulk of a man is your Kevin Costner bodyguard? Man, Bait. You hit the jackpot."

Jessica was kind and made the first attempt to draw Boston into the group without hitting on him. "Where are you from?"

"London. I'm Von's youngest brother." He settled in beside me, running his hand down my back to give me a good pull, which I'm sure made us look more like a couple than guard and charge. Some things couldn't be helped, though. "What'd you call October? Bait?"

Jordan laughed, taking a drink from his long-necked beer. "Yeah. Jailbait. She's been in the group since before she was legal. Ollie warned us all we couldn't date her until she was eighteen. It was a long couple of years, Bait," he said, winking at me. "The name only got funnier when she started working at the prison."

Boston let out a snigger, and though it was at my expense, it was good to see him smile. He leaned back in his chair, signaling to the bartender to get him a beer.

The more the alcohol flowed into Boston, the more his old self he became. He even managed to give Katrina a good leer, which mollified her frustration at being passed over for the asexual kid of the group. It was nice to see him let go a little.

Boston let go a little more, and a little more, until his eyes were red and lidded, his laugh obnoxious, and Boston was stone drunk.

9

HOW NOT TO BE A SKANK

Ollie helped me get Boston into the backseat after we packed up all the gifts into the trunk. My brother sighed heavily as he slid into the driver's seat with Gabby beside him. I was stuck in the back, praying Boston didn't vomit all over my pretty silver dress. He was a babbling drunk, which made things tense for Ollie and me as Boston started spilling the family secrets in front of Gabby, while Ollie drove us to the mansion.

"Von's a vampire!" Boston sang out, making me cringe.

Ollie forced a smile. "Yep. Von's a vampire. I'm Count Chocula, and Gabby's the Queen Fairy." He glanced over at Gabby, who giggled at Boston's mouth. "You do look nice tonight. If there was a way to crown a fairy, I'd nominate you first thing."

Gabby grinned at my brother, and it was nice to see

them being a couple, however infrequently it happened. "And you can be head Elf."

"Which kind?" I piped in. "Christmas, Keebler or Orlando Bloom?"

Gabby didn't miss a beat. "Oh, Blooming goodness, for sure, not the Keebler variety."

Ollie gusted out his faux relief. "Whew! Thank goodness. I don't know how to bake cookies."

The winter was giving its last solid effort at a snow, but the temperature couldn't commit to letting the white puffs stick on the ground. They melted as soon as they touched the windshield, but it was pretty all the same. Boston kept letting out blasts of howling at the snow, laughing to himself. At what? I'm still not sure.

I was focused on getting Boston out of the car after Ollie pulled into the driveway of the mansion, calling Ezra on his cell phone for help with the swaying twin who was barely upright. My heart broke for him when he started calling for Bishop. "Bishop's not here," I said as Ezra and Ollie each took an arm, helping him toward the house.

At this, Boston started weeping, openly sobbing as he reached the porch. I remained in the backseat of the car to keep warm because Ezra told me the ground might be slippery, and to wait for an escort. I was determined to get a hold of myself while Gabby chattered on about how big my boobs were getting, and at what point they would tip the scales and cross over into the porn category. "They're seriously almost there now. Do you have a lot of morning sickness?"

"Not anymore."

A note of silence passed before Gabby mustered up a serious expression. "I was real sorry to hear about Bev. I wish there'd been a funeral. I would've gone. Miss that old girl."

Gabby had only seen Bev outside of her trailer, which meant the curse of the stone was far less, giving Gabby and the world a far more perfect view of Bev than the rotting truth of it all.

When I said nothing, Gabby mustered up the guts to tell me how she really felt, cutting through the BS to the heart of it. "You should've told us, Bait. You both should've. I'm Ollie's girlfriend, and he didn't tell me that his mom died. I wish you two would drop that constant wall you've got up. Makes it hard. I mean, you were halfway through your pregnancy before you told anyone!"

"You're right, Gabby. I'm sorry. I think I was in denial for a long time. But you're totally right; we should be more open." And I meant it. It didn't mean I was actually capable of doing it, but she was right all the same.

The back door of the SUV flung open, and I jumped, shocked to see Finn staring at me, a scarf around his neck and hurt shining in his green eyes. "Of course you had to be beautiful when I finally get to see you. Now I can't be frustrated. Well planned on your part."

"Finn, what are you doing here?"

He held out his hand to me and lifted the rectangular package with his other hand for my perusal. His expression was closed off when he muttered, "Special delivery."

I cleared my throat to remind him we weren't alone. "Gabby, meet Finn. Finn, this is Ollie's girlfriend."

He held my hand, not even glancing at Gabby, who waved hello with wide eyes that danced at the intrigue of a handsome older man calling me beautiful. "Walk with me," he requested, the sincere look in his eyes giving me butterflies.

"I don't think I should, Finn."

"Please. I promise to behave."

Gabby motioned for me to go with too much enthusiasm, so I consented partly to shut her up, partly because I was afraid his scarf might slip and she'd see his gills, and partly because I was ashamed to admit that I missed Finn. He'd been good to me, saved me a few times, and was still trying to connect with me even after I turned him away. I couldn't even reach Von on the phone, but Finn pursued me across whole worlds.

"Okay, but just a short walk. You'll be cool?" I asked, warning him not to declare anything about his feelings.

"Best behavior," he promised, holding the book over his heart. "I've been waiting for months just to get a look at you. Come on out."

He slowly pulled me out of the car, being careful and patient as I slid out of the side and stepped onto the driveway, feeling like a whale being birthed from a car. Finn gaped at my round belly, and then finally looked up at me with too much love beaming through. "And you can't look at me like that. It'll get us into trouble."

"You're afraid of a little trouble now?" he asked with a tease as he held his elbow out to me. "Motherhood's really done a number on you. I'd hoped you'd be hideous so I could move on, but I've never seen you more spectacular."

"Okay, this is exactly the kind of talk we need to avoid. Lock that noise down, or I'm going inside."

"But why? Are you going to lie and say you really feel nothing for me?" We turned to the right at the end of the driveway, heading down the dead-end street to a path I knew just through the trees. It looped around and would land us in the backyard of the mansion.

"I have to lie, Finn. I'm carrying another dude's baby. I'm pretty sure there's all kinds of rules in the *How Not to be a Skank* book warning against that. Plus, I like you. You're in love with me. It's a big difference, and I'm not willing to hurt you like that."

Finn's lips drew in a tight line. "You're still in love with Von?" He spoke the name like it was a gross insect entirely beneath him.

"No. But that doesn't mean I'm available. I'm going to have a baby, Finn. I'm rooted here now. You're really telling me your kingdom can get along without you? You want to share a bed with me and Mason? You seriously think this can work in any way?"

"You and the baby can come stay with me in Dagat part

of the time," he suggested, puzzling through the plan I could tell he was coming up with on the fly.

"My daughter's not setting foot in Dagat." I was firm on that. "She'll have legs, Finn. Your people can't handle themselves. I didn't make it a month before I was molested."

Finn stopped, hearing nothing but what he wanted to pick out. "A girl? You're having a baby girl?" His hand flew to my belly, stroking the swell through my opened coat as if it belonged to him – as if *I* belonged to him. It was enough to rip my heart in half, seeing how much Finn actually really did love me, and that I couldn't return those feelings.

Could I? Had I really given him a decent chance, or had I written him off in the heat of being blinded by the Amazing Vanishing Von? "September," I admitted, divulging my secret to him. I wasn't sure why I chose him to break my secret to; Ollie and Mariang had been inquiring for weeks. "September Serendipity Reese. I haven't told anyone the name yet, so keep that to yourself."

He snorted at the name. "That's cute. I like it." His eyes met mine in earnest. "I could keep her safe. The country's still shifting, but Atius and his men are dead. No one's coming after me anymore. I could get a house on the island instead of on its own in the ocean. September could have her pick of any of the Kataw when she came of age. She'd be the only one of her kind. A treasure."

I tried to picture the life he was promising, wishing it

was as easy as he made it sound. The evergreens along the pathway faded, and I tried to replace them with the roar of the ocean I'd nearly drowned in. "You forget I'm an Omen. I have to live Topside to do my job."

"Maybe you can split your time. Have Mariang do a month, then you. On the off months, you could come with September and live with me." He cupped my face with one hand and pressed his forehead to mine, his eyes shut in earnest. "We can make this work."

"No, we can't! We can't, and you know it. And I'm not where you're at in this. You're way more certain than I'll ever be. We're too different, Finn. We're not fairytale characters from your books. We're not Lissima and Ricardo." I closed my eyes, pleading for him to understand. I came back to my mantra that kept me from diving headfirst into something I knew wouldn't work. "You're a fish, and I can't swim."

"You'll learn to swim. You'll learn to love the ocean."

I knew he meant that I would learn to love him. Maybe he was right, but *maybe* wasn't enough to gamble September on. My girl and I had grown pretty attached in the past few weeks. "I can't take that chance with a baby. She comes first, and you and I both know Dagat isn't safe for a girl with legs."

With each tword he spoke, he jolted my face with his palms on my cheeks to make his point clear. "I can protect her."

Our lips were a breath away from colliding in a crash

that would destroy us both, and though he could've cleared the gap with little hesitation from me, he waited for me to make that choice.

Finn was tempting in the best and worst ways. With a single kiss, I could forget that I was alone in this. I could let myself feel the warmth of being cherished by a warrior. He'd wrap his rough and tumble military arms around me and give me that shot of security I'd been desperately lacking.

Security wasn't the same as love, and though I felt a great deal for Finn, I knew it wasn't enough. I kissed his cheek, cursing myself for passing on a real kiss. I pulled back to keep my lips honest. "I told you we couldn't be around each other. It's been five minutes, and we're already too intense. I can't have one more thing making my life complicated. I have to be able to focus on September. I need to be a good mama." I shook my head and clenched my fist to my chest. "I *need* this, Finn."

Finn took a deep breath, too many emotions and retorts washing over his face in swirls of contradictions. He laced his fingers through mine. "Okay. We can talk about something else. Has Ezra been giving you the books I brought?"

A smile found my face when I realized he was trying to be good and veer to less dangerous topics. "Yes. I love them. Thank you."

"Can you read them alright? You were getting almost fluent before you left."

We neared the backyard of the mansion as we walked along the path, hand in hand. "I get what's going on, but there are words that I still don't know what they mean. If I brought the books out, could you help me?"

"Of course. Go on and get them. I'll meet you in the living room. I've got a few things to clear with Ezra while I'm here." He kissed my cheek after opening the sliding glass door of the kitchen, splitting off from me to do his grownup talk while I scampered off in search of fairytales.

10

UNCLE DANNY

*D*anny came out of his bedroom, shutting the door with that same secretive smile I'd seen appear several times for a few days now. He'd been decidedly less antagonistic since Mariang had agreed to go to the Justice of the Peace and sign their marriage license three weeks ago. Apparently, an Omen getting married in Terraway was a big deal, and took months and months of planning. Danny got irritable waiting in line to file their paperwork. They were officially married now, though no song and dance had been done to commemorate the occasion just yet. Their marriage was something of a secret that only our families knew about, with Terraway not being let in on the joyous union until the big wedding to-do. The bells and whistles would be held at Kabayo's castle in Silo, as was the tradition for Omen weddings and funerals.

I nodded to Danny in the hallway, knowing it was

usually when I spoke that his smile disappeared. "Hey, kid. I'll help Mason set up the crib in the nursery tonight. Do you want the bassinet in your room now, or wait until later?"

I blinked at him, unsure why he was being so nice. "Um, thanks. Whatever's easiest for you guys. But you don't have to, you know. I can put the crib together."

"I don't mind." Danny looked back at his bedroom door, ensuring it was shut as he lowered his voice. "Can I ask you something?"

No good can come of this. I waved him into my bedroom where I fished out the books Finn had given me, along with my notebooks where I'd translated the stories as best I could. "Sure. What's up?"

"Have you felt the baby kick yet?"

Of all the things I ever thought Danny might ask me, that was last on the list. "Not yet. Sometimes I feel something that's almost like movement, but it's hard to tell. Nothing as definite as kicking yet."

Danny's mouth drew to the side. "Oh." He glanced over his shoulder to make sure we were alone. I heard Boston snoring from his bedroom down the hall. "Can I... Would it be okay if I felt it?" He stared at my belly as if gearing up for climbing a mountain.

"Are you serious?"

"Never mind. Forget I asked."

The fog of distance settled over Danny again, and I was desperate to get the nice guy back. "No, no. You just surprised me, is all. That's fine. No one ever asks. They just up and put their hands all over my stomach. It's unnerving. Thanks for asking. Makes me almost feel like a person again." I pointed to my silk-covered belly, trying to smile through my confusion. "Go nuts."

Danny was hesitant, not sure where he was supposed to touch me. He had several false starts before his hand landed on my stomach just above my belly button. His eyes grew round with fascination. "Wicked! It's so hard. I thought it would be soft for some reason. Is it off the wall to think a whole person's growing inside you?"

"Totally freaky." I smiled at Danny, floored at how tender and precious he was being. I rarely saw him care about anything other than Mariang, and even that was laced with an edge of "don't you dare look at me while I'm being nice." I moved his hand to where I was pretty sure the head was. "Feel that little lump? I think that might be the head."

"Are you serious?" He felt around carefully, transfixed. "I've been reading up on the whole baby thing, and some books are saying the baby can hear people's voices even this early on. Do you think my niece can hear me right this very second?"

"You've honestly never been sweeter than you are right now. You're reading up on babies to get to know your niece? That's Uncle of the Year stuff right there. Ollie's going to have some steep competition." We shared a smile before Danny went back to staring at my belly as he felt along the equator. "I think she can hear you, yeah."

Danny's smile fell. "I don't want her to be frightened of me. I'm not all that great with kids. Or people."

Understatement, pal.

His eyebrows drew together. "The little ones take one look at me and run straight for Mariang. She's got a way about her."

"I'm not well practiced with kids, either. And if you don't want her to be afraid of you, be like this more often. Be sweet. Kids like sweet, I hear."

With his free hand, he rubbed the back of his neck – a thing he did when he was anxious. "Would it be okay if I read to her or something sometime? I mean, I don't know if I believe the books, but I don't want her to be born and have no idea who I am when I try to hold her."

"You really need to tell Mariang you're asking me this. It's super adorable, Danny. She'll fall head over heels in love with you all over again if you tell her you want to read to your niece. Of course you can. That'd be great. She's probably sick of hearing my voice anyways. Mason talks to her all the time before we go to sleep."

"He does? Then I'm falling behind. Yeah, I need to start doing that straightaway. What's he reading her? I don't want to read the same thing, and have her hate me because I'm boring her."

I bit back a smile at his cuteness because he was totally serious. "Mason's been running through the lineage of his father's kingdom, teaching her how to set traps and how to track the undead to bury them. Pretty boring as far as bedtime stories go. She'll probably be happy to get a break and hear a story from you."

"Okay. Thanks. Do you have a name yet? I should probably start calling her something other than 'baby'."

"Yeah, but I don't want to tell you. You'll say it's stupid, and I really like it."

Danny's eyebrows danced mischievously, erasing his monster of Frankenstein features and making him look… handsome? It was hard to tell. "I'll tell you my secret if you tell me yours. I promise not to say it's stupid, even if it is."

I sighed, waiting for the magic of our precious moment devoid of conflict to fade. "Fine. September Serendipity Reese."

Danny let the name roll around for a few seconds as he tempered his response. "That's brilliant. Really. I like the September bit for sure." Danny let out a light chuckle that quickly died on his lips. "Reese? I was hoping she'd be Vandershot."

I swallowed hard, making sure to keep my voice even. "But Von's not my husband. He's not in the baby's life. My last name's Reese, and September will be my daughter only, not his."

Danny nodded, sullen. "I guess that makes sense."

"That doesn't make you any less an uncle, though." I watched him nod, grateful he wasn't taking story time off the table. "Alright, I told you my secret. Your turn. Fess up.

And I want something good, not like admitting you secretly like wearing women's lacy underwear, or something else we already know. I want a really juicy secret."

Danny's smile revived his features as he looked down at me, lowering his voice to a whisper. "Mariang took a pregnancy test a few days ago. We agreed we wouldn't say anything, but I can't keep it in! It's still early, but she's pregnant."

I covered my mouth to stifle a shriek. "Are you serious? That's wonderful!" I hopped up on the balls of my feet, clapping my hands in excitement. I could imagine Mariang with a swollen belly, graceful as anything, an elegant knocked up ballerina. "Oh, she'll be a great mama. You guys so deserve something good for a change! Why aren't you telling anyone? Why's it a secret?"

"She didn't want to steal your thunder, what with the baby shower and all."

My nose crinkled in distaste. "My thunder? Who the crap cares about that? She's too thoughtful." I pulled his wrist to drag him out into the hallway toward her room. "Let's go tell her it's fine. Oh, I can't wait to see the look on Ezra's face!"

Danny planted his feet steadfast on my carpet. "She's napping. The baby makes her quite sleepy." He grinned. "I'm already a husband, and now I'm going to be a dad."

I discarded my caution and threw my arms around Danny, reaching up on my toes to peck his cheek. "Congratulations! That's the best news I've heard all day. September's going to have a cousin! And so close in age. Oh, I'm so happy!" I kissed his face all over, making him laugh.

"See? I knew you'd be cool. You don't care about the thunder part of life. Mariang's always wanted a sister, so she treads lightly around you, afraid she'll do something wrong and you'll hate her forever."

"That's silly. Come get me when she wakes up, so I can do a real freak-out. I've got to go downstairs now, though. Finn's waiting."

Danny frowned. "You let Finn in the door? I thought you were holding out for Von."

I returned his sour expression. "I'm not holding out for any guy. Von split, and I stopped dreamwalking with him a while ago, so either he fell out of love with me, or I did. Either way, it's over. He's not coming back, and that's that. And things would be too complicated with Finn, but we're friends, so we're just hanging out in the living room for a while. You're welcome to join us."

"Pass. I've seen the way he looks at you. It won't be long before you cave. It's the wrong move, but whatever."

I pulled back from him, affronted. "Butt out of it. I'm allowed to sit in a house full of people with a guy. I'm allowed to have friends who aren't my family or the people who get paid to guard me."

"I'm just saying."

Bev's tried and true excuse for her endless insults

smacked me afresh when it birthed out of Danny's mouth. "Quit 'just saying'."

"What about Mason? After the baby's not so much a baby anymore, he'd make a great father."

My mouth dropped open. "Are you serious? Mason and I are good the way we are. Quit trying to marry me off."

"October, you can't do this alone."

I stepped backward, looking up at him with unquenchable anger. "Am I alone? Is that what you're telling me? Ollie, Ezra, Mariang, Mason, Lynna and Boston don't count? I need a husband, or I'm alone? Screw you! That's the meanest thing you could've said to me. I'm barely holding it together most days. Don't come in and crap all over it because my life doesn't shine as golden as yours."

Danny crossed his arms over his chest. "Ollie's going to go off and have a family of his own one day. Ezra, Mariang and I will be around, of course, but we're going to have our own baby to worry about. Sooner or later Mason's going to meet someone. Sure, he'll still work for you, but one day he'll have his own family. And Boston? Really? You're counting on Bos to be a solid role model for your kid? He couldn't even make it through the baby shower sober."

"Get out! You're such a jerk, coming in all nice and pulling this crap when my guard's down. This is the best I can do, Danny. I can't make Von want to be with me."

Danny rolled his eyes, reaching for the door. "Whatever. You're getting hysterical. I'm leaving."

"You're not leaving; I'm kicking you out!" I was shaking

with rage, so I knew I needed to calm down. As soon as the door shut, I changed out of my dress and donned a form-fitting black stretchy shirt and some comfortable dark purple capri yoga pants. I didn't bother with socks as I scooped up my books and padded down the stairs, putting as much space between myself and the smackjack known as Danny.

11

THE RETURN OF RICARDO AND LISSIMA

I slammed the books on the coffee table in the living room and stomped to the kitchen to pour myself a glass of water. I was furious with Danny and even angrier at myself that I got tricked into thinking he could be a decent human being. I took my water to the living room and flipped open the first book, thumbing to one of the pages that had tripped me up.

When Finn came into the room, he frowned at my tight shoulders and scowling expression. "What'd I miss?"

"Nothing. Just Danny being his normal charming self. I'm so pissed right now; I can barely think straight!"

Finn sat down next to me on the white leather couch, leaning back and stretching his arm out to rest behind me. "Anything I should beat on him for while I'm here?"

"No. He's permanently in jackweed mode. Nothing a beating can fix, unfortunately. Though keying his car might take him down a notch." I slammed the book back on the glass coffee table and huffed. "I was looking forward to you helping me with some of the more confusing words, and now I'm all worked up."

Finn took the book and flipped it open. "Which part's got you stumped?"

I opened up my notebook I'd been translating the novels in and thumbed through to one of the dog-eared pages. "This one on page eighty-nine. It's spelled like *karagatan*, but I don't know what that means. Did I get that wrong?"

Finn smiled lazily at me, clearly pleased I was taking such a shine to his language. It was the puzzle aspect of it I craved, my OCD at its most glorious in situations like this. "It means a briny ocean. You got the pronunciation right; it's just not a word you have here. We've got something like fifty words that all mean ocean."

I scribbled in the text the translation and moved onto the next. Finn was patient as we worked through several notebooks of questions I had, taking detours when we got caught up in talking about the twists of the plot. "You really think Amafura's good?" Finn asked, surprised that we had a very different take on his favorite character in the series.

"I think she's redeemable, which is very different than being good. But you already know how it ends, so don't spoil it."

Finn chuckled, his arm having drawn me into his nook

half an hour ago. He played with the tendrils at the base of my neck, giving me the shivers every now and then that I tried to suppress.

The sun started drooping, and despite only being twenty-three years old, I yawned, though it was hardly past eight o'clock. "How long do I have you for?"

"As long as you like."

I shot him a simpering look. "I mean how long until you have to go back home?"

"I have to be home before your sun comes up. The prison's starting to fill up, now that Mathias is in charge. He's cracking down where Banak turned a blind eye. I thought Mathias would be useless on the throne, just someone to pass the time, but he's not so bad. I've got to make sure there are enough guards for the east wing of the prison."

"You should go back, then. If they need you, I should say goodnight."

Finn turned sideways on the couch and moved his leg to snake behind me, patting the space between his open legs. "I told you, I've got till sunup. Let me read to you. Show me the page you're on in the last book I gave you."

I debated internally, but eventually handed him the book, judging reading together as something that wasn't too risqué. "That would be great. I'm not a fast reader in your language, so I think some of the magic's getting lost while I puzzle it all out. I plan on rereading the whole series once I've got it all translated. See what I missed while I was in work mode."

"Come here. Get comfortable." He patted the empty space between his legs on the couch once more, inviting me in – always inviting.

Again, I hesitated, but finally gave in, curling up in the space he offered. Finn's body was warm, hard and welcoming. Despite knowing I couldn't let myself be with him for real, I missed being near him. My heart ached for the closeness we could only share for this brief time when he read to me. Our days spent lounging in his house, reading and debating were precious to me. As I scooted closer and leaned my side into his chest, we both exhaled with relief at indulging in our connection. Our closeness hadn't disappeared through the distance that the world and I tried to put between us. Finn's voice was soothing as he read to September and me, encircling us with his arms as he held the book out so I could follow along if I wanted.

Mason came home, raising an eyebrow at our intimate cuddle, but saying nothing. "You can join us," I offered, hoping that by adding a third person to the mix, the growing heat between Finn and me would start to cool. Mason came down twenty minutes later as a wolf, holding a blanket in his teeth as he jumped up on the couch and curled up on my feet to warm them. He dropped the cream colored, fuzzy, soft blanket atop me, which Finn thanked him for as he spread it out over us. Mason nodded, giving me a steady pull while he vacillated between listening to the story and sleeping. Finn continued on as if nothing was different, clarifying whenever Mason gave a confused tilt to his head accompanied by a light bark.

There was something about Mason's acceptance of Finn that gave me pause and peace all at the same time.

Ezra eventually joined us, lighting a fire in the hearth and sitting in the recliner as he listened to Finn. I could tell my dad was half-chaperoning and half-enjoying the evening with us. The firelight danced off his skin and made his worry wrinkles fade away into the nothingness of a much younger man. He gave me a tired smile as his eyelids started to droop after about twenty minutes. Ezra deserved a little respite; he'd been through enough with trying to keep his daughter alive, his kingdom safe, and Ollie and me afloat. If there was one person I wished a good night's sleep for, it was Ezra.

Finn read to us all, my forehead resting to the side of his neck contentedly so I could feel his soft gills. His body wrapped around mine as he held the book with one hand and lightly stroked my belly with the other.

My breathing evened out, and despite my misgivings of how this would end badly for both of us, I let myself feel safe in Finn's arms, in his life, and in his heart, that seemed to have a steady beat for September and me.

RUBBING MASON'S BELLY

For the next three nights, that was how the evening wound to a close. Finn came to visit and read to me after dinner, with Mason or Ezra or Danny and Mariang joining us. I almost always fell asleep in Finn's arms, but on the third night, I managed to stay awake until ten. "I think we should call it a night," I suggested, motioning to my sister who was lightly snoring in Danny's arms. "Mariang's out."

When Danny roused Mariang to disappear up the steps, it left just the two of us, with no chaperone. I nervously fiddled with one of the ruffles on the V-neck collar of my stretchy blue short-sleeved shirt.

"How are you feeling?" Finn asked quietly. "Is the baby, you know, keeping you up at night?"

"Nah, the baby's good."

"Are your feet sore? I heard Mason asking you about that earlier."

"Yeah, but that's normal. I'm alright. Just the usual aches and pains they warn you about in those books Danny keeps quoting at me."

Finn moved away from me toward the other end of the couch, his hands open like he was trying to catch a football. "Give me your foot."

I looked around to make sure we were alone. "No, Finn. You know we can't do that."

"But your feet are sore. I'm supposed to be your friend, right? A friend would offer to help if you're uncomfortable."

Finn was tempting, as he always was. "That's where this always gets out of hand. I'm off the market, remember?"

"What if I promised to behave?"

"You don't have the authority to make that promise. I should turn in." I didn't mean to be so harsh, but we'd been striking a sweet note in our friendship. He was getting along with my new family, which was something he needed more of in his life. I wanted Finn to have a family who cared if he was a good man or not. He was still in the beginning phases of his conscience, and needed a guidepost to teach him all the functions a respectable moral compass should have. "I'm sorry. I'm being crabby. That's nice of you to offer to rub my feet. I just think we'll get carried away, is all. I have to be more careful with you."

"Why is that again?" Finn leaned over and lifted my legs up, stretching them out onto the couch between us. "Hasn't this been nice, me coming and reading to you and your family?"

I nodded slowly, my eyes rolling back when he ignored me completely and started massaging my left ankle with steady pressure. He tugged my stretchy black yoga capri pants up past my knee. "Yes, it's been very nice. Oh, that's good. Right there." So much for me setting clear boundaries.

Finn smiled at me with too much victory lighting his green eyes. "I've missed you, *sinta*. My house feels empty without you in it. I've been taking to sleeping either in one of the rooms of the palace, or here on your father's couch because I don't like the sight of my home without you in it."

I bit down on my lower lip when his hands migrated to my calf, massaging the meat like a professional who was going off the grid. "We can't talk about stuff like that."

Finn was quiet a few seconds, watching me barely hold myself together through the seduction of his massage. "You're letting me in more these days. Have you reconsidered turning me away?"

I shook my head defiantly, but the swoon when his thumb rubbed the muscle above my naked knee undermined my resolve. "I'm not good for anyone right now. I'm barely holding myself together these days, Finn. You should be with someone who won't drag you down into their mess. You deserve someone with their act together." My head lolled back against the arm of the couch. "Oh, right there."

"You held me together when I was a mess, and it only made us both stronger." His tone turned darker as he stared at my toes. "Beautiful." So light, I barely recognized the touch at first, Finn kissed the heel of my foot. When his lips dragged across my toes, I tried not to give in to his seduction – though we both knew I was a puddle of "I surrender" when he pulled stuff like that.

I think we both expected me to jerk away when he sucked my big toe into his mouth, but I moaned instead, throwing my head back as my body arched to get closer, to have more of what I shouldn't want. "That's the way. Oh, just like that." I grabbed the throw pillow that had fallen to the floor and smashed it over my face to muffle my gratuitous groans and to keep my mouth from leaping onto his. Finn's lips worked their way up the back of my leg, until his tongue laved in the underside of my knee. My body shuddered of its own volition, opening to his perusal. I let out a noise of pleasure that sounded like distress into the pillow.

"October, I – Ho! Sorry, guys. I heard a noise, so I... Carry on."

Mason's voice was just the thing I needed to snap me out of my bad decision. My leg fell away from Finn as he sat back, his hand rubbing over his face to collect himself.

"Mason, wait!" I called, rolling ungracefully off the

couch and fighting with the furniture to stand. My face was beet red, and I couldn't look at Finn, even when he helped Mason hoist me up off of the floor. "Finn was just leaving. Goodnight, Finn. Thanks for coming reading and over." I shook my head. "For coming over and kneading." I covered my face with my hands, frustrated and embarrassed. "I mean coming over and reading."

Mason took a cautious step back when Finn gripped my chin with his thumb and forefinger to whisper in my ear, "Remember how much your body wants me. I'll be back for more tomorrow."

"I'm going to bed!" I shouted, my volume making me flinch. I all but ran up the stairs and slammed my bedroom door shut. Clothes were ripped off me and pajamas pulled on in record time. I buried myself under the covers, closing my eyes and hoping with everything in me that I could trick Mason into thinking I was already asleep.

"You are such a faker," Mason teased, pinching my side under the covers when he slid in behind me. "Sorry I interrupted... whatever that was. I didn't realize you'd decided to let Finn in like that."

"If I started snoring, would you pretend that I'm asleep so we don't have to talk about it?"

Mason chuckled at my chagrin. He reached his long arm around me and palmed my belly, coveting the bump and the baby inside. "Not a chance. What kind of sex are the two of you having? It looked like you were ramping up for something filthy."

I let out a mini cry of shame and covered my face, as if that would keep Mason from seeing all I'd done. "It was nothing like that! It was an accident, a total mistake. I didn't mean to let that happen."

His laughter only made me feel worse. "Does that accident happen often? It didn't look like the first time he'd... Was he sucking on your knee pit? Do you like that sort of thing?"

"Shut up! Shut up! Shut up! Nothing happened. He read to us, and then he went home. Nothing else." I groaned when Mason's laughter shook the bed. "Mason, you can't leave me alone with him. I mean it. You're my Reaper, so you're not supposed to let me wander into dangerous situations. Finn is dangerous to me. I have no self-control anymore, and that's hazardous! I say no, and then somehow I've got my toes in his mouth!"

Mason's laughter came out a howl at my admission. "Oh, that's excellent. Please tell me he's got a weird toe fetish." When my answer was a guilty shade of red that went impossibly deeper, Mason rolled onto his back and clapped his hands. "You just made my night, *hani*. The great Captain Finn likes to suck on women's toes!"

"I'm going to go sleep on the couch downstairs." I made to sit up, but Mason dragged me back down so I was tucked into his nook.

"Oh, I'm only teasing. Good for you, October. Truly. It was refreshing to see you let go. It was strange – make no mistake about that – but I'm happy for you."

"Ugh. There's nothing to be happy about. It was a mistake, and if he comes back tomorrow, you can't leave me alone with him. I'm serious. I'm pretty sure you're not supposed to have one guy's bun in your oven while sticking your feet in another guy's mouth." I buried my face in his shirt. "Oh, I'm such a whore! Gross!"

Mason's chest vibrated with silent laughter. "Tell me again. You were sitting there after Danny and Mariang left, and then what? He just starts sucking on your toes?"

"No! He asked me if my feet were sore, and then started rubbing them. It all went downhill from there. I mean it, Mason. You can't leave us alone. I need a chaperone if I'm going to stay away from him."

Mason's laughter ebbed, his eyes on the ceiling. "Is there a reason you're staying away from him? I mean, you're not in love with Von anymore. It's obvious you feel something for Finn."

"Finn's conscience is new. He only just got out from under Banak's curse. He's still learning to be a good man. Plus, it feels wrong trying things out with Finn while I'm pregnant with Von's baby. Icky somehow." I shook my head as Mason sat up and tugged off his shirt. He laid back down and placed my hand atop his stomach, and I began our nightly ritual of rubbing his belly before he took his turn stroking mine. Human Mason liked a lot of the same indulgences that wolf Mason did, including tummy rubs. His stomach was hairy again after the months since Geon had ordered him shaved. My fingers fluttered over his skin, relaxing him before we went to sleep. My voice was quiet when I finally spoke. "Von slept with Katrina two months ago. I know he doesn't know the baby's his, but that one stung. I asked him to stop sleeping with my friends."

"Von's miserable. Men make all sorts of mistakes when they're unhappy."

"A mistake is wearing two different kinds of shoes. Von wants to be with Katrina." The admission cut me anew, digging past the concrete I'd walled around my heart so thoughts of Von couldn't hurt me anymore.

Mason thumbed my cheek. "Von's miserable, and that's the size of it. Mark my words. The times when you and I have fought and I had to distance myself? It was torture. You have no idea what this feels like for us, the tie we have to you. Being apart? Von's trying to fill in the hole with anything just so he can breathe."

My hand stilled low on his stomach, and I saw goose-bumps break out across his abdomen. "You're too good to me."

"Lower," he beckoned, his hips shifting on the mattress as his eyes closed and licked his lower lip. "I love when you do this."

My fingernails dipped an inch into the waistband of his shorts, and though I knew the teasing game we played was not so smart, it seemed to work for us. "You look content," I mused, gazing at his lashes and the peaceful expression that erased his worry lines.

"I am. I know you're miserable, but I love our little

pregnant life that we've got going on here. I'm holding on probably longer than I should. I know I need to leave to take my sabbatical so you can have the baby. I've actually packed a bag twice now, but I can't manage to make it out the front door."

"Am I safe? You're not going to lose control, right?"

As if on cue, Mason's stomach rumbled under my palm. "No. I'm fine. But I'll have to leave in the next week or two. Every time I think about it, I get this hollow feeling right here." He tapped his chest. "Roll over. It's my turn." I shifted onto my back so Mason could palm my stomach. "You're so worked up. I'm going to have to call Boston in tonight if we're going to get you to zero so you can work tomorrow."

"Sorry."

Mason lifted my shirt to hitch just under my breasts, as was our nightly ritual. He stroked my belly and kissed it, instructing September and me how to best make a trap to catch a zombie. He spoke so sweetly, even when he warned her where to stab them so as best to incapacitate them for burial. Mason told the weirdest bedtime stories, but I didn't mind. It was his way of passing down his wisdom to the next generation, and I adored him for it.

The only thing that gave me pause was a tiny quirk he'd started doing this week. Instead of merely kissing my belly, he flattened his tongue against the bottom of the orb, and licked up over my navel, all the way up to my raised shirt. Every now and then, he would graze the tip of his nose across my breasts, smirking at our little flirty secret before he buried his face in the valley of my breasts. Then he would migrate back down and lick my belly again, letting out quiet "mm" noises that made me feel like I was his forbidden dessert.

"You getting hungry?" I asked him, mildly nervous. If he didn't have baby eating in his genetic code, I might like the intimate, ticklish sensation, but as it was, I didn't know which way was up. My hips squirmed with hormonal confusion that felt like misplaced desire. I clenched the sheets in my fists and prayed that I didn't moan too gratuitously.

He ran his nose down over the line he'd licked. It was so very intimate. "I'm in control. You have no idea how amazing she smells. I just want to smell the baby." He licked and inhaled a dozen more times, making me twist with my traitorous hormones in the sheets, before he went back to kissing my belly and telling September more stories about Sombi.

He called in Boston twenty minutes later when his eyelids started to droop. I slept soundly with Mason spooning me and Boston resting his arm over mine in the night. Under the covers, Mason's hand snuck under my shirt during the night, so he could press his hand to my bump, coveting September as if she were his even in slumber.

I awoke to a pinch, and then something wet on the back of my neck. I shifted, and felt Mason's human teeth open against my skin, gently raking down the nape of my neck without tearing the flesh. "What the..."

I roused Boston first, who watched with growing alarm as Mason continued gnawing on my neck in his sleep. "Mason!" Boston barked. "Go sleep on the couch, mate. You're pushing your limit on how long you can be around the baby."

"No, no," I insisted, sitting up. I kissed Mason's lips that were slick with saliva. "Go back to sleep. I'll go snooze on the couch."

Mason was barely awake for any of the conversation. He shifted and dozed back to sleep.

Boston was wide awake. "Come on, sis. This isn't safe anymore. You're sleeping in my room tonight. Let's go." Boston didn't take no for an answer, but helped me roll off the bed and led me to his room, where no one tried to bite me in my sleep.

I wasn't often alone with Boston, and didn't relish the thought of sleeping with only him, but I tried to be a team player, as very soon, this would be the arrangement. I tried to fall asleep as quickly as I could next to him, my leg draped over his thigh so he could pull from me while we slept.

The leg beneath mine started quivering a few minutes after I closed my eyes, and I opened them to find tears sparkling in Boston's eyes. They ran down his face as he tried to mourn in private. I wished that I could give him the space to do exactly that, but we were stuck together now, so I tried to make the best of it and be there for him, if he'd let me. My fingers twined through his, and immediately he swiped at his tears with his free hand. "Go to sleep," he said in a husky voice that was thick with emotion.

"Okay." I wanted to help him, but other than bringing Bishop back to life, there was no helping Boston. Instead I held tight to his hand while he wept. The sound was horrible, muffled, ashamed and alone. His tears knocked a few of my own loose, when the agony he couldn't master on his own tackled him without mercy.

"Bishop, he was... Do you think he died a hero?"

"His last words were about you," I admitted, reminding him of the message Bishop had asked me to deliver to his twin brother. "Unselfish to his dying breath. Only heroes can do that."

He turned on his side to face me, clutching my hand between his. "It hurts," he whispered desperately, breaking my heart in two.

"I know, honey. I know. You have to let it hurt for a while. How about in here, we just be sad about it all for as long as we like."

Boston nodded, and this time when he sobbed quietly, there was no shame in his tears. "It hurts."

"Hold tight to my hand, Boston. I won't let go. I'm here for the worst of it. I'm not going anywhere."

"It hurts!" he cried, his streaked face pleading with me to make it all go away.

There in the dark, we wept together. There were tears for Bishop, Bev, Allie. There was a clawing ache of loneliness that surviving, while the world crumbled around you, marked a person with.

That night, shrouded by the privacy of darkness, Boston and I became friends.

13

MASON THE MATRUCULAN

Finn came back the next evening a little earlier, sitting at the table when Ezra invited him to eat dinner with us. I could barely look at him as I pushed the food around on my plate. I wasn't hungry at all after a day of reaping. I was exhausted and queasy, which didn't make me a great conversationalist at dinner.

I pulled Finn aside before dessert, lowering my voice in the hallway. "Look, I love that you're trying to get along with my family and all, but what happened last night was completely wrong. Totally my fault, and I'm sorry. I'm not available, and I got caught up in the moment."

Finn's jaw tightened. "I thought you'd say that." He sighed with practiced patience. "This whole having a conscience thing is terrible. All I want is to carry you up to your bedroom, throw you down on the mattress and suck on your ankle until you admit that you want me with you.

Then I'd strip your clothes off and make love to you, which is what I should've done when we were living together."

I swallowed hard. "That wouldn't fall into the realm of friendly behavior. We're friends, Finn. So anything that you'd do with Mason, you can do with me." I pressed my fingers to my forehead to rub the tension away. "I've got to warn you, friend to friend, Mason's toes are very hairy, so I'd think twice before putting his foot in your mouth."

Finn's eyes hardened as he ran through his lengthy mental list and crossed off offending items. "I wanted to stay tonight and read to you."

"Reading is fine. In a group setting. With witnesses and socks and shoes on." My cheeks pinkened.

The corner of Finn's mouth tugged upward. "If you say so. You're the one who's barefoot now." He let out another labored sigh. "But I can keep myself honest, if it means I get to keep you in my life."

"Really?"

"Really. I'll have however much of yourself you'd like to give to me."

I blinked twice, touched that his love was about more than the physical connection we couldn't seem to sever. "Wow, Finn. Thank you. You're a good man." I shifted my cheery yellow stretchy maternity shirt, wishing it was a little less form-fitting so I didn't feel so very exposed. Mariang had sworn I didn't look like a giant bumble bee, but I'd still switched my black yoga capris for dark gray ones, just in case. As Finn stood before me, looking too tempting and too available, I knew I should've opted for a ski jacket and clown pants.

I was tentative around him during dessert, extra polite and avoided too much eye contact. I finally started to loosen up in the living room when Finn opened the book to start our nightly ritual. Mason stayed true to my request that he not leave me alone with Finn. He was in his wolf form, warming my feet while Finn read so that no one would suck on my toes. Ezra was my other buffer, sitting in the recliner to keep us company.

Finn finished three chapters, and then closed the book, resting it on the coffee table. I was too tired to go up the stairs, so I drifted off to sleep on the couch in Finn's arms with Mason warming my toes, guarding them so they didn't end up in Finn's mouth again.

I expected to wake to Finn jostling me gently before he left for work. The jaws that clamped onto my calf woke me with a jolt and a scream I wasn't awake enough to temper. Finn jerked awake, sitting us both up as he assessed the source of the danger. Mason's fangs were latched onto my left leg, digging deeper as I screamed. He growled with a feral snarl that started deep in his belly.

"Mason! Let go!" Ezra was upright, clearing the distance between the recliner he'd fallen asleep in and the couch. "Danny! Boston!" he shouted through the mansion, his voice carrying up the stairs.

"Mason, stop! It's me!" I screamed as the teeth dug deeper. "You're hurting me! You don't want to hurt me!"

I clawed at the couch as Finn slid out from under me. He grabbed my wolf by the snout, prying Mason's jaw open without caring that his own fingers were getting sliced. Mason wriggled his head free and lunged at my belly, jaws snapping. "Get her out of here!" Finn ordered, a determined snarl in place. "Ow! Damn Matruculan!"

Ezra helped me up and ran me to the hallway bathroom, shutting me inside. "Lock the door. Mason's not in control of himself anymore."

"Don't hurt him!" I cried, hobbling to the toilet and closing the lid so I could get a good look at my calf. Mason hadn't done a ton of ripping back and forth, but the bite had gone deep. Blood was cascading down my leg and pooling onto the hardwood floor. My lower lip started trembling as the air hit the angry bite marks. Immediately I did my best to compartmentalize the pain so I didn't lose it altogether. I bit down on my lower lip and set to cleaning out the wound, which was impossible to do properly without some kind of antiseptic.

Mason hadn't recognized me. He attacked, and even when I screamed, he didn't know who I was. I guess I'd romanticized that there would be logic left in him even as his desire to eat September grew stronger. He talked to her every night, spooning me while he stroked my belly protectively. He promised my daughter things as if she belonged in part to him. He even referred to himself as Uncle Mason when he spoke to her. Mason loved us.

And now Mason wanted to eat my baby. Ain't no shrink qualified to guide me through that bucket of nonsense.

Danny banged on the bathroom door. "Let me in!" When I unlocked it, Danny nearly crashed through to the opposite wall. "Get up. You're leaving now. We've got him contained to the basement, but the second he gets it in his head to turn back into himself, he'll be at top strength and there'll be no stopping him. Get in the SUV."

"Get Mariang! He might smell her baby and go after her instead!" I was scared of the damage Mason could do at full strength.

Danny's eyes widened when it dawned on him that there were two babies ripe for eating. "Oh, shite! Get in the car!"

I grabbed the hand towel off the rack and limped as fast as I could to the driveway. I was barefoot and cold as the light dusting of snow that had been accumulating after the sun went down iced my toes.

"October? October!"

The voice that reached me cut worse than the teeth marks and stiffened me more than the snow on my bare feet. I turned as if in slow motion and saw none other than Von tearing up the driveway toward me at full speed.

I reared back in shock, my butt bumping against the side of the SUV. My mouth fell open at the sight that had once been beautiful, but now was only painful. The man with messy black hair, lips meant for kissing, a tall, lean and muscular body, but totally devoid of the smirk I adored stood before me, taking my breath away and shocking me even more than an attack from Mason.

He reached for me, but then inhaled sharply the scent of my blood. He looked down at my leg in alarm and recoiled.

"No!" I cried, cocking my fist and taking a wide swing. I didn't want to make contact, only to show him I was ready to defend myself if it came to it. "Back up! You can't have my blood! It's mine!"

"I'm completely under control. I don't care about your blood; I care that you're bleeding." He gripped my shoulders, looking down at my belly in fear and wonder.

I recoiled from his touch, pushing him back and putting up my fists in preparation to fight my ex-vampire if he attacked. "Don't bite me. Don't even think about it. Dad!" I shouted, hoping anyone heard me.

Von voluntarily took a step back, his arms raised. "I'm not thirsty at all. I promise you, I'm safe. Why are you bleeding? And you're barefoot and pregnant! Get back inside!"

"Mason bit me!" I wailed, shivering. I was wracked with pain from the freezing snow on my feet and the bite that was still oozing on my leg. "I have to get out before he hulks out and tries to eat the baby!"

Von's eyes widened, flinching at my shriek when he lunged forward. I didn't realize he was just opening the car door to usher me inside. "Get in and warm up. I'll see if I can lend a hand with Mason." He ran into the house before I could respond, though what I might've said, I couldn't tell you. I was reeling, shocked that Von was here, and that my Mason wasn't.

I shoved myself to the backseat of Ezra's SUV, knowing Danny would never let me drive, bloody as I was. Plus, I didn't have the keys anyway. I buckled up, shivering in the freezing temperature that the last days of winter just refused to give up on. I wrapped the towel around my calf, scared that at any moment, Mason could come out as his human self and rip the car door off its hinges. I held my belly, singing softly through my panic to September, assuring her that Mason still loved us, and that I'd keep her safe.

14

VON, IN THE FLESH

Von was back, in the flesh. For what purpose, I couldn't begin to imagine.

One by one, everyone came running out of the mansion, piling into the car in various stages of shivering and disarray. Ezra had his arm around Mariang, who was wild-eyed in her pajamas, hair in a messy bun, but luckily unhurt. Still I clutched her to me protectively while she cried out her fear at being awoken for such a terrible reason. Danny flew us out of the driveway once Boston clumsily shut the door. I didn't know where we were going, but I knew we couldn't stay and wait to see if Mason could calm himself down.

When Von tried to sit in the empty spot next to me in back, Finn barked, "No! You're up front. She's bleeding, and you're a whore for blood."

Von snarled as Finn slid in next to me. "I'm in control!"

"I've been reinforcing the charms around the house while you were off doing who knows what. I've done everything I could to protect her from you. You'll do as I say, *kendi*. Stay up front with Ezra."

Von obeyed, angrier than ever. "Oh, I could've bet it was you who reinforced the charms. You made it so I couldn't find the house! I'd get close, and the address would slip out of my head. I'd try to call Ezra, and the number would be gone. I've been trying to get back for a month now, but I couldn't because of you!"

My mouth fell open as I blinked up at Finn for confirmation.

Finn was unperturbed at the accusation. "The charm didn't work on people who were in the mansion at the time I put up that particular protection, or on members of the council. Had you been around instead of running out on your responsibility, you wouldn't have needed to fight through the charm at all. How'd you even get through it?"

"I'm brilliant, that's how. I'm brilliant, and you're getting old. I've been working nonstop to try and break through. Then I do, and this is what's happening? This is how you protect her?"

"My job isn't to protect her; that's your job as her Duwende. I'm looking out for October because I love her."

"I will end you if you say another word like that about her! She doesn't belong to you!"

"Shut up, both of you!" I shouted, holding my hands up

to stop the stupid fighting. The car jerked, and Finn's arm settled around my shoulders to anchor me.

Ezra's tone was clipped. "We knew this was inevitable. Mason was doing so well. I thought we had another week or two with him."

"We're just leaving Mason in the house by himself?" I asked, watching Ezra take his cable knit sweater off and hand it to Lynna, so she could tug it over her white hair. Even in a crisis, Ezra was a gentleman. Gotta love him.

"I put a twenty-four-hour charm on the house to seal it. Mason can do all he likes, but the worst he'll do is upset the house. I don't care about that. We're all out. That's what matters." Ezra was buckled with Lynna in the middle row of seats, moving his feet so Von had a little more room on the floor where he sat, fuming. "Drive to the nearest hotel, Danny. Does anyone have a phone? We have to make sure Ollie stays away."

Boston belched loudly, his weighted hand landing on Von's shoulder from his place in the front passenger's seat. "Good night for you to come back, mate."

"Get off me," Von sneered at his brother. "You're drunk on the job? You're supposed to be watching her for me."

Finn's arm was around my back while his other hand clutched at his long, crooked knife. "How's the baby?"

I cupped my hand to where September's head was, doing my best to calm down. "Okay, I think. Mason only bit my leg a little. It's fine. No big deal." I was scared and in pain, but we would live. I wouldn't make a big fuss about it, so help me. I didn't want Mason to feel the guilt of this misstep.

"I'll patch it up once we get to the hotel. Can you hold on till then, *sinta*?"

"Call her that again, and I'll kill you where you sit!" Von shouted back at Finn.

"Would you two shut up? Finn, you don't get to call me anything that I don't know what it means anymore. And Von? You don't get to care about who calls me that. Both of you need to chill out. There are bigger things going on right now. Ezra? How're you holding up?"

"I'm fine, sweetheart. Mason didn't bite me at all."

"No, I mean are you jonesing to eat my baby right now?"

Ezra exhaled, hanging his head. "I'll get something to eat once we're settled. I feel the pull, but it's nothing I didn't master when Mariang's mother was pregnant. I'm much older than Mason, so I control my urges better. You've nothing to fear with me around."

"Okay. Sorry if that was rude to ask. I just have to be sure."

"No apologies needed. Your daughter's safety comes first. You've got good mothering instincts."

Von perked up. "You're having a girl?" His eyes fell on Finn's arm around me, and the flicker of tenderness dissolved into a sneer. "Congratulations. Though I do hope she won't get her father's fetching gills."

Finn scoffed as Danny reached down between his seat

and Boston's and whapped Von upside the head. "Finn's not the father, you wanker."

I put my hand on Finn's knee to steady his temper. "Finn's not the father. You don't know who the father is. He's a friend of a friend I met up with one night. Casual one-time thing. I didn't know how to tell you."

Von looked over the middle seat at me and mimed stabbing himself through the heart. "You cut me, Peach. You cheated on me. If I had to put my money on who'd be the one to step out of line, I never in a million years thought it'd be you."

Danny glared at me in the rearview mirror while Mariang squeezed my hand. I held my chin up, flipping Danny the finger. I hoped September wasn't listening in. "Yup. I'm a big, giant slut. Boston can pull for me, and when Mason gets ahold of himself a month or two after the baby's born, he can reap with me. You can go back to doing whatever you were doing before this. We'll drop you wherever you like. You're off the hook."

Von turned and glared at me, speaking through gritted teeth. "I came back for you, no matter what or who you did."

I had an angry retort all ready for when he told me off, but when his reply came back loyal, I deflated, not knowing what to make of it.

Boston let out a snort of derision through his buzz from too many nightcaps, his chuckle interrupted by a hiccup. "You two are terrible at this."

No one spoke as Danny drove us to the nearest hotel, passing up on two gross looking motels, thank goodness. Ezra checked us into adjoining two-room suites, shaking Finn's hand in silent warning. "Thank you for your help, Captain, but it's time our family had a few hours to sort things out, yeah?"

"Yes, your majesty." Finn was rigid as he waved goodbye to the others, but soft when he said goodnight to me, though there was only an hour or two left until dawn. There was a hardness in his eyes, but his words were gentle. "Be safe. I'll come back in a week to check on you two." His finger traced the outline of my belly, as if silently promising September he'd be back for her, as well. Then he pulled me into his arms, holding me for a moment before we parted to brave our separate storms.

"Thank you for helping with Mason. Go on home; your country needs you."

He snapped his fingers at Danny. "You. Her leg's still bleeding. See that it's wrapped up before the vamp destroys an Omen."

Danny nodded with a scowl. I knew he hated anyone telling him how to do his job, with the exception of Ezra. Danny shoved Boston into the suite on the right and corralled Mariang, Lynna and Ezra to the room on the left. He turned to me with a business expression. "Go into the room and wash your leg off. I'll get a first aid kit from the front desk and be right up." He jabbed his finger at Von. "Stay in the hallway until I get back. Her blood's still too fresh. And if you so much as step a toe outside of this hotel, it'll be the last thing you do. You're done running out on your life."

When Danny skulked off, Von jabbed his thumb over his shoulder. "He's gotten cheerier since I left, yeah?"

15

DANNY'S INTERVENTION

Danny broke his eyes from dressing my wound in the cramped beige bathroom to glare at me every so often. "You should've told him."

"I don't see why. If he's going to run, might as well be now. I don't want him to stay out of obligation."

"Would you wake up? You *are* his obligation, even before the baby came around. He's your Reaper. He's bound to you for life. So is Mason. Baby or not, he ditched his responsibilities."

"A baby won't fix that. Von is who he is; you've been telling me that from the beginning. Now that I'm listening to you, you want me to let him in and cut him some slack? *Now* who's the one with mood swings?"

"Yes, well," Danny grumbled, pulling the bandage a hair too snug around my leg, "you should still tell him."

"I'm sorry, Danny, but that's just too tight."

Danny harrumphed like I'd told him he was an idiot or something. He fiddled with the bandage so it was on correctly, and stood, helping me up off the toilet lid. "Von's better than no one. Not by much, but still."

"Go worry about your own fetus. When you pretend to care about what happens to me, you come off sounding like a jerk. Practice growing a heart elsewhere. I'm not interested in investing time in your learning curve."

Danny stomped off, glaring at me. He flung open the door and looked down the empty hallway. "Well, it's a moot point anyways, because your prince charming split already." His shoulders relaxed. "Oh, there he is."

Von's voice forced lightness, but I could hear the strain. "Miss me already? I can't say I blame you. How you all got along without me to brighten the mood around here is beyond me."

"We managed." Danny shoved his brother into the suite with me and Boston, and left us with a bang of the door. Boston was snoring in the queen-sized bed atop the thin burgundy comforter, shirt twisted around his torso. He had his hand over his belly, and his lips were parted as he slept off too much vodka and far too much grief.

Von and I just stood, blinking at each other in the dim lamplight. To break the building tension, I reached for the phone, calling down to the front desk for a cot.

"You're pregnant. You're not sleeping on a cot," Von said, his insistence gentle, but firm.

"I know I'm not. You are." I focused on Boston, who

was in the dead center of the bed. I scooted him gently over to the side so I had a place to sleep, not that I'd be able to calm down now.

"I'm not tired. I want to talk."

"There's no need. I got pregnant, and you split. Anything else to add?" The whole lie of me cheating on him and sleeping with some random guy made me feel even more alone than usual, but I was firm that Von didn't need to know what he didn't want to know. If he wanted to be a dad, he'd have to be around first. Once he managed that, then I had options.

No, this was not covered in any of the baby books. I was winging it, for better or worse. I'm pretty sure Mrs. Brady had never been in this situation before, so I had no role model to pull from who'd been psychically knocked up and abandoned.

Von's red garage rock band t-shirt was thin and stretched across his torso, giving me a hint at the musculature beneath. It would be a lot easier to keep him out of my head if he didn't look like that.

Von sighed, shoving his hands into the pockets of his jeans. "No. That's about the size of it. You want to tell me who he was? Who was so great you threw us away for?"

"There was no 'us'. You were clear that you didn't want anything serious. There was no one to cheat on, because as you made it abundantly clear, you were never my boyfriend." I stopped myself and held up my hands. "I'm not doing this. I've got enough on my plate. You want out? You already know how to make good use of the door."

"You're not even giving me a name?"

"What for?"

Von's hands flew out animatedly. "He should be here! It's his baby you're carrying. I'd want to know if it was my child."

"You would?"

Von blew a loud raspberry, and I could tell he was nervous. "I didn't even really know Angela, but the day I found out I was going to be a father was the happiest day of my life. Even though it was all a lie, and Penny was never mine, it was the best lie that ever happened to me." He stared at his sleeping brother, taking a beat to collect himself. "Penny's the best thing that ever happened to me, apart from becoming your Reaper."

"Weren't you scared?"

"Of course I was scared. I didn't even know if I could be around her. What if she skinned her knee and I lost my head? But I've learned how to be there for them as best I can."

"What about my girl? I mean, you're stuck with me. Should I be worried about you losing control around her?" I hugged my belly with one hand, drawing Von's eyes.

"Not in the slightest." Von sat down on the chair by the mahogany desk in the corner of the room, facing me with his elbows resting on his knees. "Let me get a few things off my chest, yeah? Let's get it all out so we can move on. Can you handle that?"

Not really. "Hit me." I sat on the edge of the bed carefully, my back stiff and my leg so sore, I had to limp on my way to the mattress.

"What you did? Sleeping with some random bloke? It broke me, Peach. I loved you, and that's not something I do on a dime. You were my best friend, and you knew how hard it was for me to stay in one place."

"Stay in one place? You were never in one place. After we had the best kiss of like, all my lives, you said you still weren't ready to settle down. If you wanted to lock this down, you should've. I would've stayed with only you if you wanted me, but you wanted one foot out the door, so I let you go, because that's what you asked me to do."

Von narrowed his eyes at me, frustrated but determined to keep his cool. "I was getting used to the idea of being exclusive, and you cheated on me. That's low. I asked you for time, and you gave me all of five minutes. And Finn? Of all people for you to cozy up with, that one hurts the worst. You know what a dirty tosser he is."

I swallowed, knowing he was right on that last point. "First off, I'm allowed to be friends with people, especially the ones who need a little help. Finn was lost, and you're right, he was a bad guy. But he's grown since you knew him. He's a different guy off of Banak's curse."

Von rolled his eyes. "Please, spare me the details of your love for him."

"Finn disbanded the harem and helped take down Banak. He saved my life a few times. Last month he kicked out the head of the Kataw Academy who was beating children and replaced him with someone better." I motioned to September. "And even though he knows who the father of my baby is and hates his guts, he still stuck around for me. I've been sending him away for months, but he still comes back. *That's* love. What you did? Something's off with our kiss-o-meter, because I'm pretty sure you never loved me." The words were harsh, but since we were being honest, I threw away any semblance of peace to get to the guts of it all.

Von's eyes were practically slits. "If Finn's so grand, then why aren't you with him?"

"Because he's in love with me, and I don't feel the same way. I like him, but a crush isn't enough. I've got too many problems without adding more relationship drama to my life. I can't afford to bring someone into my daughter's world who I know I can't make it work with."

"Don't you get that I wanted to be that guy? The bloke you're in love with? Now I can't even find you in my dreams!"

"How long was I supposed to wait and pine? For September to grow up and graduate college? Then you'd for sure come home to me after sleeping your way through my phone book?"

"September?" His nose crinkled. "Is that the baby's name?" He softened, his shoulders lowering as the name cradled on his sculpted lips. "September. That's really perfect. Because September comes before October. You're putting her first. It's brilliant."

My mouth fell open in surprise, my heart pinging unexpectedly. "I can't believe you guessed that. Even Ollie just thinks it's cute because it's the name of a month."

"Yeah? Well, I know you."

I swallowed the lump in my throat, my voice quieting. "I didn't know that you'd ever come home, Von. I tried to reach you in our dreams for the longest time, but you kept me away."

"That's not fair. You hurt me. I've got every right not to be with you when you step out on me."

I took a steadying breath. "Then why are you here?"

"Because after everything you did, I still love you!" He stood and started pacing, worrying his messy tresses and making them stand on end even more. "I wanted to make a clean break, to leave and never come back, but the thought of you raising this baby on your own? It broke me all over again. I knew I needed to find a way to come home, even if it was painful. So I found a new blood supplier who can guarantee I never run low. I quit smoking. I did everything I could to clean myself up so I could come back and help you raise this baby that's not even mine! That's how much I love you!"

My mouth dropped open. "You quit smoking?"

"That's all you got out of what I just said?"

"But you love your cigars."

"No, Peach. I love *you*."

A fist pounded on the door to the adjoining suite, and Von moved to open it. Danny stormed in, his monster of Frankenstein eyebrows pushed together and fists clenched. "I can't take it anymore! We can hear everything through these paper-thin walls. She made it all up to keep you from feeling trapped. There's no other bloke, Von. Not even Finn, though he's tried everything. You're the father."

I groaned. "Shut up, Danny! This isn't your call."

Danny ignored me. "When you had sex with October in your vision, it knocked her up in reality. I don't know how it works, but Mariang and I have flukes like that, too. Not as big as this one, but I fell once in our dream, and woke up with a scraped knee that matched the injury in my dream." Danny grew frustrated trying to explain it all and threw out his hands. "Point is, you're the father. Not some random bloke. She's not telling you because she doesn't want you to stay only for the baby. She doesn't want to trap you. Plus, she's afraid you'll freak out and split again, so man up, quit mucking about, and stop being a child about it!" Then he turned to me, and I couldn't tell which of us was angrier with our matching sneers. "And you, Von left. Get over it! He thought you cheated on him with his worst enemy. He came back to help you raise what he thought was Finn's baby! That says more than him checking out and leaving over something that makes no sense to any of us. You can't nail him to the wall for this."

"You suck, Danny!" I shouted.

"Yeah? Well, get over it. We're trying to sleep over here. You don't want to know me when I'm sleep-deprived."

"Really? I don't want to know you *then*? Is it because you become even more of a pain in the butt than you are right now?"

Danny turned to his brother. "You're welcome. Don't say I never did anything for you." Then he left, slamming the door behind him.

Von was thunderstruck, mouth agape and eyes like saucers, staring at me from his corner of the room. Neither of us spoke as we balked at each other for several long seconds in which I very much wanted to run away from him. When it looked like Von was about to break the silence, I scooted to the right, aiming for the door. "I think I forgot something in the car."

"Oh, no you don't! Get back here and settle this, you big chicken."

"I really need to go!"

"With no shoes? In winter? It's snowing out!"

"I'll run."

"Pregnant women don't run."

"Yes, we do! How would you even know what pregnant women do? Watch me! I'm pretty fast."

Von clutched my shoulders, anger and wonder clashing on his handsome features, making him look unbalanced. "Is it true? Is all that true?"

Danny, Ezra, Lynna and Mariang shouted from the other room, "Yes!" and I cringed. Mariang's voice sounded like she was bumped up against the wall, her ear pressed to the drywall to take in every syllable.

I nodded, unable to look at him for fear of spontaneously combusting and leaving in my place a pathetic pile of ashes for Von to reason with. "I tried to tell you, but you were gone. And then you stayed away, even in our dreams. I didn't want you to be with us because you felt some sort of obligation. I wanted you to be with me because you wanted me, and now it's ruined!"

Von fell back, grasping at his chest as if his heart was in danger of failure over the too much that crashed around him like so many unruly waves. "I'm going to be a father? You're... My peach is having my baby?"

I choked out the truth, unsure of all my reasons for keeping him away, now that I could see his sincerity. He fell to his knees before me, ripped my stretchy yellow shirt upward to expose my belly and pressed his cheek to the skin, giving me the shivers and forcing tears out of me as he hugged my hips. He rubbed his nose across my navel, peppering tiny kisses across the equator of my stomach. "Baby," he crooned, attaching to the idea far easier than I'd anticipated.

It was at that exact moment I felt September's very first kick. It was square where Von's face was, making me jump. Von fell backward in shock. "Whoa!" I gasped. My hand felt around to replace Von's face in case she decided to go at it again. "That was her first kick!"

"That was incredible! September?" Von was on his

knees again, face pressed to my belly, laughing when she kicked again and again, as if trying to get at him. I let out a muffled laugh into my palm. Von held my hips tighter to keep me from bolting. "It's like she knows it's her daddy. I'm here, baby. I'm here and I'm not going anywhere. I didn't know it was you, or I would've been here the whole time." She kicked him again, and I was afraid if the two of them kept this up, I'd be an idiot and make an emotional decision. "How pregnant are you? How many weeks? Twenty-eight? Twenty-nine? I've been trying to keep track, but now my math's all off. Man, my sperm is amazing. I got you pregnant with my mind!"

"Twenty-eight." I covered my face to keep from seeing the sight I didn't think I'd ever get the chance to indulge in. Von was clinging to my baby, trying to get as close as he could to the both of us. "You can be as involved as you want, but you don't have to. Ollie and I have a plan, so I'm not up a creek or anything if you decide this isn't for you."

"It's for me," Von growled, his lips stilling on my stomach. "It's all for me. I'm in. You should never have kept this from me."

"I called you. I tried to tell you, but you were gone."

"Today. With your daft story. All I kept thinking was you slumming it with some lowlife at a truck stop named Bubba or something. I didn't get the chance with Penny. I wasn't as good at controlling myself when she was born as I am now, and then when the paternity test said she wasn't even mine? It killed me." He kissed my stomach, jerking my heart around like it was his plaything. "I want in on all of it. Doctors, backaches, Lamaze classes, everything."

"You're sure? I'm really not trying to trap you. I didn't even know this was possible!"

"Of course you didn't. The whole thing is beyond anything any of us could've guessed." His eyes widened as he stood. "You're still a virgin, then?"

I glowered up at him. "Why does everyone keep fixating on that? No, I've never had real life sex. We even had that little fact confirmed by the doctor. I've been a little too busy growing a human to worry about who I'm going out with on Friday night. I called Truck Stop Bubba, but he didn't seem up for a piece of this hot mama action." I motioned to my ballooned form.

Von leaned in and fingered the edge of my face. "Me. You're going out with me Friday night. Every Friday night. I should've listened to you when you told me you hadn't had sex with anyone. You must've been so confused. So scared."

I bit my lower lip, nodding slowly. He traced the slope of my cheeks as if I was precious to him. As if nothing had changed in the months we'd been apart.

But it had. *I* had. I closed my eyes. "You left me. You left me to raise a baby and bury my mama."

"I was confused, too. And I didn't hear about your mum until I saw her obituary in the papers."

"You should've fought harder for me – for us. You got scared and you ran. I don't need that kinda guy in my life. Parenting is scary, and I seriously can't gamble on you anymore."

Von pursed his lips, chewing on his words before they came out. "You're right. I shouldn't have run. And I shouldn't have been so hung up on keeping labels off our relationship. I was yours from the start. I don't know why I tried so hard to resist it. I got used to the idea that I was temporary after I was bitten. I was convinced that I couldn't keep you, or I might accidentally drain you, and kill the woman I love. Can't you understand that I pushed you away because I was in love with you, and was scared I might be the monster who ended you? Do you know any other half-vampires who grow to be husbands? Most don't make it a week before they turn."

My mouth fell open at the depths of agony Von had to go through just to be in a relationship. I probably knew it all before, but to have it all put so plainly shed new light on my anger, lessening my pain by necessary degrees. I massaged my temples as I factored this in to the constantly shifting puzzle that was Von and me. "You took on this job – a permanent job – knowing that same logic. Why did you take up the position of being my Reaper in the first place, if you were so scared of the permanence?"

Von's eyes shone with sadness and longing. "Because I couldn't not be near you. Even back then, the first day I met you, I knew that no matter how painful it was, and how much I might have to fight everything wretched inside of me, I had to be the one who made you laugh. I knew any number of Duwendes could do the job, but you were still so innocent, even after being completely beaten over the head by life. I don't know how you managed that, but I knew that no matter how hard it might be to put myself by your side for the rest of my life, being away from you would be impossible."

I shook my head, angry that I felt parts of me caving and leaning closer to him. "No! You don't get to come in here, shrug off all you put me through, and expect me to come back, like some lovesick teenager. You left me dangling, and I'm not interested in a lifetime of that."

"But I'm here now, and I'm fighting for us."

I tried to keep the hurt out of my voice, but when I opened my mouth, my words dripped with pain that I couldn't reconcile. "You slept with Katrina after I asked you to stop sleeping with my friends. You said you would stop sleeping with my friends! You made me a joke, Von." I closed my eyes, voicing the hurt I still hadn't made peace with. "Judge said I'd disappointed him. Do you know what that feels like?"

Von nodded, no hint of a fight on his sincere features. "It was one regrettable night with Katrina. I was drunk and lonely. I called her November smack in the middle of the sheets. I couldn't even finish." He ran his finger over my cheekbone. "It's you. It's always been you."

I closed my eyes to fend off the pain of his earnestness. "It's too late."

He pressed my back to the wall, bringing my face to his so our cheeks were touching. He whispered with a fierce anger in my ear, "Then I guess I'll just have to keep fighting for us."

JUST LIKE THAT

I slept next to Boston, and by "slept" I mean I closed my eyes and touched my toes to Boston's leg so he could pull in his sleep, while Von fidgeted on the squeaky cot. It took me until the sun rose to actually drift off.

Philip came to me in my dream, though I almost wished he hadn't. He brought that same shriveled weed for me to eat, acting like it was some grand present I had yet to understand the significance of. I ate it to be polite while we sat at a table at a café in Paris, staring at the beauty of a bridge I'd researched once upon a time when I'd thought about things like vacations and fun. It was an old structure made of stone, surrounded by sporadic bursts of nature. Philip and I sipped tea and watched the ducks swim in the river while we caught up. "How's work?" I asked nonchalantly. Philip was a manager, and we sometimes chatted about his job.

He touched his pressed collar and sat back in his chair with his ankle crossed over his knee, the slight breeze ruffling his white-blond hair. "Better than usual. Got a few new employees that are looking promising. The training's taking a little longer than I would like, but it is what it is."

"Anything I can help with?"

Philip turned his head to look at me with a mixture of satisfaction and supreme accomplishment. "Just keep our baby safe. That's what you can do for me."

"On it, chief." In my dream, the baby was Philip's. He had no problem owning up to it, and claimed both September and me easily. As the days progressed, he grew more and more protective of us, which I guess was what my subconscious craved.

"Are you still at Ezra's?"

I sipped my tea, which tasted like honey and lavender. "Nope. Had a bit of a run-in with one of my favorite Matruculans."

Philip froze, his teacup midway to his mouth. "The baby, is she safe?"

I nodded. "Of course. We got out before anything too terrible happened. But we're staying in a hotel until Mason calms down enough to go back to Terraway. It was the plan all along. He thought he'd last a little longer, but it's time. It's no big deal. I'm fine." I didn't mention my leg. I didn't want to talk about that. I cleared my throat. "Von's back."

Philip gripped his teacup harder than the delicate vessel was meant to be held. "It's not his baby, October. She's mine. No matter what you think, she's mine. You and September are both mine."

I chuckled at his sudden upset. "Oh sweetie, most days *I'm* barely mine. Can't exactly give myself away if I don't have me. But no, Von and I aren't getting back together. It's me and September, and that's the tune of that sad song."

He set his cup down and reached his hand out to lace his fingers through mine. I was so normal in my dreams – I didn't even itch to wash my hands. "I want you to deliver the stone next, not Ollie."

"Ollie finished up with Hayop not too long ago. We've got only Sombi left. You know I can't exactly go into a land full of zombies in my condition. Plus, I'm doing well. I haven't been scratching my hands up so much. Aside from the crippling depression, I'm much better off, now that I don't have the stone near me."

"Where's the stone now?"

I shrugged. "Ezra won't tell me. He put it somewhere only he knows so no one can torture Ollie or me for information."

Philip's shoulders deflated. "I guess that makes sense. Ezra thinks of everything."

"That's the thing about dads, I hear."

We watched the ducks while holding hands for a while, leaning into each other and enjoying the boring couple stuff I didn't get much of. Everything was always so harrowing. Philip sat where I put him and was the comfort I needed to get through the night.

In the morning, I laid in bed until I could no longer pretend to be asleep anymore. Boston was in the shower, and Von sat next to where I lay. "What do you want for breakfast?" Von asked, kissing my cheek to rouse me.

"I usually don't eat until like, ten o'clock. My stomach's too uneasy before then."

"Did you have much morning sickness?"

I nodded. "Buckets of it. I haven't puked in a few weeks, though. Just general queasiness."

"How do you do it? You say vile words like 'puke', but I only want you more."

"It's a gift. Wait till I start throwing around words like 'placenta' and 'mucus plug'. I'm absolutely ravishing."

"I have no doubt." His hand draped over my hip and squeezed. "I was thinking next weekend for the wedding."

My nose scrunched. "You know about Danny and Mariang? Their official wedding's not until after the baby comes. Mariang wanted a flower girl." I frowned, wondering if her own pregnancy might move things up.

Von gaped at me. "Boy, did I sure miss a lot. I didn't know they were engaged. She finally caved, did she?"

"Yeah. They're technically married, actually. Went to Justice of the Peace not too long ago. They're keeping it secret, though, so Terraway can have their big to-do to celebrate."

Von guffawed. "Are you having a laugh? They got married, and I missed it?"

"When it dawned on them that Mariang wasn't going to die anytime soon after the healing waters did their magic on her, Danny didn't waste a minute. Like, literally not a minute after he put it all together. It was sweet. Got down on one knee and everything."

Von smiled, the edges of his eyes crinkling in that way I always found cute. "Good for him. She could do better, though."

"I think I said something similar in my congratulations toast."

"I wasn't talking about them, though. I was talking about us getting hitched next weekend." He pulled a cinnamon stick from off the nightstand and started chewing on the end of it.

"Hitched to what?"

"Married," he said slowly, as if I was stupid.

My mouth fell open in shock as I sat up. "Are you high? We're not getting married. We're not even dating!"

"Yet," Von countered, unperturbed. "We're not dating *yet*. It's inevitable, don't you think? We're already head over heels for each other. We were together before our little strawberry came along. It just makes sense."

I tried not to soften when he referred to our daughter as a strawberry.

Our daughter.

I straightened, my chin in the air as I fought for

composure. "Hello, you couldn't even call me your girl-friend before. Try choking on the word 'wife'. We're not getting married."

"That was the idiot version of Von. I'm going to have a baby with you soon, so I'm all grown up now."

"Just like that?"

"Just like that."

"That's a pretty impressive growth spurt. Forgive me for not trusting it."

"Forgiven. Now when are we going on a date? I assume you'll want your shoes for that?"

"We're not dating. I'm not dating anyone. Not you, not Finn, not Truck Stop Bubba. I'm a mama only right now. That's enough to take up all my Friday nights."

"What about this Friday night?"

My head swiveled with too much attitude. "All the Friday nights until the end of time are booked. You had over a year to ask me out for any of those Fridays, and you couldn't be bothered."

"Playing stubborn, are we? Very well. I can wait it out while you pretend you're still furious, as if you have a leg to stand on."

I guffawed, leaning against the headboard to gape at him. "You're saying I shouldn't be mad that I told you I didn't cheat on you, and you left anyways?"

"Think it through," he began, chewing on the stick as he held it like a cigar. "Do you know of any other virgin pregnancies? I mean, I assume it's not a deity growing in your womb. I had very reasonable doubt. Add to that you kissing Finn, of all people."

I didn't have a solid enough argument, so I changed the subject. "Why are you chewing on that?"

Von pulled it out to show it to me. "Cinnamon stick. Almost as good as the real thing."

I rolled my eyes. "You can go outside and smoke. I'm not stopping you."

"I told you, I gave it up. Even if you were carrying Bubba's baby, I was working my way up to coming back, but I knew I couldn't if I didn't get myself together first. So I quit smoking and found a more reliable blood provider."

"Just like that?"

"Just like that."

"You're a dork if you think that's all it takes."

"Oh, you love it." He took the stick out of his mouth and held it out to me, as if to offer me a smoke. "Try it. It's not bad."

"No, thanks. I'm trying to quit. I try not to put things that have been in other guys' mouths into mine."

"I hardly think that matters when it's me. You've sucked on my tongue on more than one occasion."

"Gross! Don't say it like that."

"Like what? Like I didn't make you melt for me? Like we didn't make that baby in our minds over and over again? It's only a matter of time. Though, you're right. Next weekend might be problematic for a wedding, especially if we want Mason there."

"Oh, you're hopeless."

"Actually, I'm hope*ful*. Quite the distinction."

Despite my aversion to him sliding back into my life too seamlessly, I gave in to a small smile. "I missed this. Us. The back and forth. You were my favorite friend before it got all tangled."

Von put his stick on the nightstand, got comfortable in the bed and sunk down next to me, inviting me into the haven. He slid under the covers and pulled the comforter up over our heads, like we were children hiding in a fort. "Don't you know? Untangling damsels from life's snares just so happens to be my specialty."

"Oh, Von. *You're* the snare. You're always the thing that gets me twisted."

"Then why are you resisting me?" Von pulled me closer so September was smooshed between us. His nose brushed lightly across mine. His cinnamon breath that had no hint of cigar to it sweetened the air in our fort, leaving me a puddle of malleable clay that begged for his hands to shape me.

"Von?"

"Tell me you don't want me."

How I desperately wanted Von. How I wanted to kiss him and make a perfect mess of the sheets. How I wanted to do what we'd done in our dreams together right here on the bed. "You know I want you," I breathed, and then rolled onto my back to break our closeness. "You should also know that's not enough. You split on me. And Danny was right – which you know I hate saying."

"What did my petulant little brother say this time?"

"He said you ran out on your responsibility even if the baby hadn't been yours. Your duty's to Terraway, and you screwed Mason over by ditching us. You have a job, Von. Mason bit me because he was pulling for two by himself. He got too hungry. It was too much to ask of him in the first place, and you didn't actually even ask him. You just left him with all the work. That's on you. This bite on my leg? It's on you. I reaped through morning sickness, through Bev dying, through swollen ankles, through every-thing because it's my job. It was every bit as much your job too, and you decided the whole thing was an option you could elect not to show up for." I chewed on my lower lip, swinging the final punch. "You left me with a Matruculan, knowing I was pregnant. You didn't care if I died, Von."

Von pulled the covers down and sat up, frowning. "You're not serious."

"I had to give up my whole life for Terraway. I can't even live in my own house! You think it's rough to have to stay with a woman you assume cheated on you? It's even harder to carry a baby by yourself, still work a normal day, and have nothing in your life that's actually yours." I shook my head. "I have to get my life together. September needs me to be on my top game. I can't do that with a guy who doesn't understand the job. We're feeding starving nations,

Von. You cared about your drama more than you cared about people starving to death when you ran out on me."

Von's mouth dropped open. "You're kicking me out? I come back, and you kick me out?"

"Of course I'm not kicking you out, you drama queen. But we're not getting back together. Not until I have some reassurance that you won't ditch September again. I meant what I said; you can be as involved as you want – with the baby. But you and I are coworkers."

"So that's the size of it? After everything we've been through – just friends?"

"After everything *you put me through*, yes. That's the size of it. You're lucky we're friends. I wouldn't turn your nose up at my friendship. I'm an excellent friend."

He rubbed the back of his neck, looking confused, like he'd suddenly taken a wrong turn and couldn't get back home. Boy, did I know that feeling. "You're serious, aren't you."

"Very. Date whoever you want, but I'd still appreciate it if you stopped sleeping with my friends. It kind of makes me the pathetic joke on my own turf. Not only could I not keep the father of my baby around even after I got knocked up, but I also couldn't satisfy him. Now he's out populating the planet with the nearest piece." I mimed stabbing myself in the heart. "Hurts on a level I can't really take right now. Friend-to-friend and all."

Von nodded, though his eyes were a million miles away. "Sure. I can stay away from your mates. Wasn't planning on going back to Katrina anyway. That last one was a drunken mistake."

When Boston got out of the bathroom, I took my turn in the shower, using the steady sound of the water to muffle my pathetic tears that couldn't be helped. Did I want to be with Von? Of course. I wanted to be with the loyal, fun one who got me and loved me even after knowing my quirks. The one who made fun of my scar in public and treated me like a stranger? The one who ditched me when things got super dark? Him, not so much. What would happen one day when September threw a fit and he decided he just couldn't take it? He'd leave all over again, and I couldn't afford to be hurt or surprised anymore.

My shower took longer than usual because my tears had no self-control, shameless as they fell faster than the water could sweep them away. Mason was gone, and Von was back.

For now.

17

MORE OF ME, NOT LESS

It was a couple mornings of checking the bed to see if Von had split in the night before I started to sleep without that worry. At night, I was swept immediately into a dream with Philip, where he gave me that same weird shriveled weed again from the black leathery hard box. Whatever. It made him happy, and then we got to go to the pyramids of Giza. That's right. My dreams are cultured. Not my real life, mind you, but in my dreams, I've seen the world.

I went from admiring ancient architecture with Philip to being gently woken by Von nuzzling my neck. His nose climbed from my clavicle up my throat when I rolled onto my back. "Did you sleep well? You were making these little 'hmm' noises."

"Good dream. You?"

"I don't need good dreams. I have you. That's dream

enough." His nose scrunched. "Too much cheese this early in the day?" He nodded and then shook his head at himself. "I meant it, but it came out like a greeting card."

"I like greeting cards, even when they're dorky."

I'd tried to make Von sleep in a different room when we got back to the mansion after Mason retreated to Sombi, but Ezra was firm on following the strict pulling for two rules. That also meant that Boston slept with us, which neither brother was all that thrilled about. We'd submitted to the arrangement for weeks now, and it wasn't all that bad. Our pattern was slowly being established: Von spooning me and September while Boston held my hand in the night. It was so uncomfortable and claustrophobic – especially when Boston first climbed clumsily into the bed after his nightcap. But he was a good third wheel, for which I was grateful. I couldn't cave and fall back into a rhythm with Von if his brother was in bed with us.

It took Von a solid fifteen minutes every night to let his hand move from its anxious, shielding hold on my belly to a relaxed stroke down my navel. It was like the second Von knew the baby was his, he turned viciously protective. Not a bad thing, but it was a steep learning curve going from him not being around at all, to being everywhere I turned.

He was best behavior Von, which was a whole new experience for me. When I got out of the shower that morning, I found he'd laid out fresh clothes for me. Then I migrated downstairs to find he'd made breakfast for me.

"You made this?" I asked of the oatmeal, bacon, eggs, fruit bowl and orange juice.

"You say that like you're surprised to find I can walk upright. Yes, I can cook. I used to cook for you every now and again when we stayed at your house in the beginning, if you recall. I lived on my own for years before Ezra took me in, and before that I took care of my brothers while Mum was at work. The boys would only tolerate cereal for so long." He narrowed one eye at me. "I've cooked breakfast for you before."

"Sure, but not like this. It's a whole spread." I sat down at the table, my eyes wide at the options. "Where's everyone else?"

"Danny and Mariang are sleeping in. Though when I passed their room, the sleeping seemed more acrobatic than restful. Making up for lost time, I assume. Boston already ate; he's in the conference room with Ezra. I'm guessing they're discussing topics like what to get me for my birthday. I told them I wanted things simple this year. A roller coaster. That's all I want."

Von had made mention of his upcoming birthday no less than five times a day since he'd returned. I was pretty sure my present for him would be a letdown, but I wasn't all that practiced with the whole birthday tradition. Birthdays hadn't been a thing growing up. Bev didn't remember which day in October she gave birth to me, so the whole month was taken up with morose anecdotes of how my father had left her because of me. I didn't much care for my birth month. Allie and Ollie knew better than to wish me a happy birthday when it inevitably rolled around on October 30th every year. I usually tried to bury myself in work and pray the day would pass without anyone telling me I'd ruined their life by, you know, being born.

Von had been loved by his mama, and it showed in how geeked the guy got thinking about his birthday. The big day was due to be celebrated tomorrow first thing, and I'm guessing would last all day long.

"You want to go to an amusement park?" I asked, spearing the eggs that tasted like butter, cheese and something amazing. "Oh, these are incredible. Thank you for cooking."

"I don't want to go *see* a roller coaster. I *want* a roller coaster. Preferably one that starts in our room and goes throughout the mansion. We could call it The Half-Vamp at Full-Speed." He waved his fork around in the air as he sat across from me at the dining room table. It was such a big table for just the two of us. "I'm still working on the name."

"I'll make sure Ezra knows, so he can paint the name on the side."

"See that you do. I mean, you won't be able to go on it for another month or so, but I'll save you the best seat for when you're ready." His lazy smile was in full swing. It was a dangerous contagion, Von's smile. It made me forget that I was still trying not to get used to having him around. He gazed at my face dreamily. "Do you think

September will have my blue eyes, you know, back when both my eyes were blue instead of just the one?" He motioned with disdain to his gold eye that now had blue speckles.

"I hope so. She'll be able to get out of all sorts of things the more she looks like you."

"My eyes, your hair. Is it wrong to hope she has my figure?"

I frowned. "There's nothing wrong with my body, Von. I'm pregnant. This is how I'm supposed to look."

Von waved off my affront with a flick of his wrist. "If she has your figure, it'll be a full-time job keeping the more sordid blokes away from her. I'm hoping she has a flat chest and mannish arms. That might buy me a little relief from worrying all the live-long day."

"Oh, I see." I chuckled through my next bite, grinning at Von's joke. "I just hope she's happy. Do you think there's a chance? I don't want my childhood for her. Or yours, actually."

Von speared his fruit in contemplation. "You're nothing like Bev, so we're cleared on that front. And I won't be leaving ever again, so she won't have my childhood, either. I didn't know the baby was mine, Peach. I thought you'd cheated on me, so I took off. Now that I know you're still mine and so's September? Good luck getting me to leave you alone ever again. I hope you enjoyed that space you had, because it's gone forever."

"Love the sentiment, but I'm still not yours, Von. Stick

around for September. That's good. You should stay for her. But I'm still mine, not yours."

Von had a hard look of defiance that twisted his handsome features, but it quickly was replaced with his usual lackadaisical "whatever" face. "Whatever you can live with, Peach. If you can keep yourself from falling in love with me again, then all the more power to you. I'm a patient man. I see what you pretend not to notice, and I can wait."

"Can we talk about something else? When are we reaping today?"

"Later this evening. Boston and I were talking to Ezra, and figured that since reaping three souls now leaves you exhausted because of my sweet little bun in your oven, we should try to reap in the evening instead. Maybe then you can be more awake for your life."

"That makes sense. So I have the whole morning to myself?"

"Actually, I have a few errands to run that I could use your help with. Do you mind?"

"That's fine. But then afterwards I'd love an hour to read. It's been a while since I've had the mental stamina to stay awake for anything when we get home from reaping."

Von raised his eyebrow. "You're reading those books from Finn?"

"Yeah. I'm right where the Mermaid main character figures out that her Merman boyfriend's really a jackweed, so I think she's going to break it off with him to go sort things out with Ricardo, the two-legged guy she's really got the hots for." I shrugged. "Or maybe the whole story's about old socks and dancing rhinos. I'm translating as I go, so I'm not totally sure I'm getting it all right."

Von's fork stilled on his plate, watching me through narrowed eyes as he sat back in his chair, feigning laziness while being totally alert. "Are you in love with Finn?"

I gaped at Von. "Jeez! Well, lay it all on the table, why don't you."

"Seems like a fair question to ask. Got to know what I'm up against."

"You're up against no one. I'm not in love with Finn, no. When we kissed, I didn't have a vision. I had a crush on him and have a deep respect for him, but nothing more to grab onto than that. He's good to me. He stuck around knowing the baby wasn't his." I knew I shouldn't have thrown in that jab, but it was the truth. I did like Finn for that very reason, among many others. "I get him, and not many people do."

"There's nothing to get. He's an opportunist. He's in it for himself. Don't ever forget that."

I drank down my juice. "I don't really think we're the kind of friends who need to talk about who we're interested in. I don't ask you about your love life. I don't want to know how many women you slept with while you were gone, enjoying your penis while I was celibate, and my head was in the toilet because I was carrying *your* baby."

Von winced at the mark that hit the bullseye. "Yes, well, the woman I degraded myself with isn't here. Finn's still around. I deserve to know who's around my baby. Violent slave drivers aren't my top pick for who I want my daughter near."

"He's been nothing but good to me and September, and I told you I don't want to talk about this with you. We've got a long way to go before we're actually friends again. You broke my heart, Von. You don't get a backstage pass anymore."

Von threw out his hands, casting aside his feigned coolness. "Yeah? Well, you stole my heart and now you're keeping it, even though you're pretending you don't want it. So we're even there."

"You told me you didn't want to settle down yet, so here we are, not settled. You took off after a long pattern of pushing me away. You can't blame me for moving on."

"I asked you for time."

I leaned forward, glaring as I took the gloves off and went for the heart of it all. "You should've asked for *more* of me, not less. So now you're getting less, just like you wanted. Don't pout about it. You're being a child, getting exactly what you asked for, and then throwing a fit when it's not as shiny as you thought it'd be."

Von gaped at me, searching my argument for signs of weakness, and finding none.

I closed my mouth immediately when Mariang flitted down the steps. She was starting to put on a healthy five pounds, making her seem less like she might blow away if Danny sneezed. It looked good on her. So did the healing waters, which made her smile more vibrant. She was lighter than air, and passed her gratitude for a sustained life on to everyone she came into contact with.

"Good morning, big brother," she almost sang as she all but danced into the dining room to peck Von on the cheek. "Isn't it a lovely morning?"

"Peachy," Von replied with a closed expression.

His frostiness began to melt under Mariang's sweetness as she grabbed a piece of bacon off his plate and munched on it, groaning gratuitously. "Mm! This is delicious. Lynna really outdid herself this morning."

I decided to play nice. "Actually Von made it. It's incredible. You want the rest of mine?" While I wouldn't be able to eat off someone else's plate, Mariang had no such qualms. She sat down next to me and grinned when I slid my plate and fork over to her so she could eat the other half of my breakfast.

Von sighed heavily. I knew he was upset that he'd made me breakfast I wasn't finishing. "Can you be ready to go in twenty?"

"Of course."

18

VON'S PLANS FOR THE FUTURE

I didn't know exactly what to make of Von; his mood swings were worse than mine. We'd just been frustrated with each other over breakfast, but when we got into the car to go run his errands, he'd collected himself, presenting me with a kind, thoughtful man who reached across the console to hold my hand. He had on a classical station, which wasn't at all like him to forsake his random garage bands in favor of string quartets. "This is nice," I said of the music.

"This website on how to birth the best babies in the world mentioned bathing your home in classical music."

"Best babies in the world, eh? That's quite the recipe. A little Mozart, a little baby powder, and out pops a genius? If only other parents knew how easy it was."

"If only." He was quiet a moment, and then chuckled softly under his breath. "Parents. You called us parents.

Can you picture it? You going to Mummy and Me classes with September. Me smoking a pipe and wearing a cardigan at the dinner table while September tells me all about school. We'll say things like, 'make sure to do your homework' and 'eat your vegetables.'"

Despite our earlier antagonism and the too many things between us, I let my lips curve into a soft smile. "I can picture all of that except the cardigan part. I may need a visual."

"You like picturing me in a cardigan?" he asked in a teasing tone.

I cleared my throat at the very Mr. Brady image of perfection. I knew the trappings of my ideal man would look all too good on Von. "So where are we going?"

Von squeezed my fingers as he turned off the freeway and onto a side street. "You're blushing. If I'd known you had a cardigan fetish, I would've bought one long ago. That's a new one, for certain."

"Oh, shut up. Where are we going?"

"To the nearest store that sells clothing for the elderly. Can't allow this heat I've roused in you to go to waste."

"Mr. Brady wasn't elderly. He was handsome, responsible and kind. And it's not a fetish. Jeez."

Von's eyes widened. "Oh, my. I had no idea how deep this Brady Bunch thing went with you. You're one sick kitten." He turned down a side street and pulled up to a small square house that looked like it had probably two bedrooms at most. He cut the engine and turned in his seat to me. "So I'm back now, and I'm trying to do things differently. Ezra had a terrifying little chat with me. He's got a temper, that one. He convinced me it's high time I started looking towards the future. I never really pictured one for myself because I thought I'd lose my mind and turn full-vamp by now. But I'm still me, and I'm only getting better at controlling my thirst. Your kiss broke a fair amount of my bloodlust curse. I barely want to tear open your veins at all now."

I skated over the gore. "You really are doing a good job, Von."

"Thank you, love." He cleared his throat to continue on with the speech I could tell he'd rehearsed. "Ezra and I made a list of all the things I used to want before my stint in Dagat, and before I was bitten. It's time I started pursuing those things, instead of throwing it all away because I don't think my life will last long enough to get them."

My lips pursed, unsure of what to say at the very grownup thing Von had done. "Okay. I like everything about that. So, what's on that list?"

"I always wanted a child, and now that we're going to have one, I don't want to muck it up. I don't know why I tried to keep my life with you separate from Penny, but I know I can't if this is happening." He motioned to my belly. "It's her spring break from school, and Angela asked if I'd play with Penny for the morning while she goes to work. I want her to meet you, to know her... sister? Cousin? I want her to know September. I don't want two separate lives. I want you in all of it."

My mouth dropped open, confused and flummoxed that Von was giving me the golden keys to his life with no hesitation. I hadn't pushed. I hadn't even asked. I knew Von wanted his personal life separate. I understood. If I'd had the option of keeping Terraway out of my home, I would've jumped on that chance. "I don't know what to say."

"Say you'll meet Penny."

"I mean, of course I'm happy to meet your daughter. I just thought you wanted me out of that part of your life. You guard it kinda tight. Not that I blame you. Kids shouldn't be near Terraway. I'm just surprised, is all."

"I told you, I'm in this. Ezra made me see that it wasn't fair to ask you to wait for me if I'm not willing to do the same. So I'll wait as long as it takes for you to see that we should be together. I'll be more patient. In the meantime, I want you in my life."

Another jaw-dropper. "Wow. Um, are you sure? I mean, I don't even know any kids. What if she hates me? I'm the woman taking her dad away."

Von's grin couldn't be contained – and as I'd learned by now, *Von* couldn't be contained – not by my expectations, not by my distance, and not by my inhibitions. Von was a force of nature, and I was merely holding on for the ride. He unbuckled my seatbelt, leaned over the console and cupped my face. He placed tender kisses on both my cheeks just to draw out my blush. "Don't worry, she doesn't know you'll soon be her stepmum. I've only told her she'd be meeting my special friend."

"What?!" I screeched, shaking my head. "Oh, no. No, no. I'm not a mama. I mean, you have to be a real adult to be a mama. I'm only twenty-three! What do I know about kids?"

Von raised an eyebrow at me and looked down pointedly at my stomach. "Hello, you're going to be a mum in another couple of months. And Penny's not living with us or anything. Think of her as your niece."

Panic gripped around the throat. I'd gotten better at handling the anxiety when it dawned on me that a baby was coming, but every now and then, the fear strangled me afresh. "I'm not ready to be a mama! I can't do this!"

Von's eyes widened, taking in the scope of what Mason had grown used to over the last few months. He leaned toward me and kissed both my cheeks, as if that might infuse me with calm. "The baby's not coming today. Today, it's me and you." He kissed my nose. "Don't you know, Peach? Together, we can handle anything." He brushed his nose across mine, his cinnamon breath making me dizzy for him. "You are strong and capable. You'll make a brilliant mum, when the time comes. Until that day, I'm here. You're not alone. We're in this together."

I gulped and finally nodded. "Okay. But don't let me do anything to screw this up. Don't let me say anything stupid. Oh, what if I accidentally swear in front of her?"

Von caressed my cheeks with his thumbs. "Then you won't have done anything I haven't." He paused and then pulled his face back an inch to look at mine. "Wait, you said you're twenty-three. That's not right. You're only twenty-two."

"I turned twenty-three in October."

All color drained from Von's face. "Truly? I missed your birthday? I've been going on and on about mine, and I was gone for yours? Oh, Ezra was spot on; I should never have left you." He leaned over the steering wheel, resting his forehead on the top, utterly morose. "You were pregnant and alone on your birthday?"

I shrugged. "It's fine. It's just another day."

"No, it's not. You should punish me far worse than this for that. Tell me Mason took you out at least."

"Why would he do that? He didn't know about it."

"Well, when was it? I'll set an alarm on my phone right now so I don't muck it up next year."

"'*Muck* it up?' Save the barnyard language for another day. There's a child in that house," I teased. When Von was not deterred from his angst, I sat back in my seat. "I don't celebrate my birthday. I'm twenty-three now, and that's the end of it. I don't need you to know the day."

Von's nose scrunched. "You don't have to be evasive. I didn't know, and I promise to make it up to you."

"There's nothing to make up to me. We don't celebrate birthdays in our house. I'd just as soon forget the day I showed up and ruined Bev's life."

Von grabbed his chest like I'd shot him through the heart. "Why would you say that?"

"Are you serious? From October first to the thirty-first, Bev was mostly drunk and telling all three of us that her life ended when I came along. She doesn't actually remember which day was my birthday, so I got the whole month. I'm the reason my dad left her. I'm the reason there isn't food in the house. I'm the reason she's miserable. I'm the reason there's global warming. Blah, blah, blah." I shuddered, recalling a particularly bad beating I'd gotten when I'd asked for a birthday cake to take to school in kindergarten. All I wanted was a cake like I'd seen in commercials, kids gathered around and smiling at the birthday girl who got presents just for being alive. I mean, just for stinking being alive. "Ollie and Allie got it bad on their actual birthdays, which Bev remembered. Since she forgot the date of mine, I got the whole month."

"I probably shouldn't say that I despise that foul woman."

"It's fine. Birthdays just aren't really my thing."

Von was overcome with a determination that turned his whole body tense and serious. He separated my left hand from the clawing it was doing to my right, and moved our palms to my belly. He spoke to me in a voice that had the edge of a vow to it. "September's going to love her birthday. She's going to get presents and pony rides and cake and streamers every year, even after she's too old to care about them. We're going to celebrate our girl every year, and every day." He looked deep into my eyes with so much earnest passion, I held my breath. "We're going to do everything possible to give our daughter a good life. No more fathers running out. No more mums who can't handle their life. It ends with us." He nodded once to punctuate his pledge, and when I finally closed my jaw, I nodded too.

"I like that, Von."

"Good. I'll not negotiate on the ponies."

19

PEPPER, CHOCOLATE AND KETCHUP

I made it into Angela's house without kissing Von, which I feel like there should be some kind of medal for. Angela was... interesting. She seemed hotwired for scoffing, which she did whenever I opened my mouth. I made it a point not to speak after the perfunctory introductions.

Von went to go see Penny's new goldfish in her room, leaving me to sit in the kitchen at the breakfast nook with Angela. She stirred cream into her coffee, sizing me up like she was a cat ready to pounce. "So you're the new Omen? I mean, can you even work in your condition?" She tossed her iron-straightened brown hair over her shoulder, her red painted fingernails combing through her locks as she looked down her thin, pointy nose at me.

I nodded, offering nothing more.

Her voice was nasally, and she sneered at me when I

refused to be baited. "Kind of selfish, getting pregnant when Terraway needs you. I mean, it all rests on you and Lady Mariang."

Selfish? Um, okay. "Uh-huh." I knew better than to argue with someone who obviously loved to fight.

She wore blue eyeshadow and gobs of mascara that framed her smaller eyes. "What're you having, triplets? You look like you're carrying a litter."

"Shut it, Angela," Von sneered, poking his head around the corner to whisper-shout at the snide woman. "I told you I'd be bringing October by, and you said you'd behave. You're speaking to an Omen like that, mind you. She's not some skank you can mouth off to however you wish."

I waved off his concern. "It's fine, Von. Go be with Penny. Let Angela get it all out of her system. I mean, clearly I'm a threat, whale that I am."

Von smirked at my moxie and scowled at Angela. "Behave," he warned her. "This right here is the love of my life, and she's carrying my baby. You'll mind your manners around my future wife."

I wanted to correct Von, but staying quiet seemed the way to go.

Angela lowered her voice and leaned across the table, her red fingernail jabbing in my face the second Von left to go find Penny. "Listen to me. I know you're trying to trap Von with this situation you've got going on here. We've got a good arrangement, he and I, and I won't let you come in here and wreck it just because he knocked you up and not me."

"You're every bit as lovely as he described you," I simpered, knowing I was being a jerk. "I think I'll go see what Von's up to in the other room." My maternity jeans were cute when I'd put them on that morning, but now I felt like a cow in them. I wished for a hoodie, but none of my favorites zipped up over my enormous belly anymore. Mariang had bought me all form-fitting clothes, which showed off every curve that I really didn't need a mega-phone for. I tugged the hem of my stretchy lavender blouse down over my belly, wishing the small ruffles around the V-neck weren't so eye-catching.

I rounded the corner and found Von on the floor with Penny in all of her yellow-pigtailed glory, playing with her dolls and using overly girly voices while she poured his dolly fake tea. I took a deep breath and dove in. "Hi, Penny. I'm your dad's friend, October." I ignored Von's disparaging look at my platonic label, but accepted his help in getting myself situated on the beige carpet that was littered with stains. It was harder to get down on the floor, now that I was so very pregnant, but I managed. There's another YouTube-worthy thing – pregnant women trying to grace-fully sit on the floor. You'll laugh your socks off.

Penny looked over at me, her round face showing off her freckles and the gap between her teeth. "Hi. I lost my tooth!"

I did my best 'holy crap on a stick' face and covered my

mouth with my hands. "Let me see! Whoa. That's awesome! What're you going to do with all that extra space in your mouth? I'm thinking you can probably fit more cookies in there with one less tooth crowding things."

Penny lit up. "I didn't even think of that!" She picked up the doll nearest her and handed her to me. "We're having tea. My daddy knows all about tea. He's from British."

Von smiled at her indulgently. "Yes, Daddy's from British. It's a land of adventure far, far away."

I couldn't help but fall in love with Penny's cuteness. "Your daddy's very smart. Did you know that his birthday's tomorrow?"

"What? It's your birthday?" She tilted her head at me. "Do daddies get birthday cakes?"

Von sat up and waved off Angela, who was watching us from the doorway. "You can go to work now. We'll stay until your mum comes to pick up Penny."

I leaned in with a conspiratorial smile. "I think we should make your daddy a birthday cake. Do you know how to bake?"

"I'm *so* good at it!" Penny exclaimed, already on her feet.

"I thought you might be. You look smart and capable. Go wash your hands, and we'll get started." Penny scampered off to the bathroom.

Angela sneered at me when Von stood and bent to help

me up. "Cake? Really? You think *more* fat is what you need?"

I don't know why I let that one hit me, but it sizzled where my armor fell slack, piercing my soft parts. The stupid pregnancy hormones made me emotional on a dime. Horrifying tears welled in my eyes, so I ducked my head and made my way to the kitchen while Von tore Angela a new one in a whisper, so Penny didn't overhear.

Von was in the kitchen in the next heartbeat, his arms around me to stem my tears. Of course, that only made them fall faster. "I'm sorry. It's fine. It's just that Bev always made those fat cracks at me, and she's gone now. I don't know why I'm upset. I keep thinking that if I'd had more time with her when she wasn't poisoned by the stone, maybe she wouldn't have thought I was a cow. Although, I am a cow now, so maybe it wouldn't have made a difference after all."

Von used his t-shirt to dry my eyes, keeping his arm around my back to comfort me and give me a mild pull. "It's got nothing to do with you. Angela and Bev were miserable. You're wonderful, and that makes miserable people insecure and angry."

I sucked in a deep breath as I straightened, pulling myself together as best I could. "Sorry. I don't know why I'm so emotional about such a small thing. I used to have thicker skin about stuff like this. I'm cool now, I promise."

"You want to lie down and put your feet up? You don't have to bake me a cake. I'm sure Lynna's seeing to that."

"But Penny's *so* good at baking." I tried to shirk out of his embrace, but melted a little when he kissed the back of my hand, holding it between us. "I'm okay, Von. Just hormones."

"I love you, November," he whispered.

The pleading for me to believe him covered my sore spots like a warm blanket. His lips were so close to mine, and the look in his captivating eyes was too earnest. I didn't mean to study his sculpted lips. I didn't mean to lean in. I didn't mean to lift myself up on my toes. I didn't mean to...

"I'm ready!" Penny called, giving us a two-second warning before she skipped into the kitchen. We broke apart, Von's wild eyes cluing the innocent little girl into none of our almost-kiss.

Von's voice came out pinched and squeaky. "Hun, can I see you in the other room for a moment? Penny, we'll be right back."

I turned away and started fishing through the cupboards at random, my face pink and my palms sweating. "We're baking a cake, Von. What kind of cake is your favorite?"

He ran his hands through his hair, swallowing thickly a few times before answering. "Any kind of cake my girls make me is the one I adore."

"Daddy likes pepper!"

I quirked an eyebrow at Penny. "He likes pepper in his cake?"

She shrugged. "He puts pepper on his burgers and fries."

I nodded, deciding to go with whatever distraction Penny provided. "Pepper in his cake for sure, then. What else does Daddy like?"

"Ketchup. He's always drinking bags of ketchup."

Von grimaced, and I knew she'd seen him drinking blood. "That's right. Daddy loves ketchup."

"And chocolate. He always has candy in his pocket for me, so I know he likes chocolate."

"That settles it. We'll make a chocolate, ketchup and pepper cake. Can you find a big mixing bowl for me?" I shook my head at Von when he gave me a look with too much smoldering love in it, warning him that he'd caught me in a weak moment, and not to make a big deal about it.

But I think we both knew it was too late. I was caving, for better or worse.

20

HIMILA WEED

"I can't believe that cake actually turned out alright. And you were worried Penny wouldn't shine to you. What a great way to spend the last day of my roaring twenties. Thank you, Peach. Truly." Von turned off the freeway, a piece of his cake wrapped up in the backseat of the car.

I'd snapped a picture on my phone of Von with a princess crown on and Penny in his lap, the two blowing out his birthday candles on the lopsided cake we'd made him. "Thanks for introducing me to Penny. She's just as great as you told me she was."

"Well, she adored you. All your worrying that you wouldn't know how to be a good mum is overruled now." He cleared his throat, and I knew he was about to bring up our almost-kiss in the kitchen.

I confiscated the conversation and veered it to a less

dangerous topic. "I'm thinking of spending a little time with Boston, just the two of us. He's been depressed, and I wanted to take him out to cheer him up. We haven't been to the bar in a while."

"You and Boston go to pubs together? I can't picture that."

It was one of our little rituals we'd swung into the habit of while Von was gone. "We've gone a couple times. I'm a pretty good wingman. Girls flock to me to rub my belly, and Boston plays the whole, 'I'm taking my pregnant sister out before she has her baby' line. He mentions helping me raise the baby, and they can't stop themselves. It's a pretty good system."

I could tell Von didn't like the idea of Boston helping to raise his baby, but he tempered his response. "That's nice of you. Mind if I tag along?"

"Now how am I going to buy you the roller coaster you wanted if you're right there with us? Where's the surprise element? Where's the birthday cheer in that?"

Von forced a grin. "Alright. Clear it with Ezra, and that's fine by me. Though I prefer my presents giftwrapped, so I'd buy a few dozen rolls of wrapping paper just to be safe. I bet the upside-down loops are absolutely wicked to wrap."

I all but ran into the house the second Von parked the car in Ezra's driveway. I knew if I kept spending alone time with Von, I'd kiss him, and I wasn't ready for the fallout of that. I hid from him in Ezra's study like a child, reading and translating the newest book from Finn, while I tried to keep my mind from wandering to the passionate fervor in Von's eyes I couldn't shake. It was too real. Too convincing.

I lost myself in Finn's book, but as this pregnancy went, I nodded off two chapters in. Unless I was moving, I was having a hard time staying awake these days. My dream swept me under as I lay curled up in Ezra's leather armchair, plopping my dream self at the beach. Behind me was a forest of stripped, barren trees. They stood like long, thick pillars stretching toward the sky with no greenery to break up their beige and brown innards, which were exposed from the bark being peeled away. The waves gently lapped at the white sand a safe distance away from where I sat between the naked trees and the ocean. I didn't much care for the water anymore, even in my dreams. The waves could all too quickly turn into a nightmare, with the Mermen dragging me under to tear at my clothes.

I clutched my shirt to my breast as I sat on the beach, vacillating between fear and peace. It was a safe place to go to puzzle out all that happened between Von and me, Bev dying, Bishop dying, and Finn dangling. I shifted the sand before me, and it started to mold together like lightweight clay, letting me reform it easily into small castles and animals and shapes. It was mindless, letting my brain relax as it created and destroyed, created and destroyed. With every creation, I breathed. With every destruction, I felt the hopeful possibility of something new and refreshing just around the corner, and at my very fingertips. There were no expectations for an entire world's survival on my shoulders here. There were only waves, only sand, and only me.

"I don't usually see you this time of day," came a voice I knew without having to look up.

"Hey, Philip. I didn't expect to see you here. I was kinda hoping for some alone time."

Philip paused before taking the spot in the sand next to me, affronted. "Is that any way to talk to the man who's bringing you a present?"

I looked up, my face stoic when I saw that same black leather hard box, about the size of a shoebox, clutched in his hands. "No, thanks."

"'No, thanks?' You're saying no to my gift?"

I sighed heavily, reminding myself that I didn't have to be polite in my own dream. I could take up space in my little imaginary world and not apologize for it. "I know I'm going to sound ungrateful, but I'm not a fan of getting a shriveled weed as a gift. It's not really a gift, you know. The classics, like chocolates, and flowers that are actually still alive? Those are always a solid win. When in doubt, don't reach for mulch. You heard it here first."

His knuckles whitened around the box. "If you had any idea the lengths I went to for this, you wouldn't say that."

"You're pretend. You don't go to lengths. You're my subconscious trying to make me feel guilty, and I gotta say, I get enough of that while I'm awake. No, thanks."

"I'm not pretend. I'm right here." Philip sat next to me

and placed the box in front of my crossed legs in the sand. He palmed my belly without asking permission first, which after the fifty-thousandth time, was starting to get a little irritating.

"Yes, and you can go. I've got a lot on my mind, and I'd love a little personal space. Real life's getting claustrophobic."

Philip pulled back. "It's that half-vamp you have feelings for. I can't get to you when you love him. I'm glad you seem to have come to your senses."

"Shut up about Von. This is supposed to be my dream time. Go away."

"Eat the *himila* weed, and I'll leave. It's been too long since your last one."

"I've got news for you, buddy; I don't actually need a weed to survive."

"That's where you're wrong." His hand migrated to my stomach again, rubbing tenderly as he kissed my shoulder. "The baby needs the *himila*. She's part Terrawayan, which means she's out of her element, Topside as she is. And Omen work is hard on your body. *Himila* helps strengthen the mother. It thickens the placenta and keeps the baby's heartbeat steady and healthy. I need both of you to stay alive." Philip's palm circled my belly again. "She'll be a princess above all others, which means she'll need extra magic to keep her as strong as I need her to be, if she's to rule with us."

"Wow, I'm a total megalomaniac in my dreams. Who

knew?"

Philip was earnest. "You and September need the *himila*. I can't protect her from where I am in Terraway. Meeting you here is the only way I can keep you safe. Omens die in childbirth far more frequently than other women do. Something about the wear and tear on your body from reaping makes the chance your heart will give out during birth that much higher."

I gaped at him. "Why are you putting that in my head? I'm freaked out enough as it is."

"I'm trying to keep you safe. You need the *himila*."

"How are you keeping me safe? You're fake!"

Philip glowered at my apparent insult. "Do you know how rare the *himila* is? Most think it's a myth! I sent someone to the top of Mount Malubha for this."

"Yes, you scale all the fake mountains for me," I simpered. "Well done."

Philip's voice lowered to a steady thrum. "You told me the Manas attacked you, so I sent one of my men to take care of them. I made sure Serena could never hurt you again."

I let my subconscious make up a valiant story of vindication where Philip was the feared king who avenged me. "How'd you find Serena? Ezra looked everywhere. He only found her because she was dead."

"I had a few moles in her ranks. I've got spies everywhere. They know who I am to you, who you are to me. They know it's my baby you're carrying, and they're helping me to protect you. How do you think Ezra *really* got into the house you were being held in by the Manas? They had charms all around the building, but my spy found a way through. Ezra got you out because *I* was protecting you and our baby."

I almost started to believe him, but then deflated. "At least tell me this nonsense with your shirt off. I mean, come on now. If you show up with a dead plant for me to eat, at least give me some eye candy."

Philip took his shirt off with a devious smile, reaching for mine as well, and casting them together onto the sand behind him. He kissed me, reaching into the box and pulling out the *himila*. "Eat it, and I'll do whatever you ask."

"What if my fantasy is for you to dress up like a chicken?"

"Whatever you ask. Only eat it first."

I went to grab the weed from him, but he pressed it to my lips, feeding it to me with too much anticipation. This was too important to him, and I didn't understand why my brain was so insistent I eat a shriveled green and brown twisted weed. I swallowed it down, and watched as Philip's nerves decreased while he played with my body. "That's good. That'll keep our baby safe until I can come for you."

"Uh-huh. Time for that chicken suit."

"I think we both know what you want." We made ourselves at home in the sand, rolling carefully as we made love to the sound of the gently lapping waves.

21

IT HURTS

Reaping that evening was short, since Mariang insisted on me taking it easy and only reaping two bodies, instead of my usual three. "You fell asleep in the middle of the afternoon," she insisted. "It's time you slowed down and let me pull my own weight. You can be the hero when I'm in my third trimester and need a break."

I wanted to argue on principle, but girlfriend was right; I was beat. Plus, I still had to finish Von's birthday present. Boston and I had skipped the bar and gone to the store after work that evening, picking up the necessary tools. Von promised to stay in our bedroom so he didn't spoil the surprise, but I insisted we work in one of the guest rooms just in case he got too curious.

Boston and I worked for hours that evening, putting together the pieces of the project until Boston insisted we call it a night. "It's done. Plus, I'm beat."

"But we can do more! Von will want it bigger than this."

"Bigger than *this*?" Boston was incredulous, motioning around the room that had barely any space to walk. "Why do you think he wants anything other than you? All of this won't make up for the fact that he's smitten, and you're putting him on hold."

"Oh, go to bed. I'll be right behind you." I waved Boston off and went back to my project with the tools I'd borrowed from Danny. I hammered and worked for another two hours, not tiring as I put my hands to use, hoping I could escape all the feelings I couldn't manage to get a wrap on.

When I finally went to bed, I climbed into the middle as I always did from the foot of the bed, so I didn't have to squish anyone getting in. Von's chest was moving evenly, but Boston was gathered into a ball of nerves. His eyes were squinched shut, and on closer inspection, I saw that his lashes were wet. I leaned over him, my hand on his shoulder. "Boston? Honey, you alright?"

"'m fine. Just go to sleep." His voice was laced with emotion, his face red.

"Do you want to go downstairs and talk?" I offered, knowing Boston wouldn't want this the second I said it.

"No. It's just been a long day."

I gazed down at the man who was shaking like a scared boy. My heart clenched in my chest for the stiff upper lip he'd attempted too many months in a row. Gently I rolled him over to face me, taking the edge of the sheet and wiping at his tears with the green material as he avoided my eyes. He smelled like his nightcap, which always had too much alcohol in it. "Sweetheart, I'm here." I sunk down next to him and wrapped him in a gentle hug that set more tears loose as he clung to me, weeping into my breasts. He hadn't broken down in a while, since Von now shared my bed with us. I ran my fingers though his hair, tenderly holding him so he could feel safe in my arms.

"Bishop, Bishop, Bishop," he moaned in a tight whisper. "It hurts!"

Boston had been lost without his twin, his whole personality on mute as he waded through life like a lost puppy. I held the puppy while he broke in my arms, howling his pain to the universe. "Let it out," I cooed, tucking his head under my chin.

Though Boston had kept his sobs quiet, Von stirred, sitting up to examine the situation with rumpled hair and puffy lips. "What's going on?"

"It hurts!" Boston wailed, now having no reason to quell his mourning. "Bishop's the other half of me, and he's gone! Don't let it be real!" Boston's tears multiplied, and then he started getting even more worked up until he let out painful howls into my cleavage. He gripped my shirt hard, holding me to make sure I didn't leave him in his dark hour of vulnerability. I anchored him to the earth as the waves rocked him, promising him I wouldn't let go.

Von reached over me and rubbed his baby brother's arm. "We're here. We're all here."

"Bishop's not here!" Boston wailed, his cries of distress reaching new heights. I was scared for him, worried at his level of grief that swung hard and fast. He was shaking in my arms, a shiver that started and wouldn't stop.

"Von, can you pull for him? He needs help!"

"I am, but it's hardly making a dent. Hold on. I'll get Danny." I barely heard Von before he ran out of the room. I did my best to hold Boston together while he grieved. He was howling like a madman into me, and I worried at what point his panic attack would become physically damaging.

Von ran back in with Danny, who was bleary-eyed and wearing only red flannel pajama pants. "Okay, mate. Hold on. We'll help you calm down." Von knelt on the bed beside Boston. He gripped the back of his baby brother's head, and snuck a hand between us to palm his chest. Danny held his baby brother's calf and waist from his position at the foot of the bed. Boston realized hands were on him, but he was too disoriented to make sense of why or who. He clung to me and started thrashing around like a fish out of water, struggling and fighting with weighted hands. Von cried out, "October, get back!"

It was hard to do anything fast, but the unexpected hands behind me slid me away from the mayhem. I looked up and found Ezra, messy-haired and surprisingly focused, despite the late hour. He managed to extract me from Boston for the few seconds it took the pulling to ramp up to the dose Boston needed. Slowly he stopped fighting, his howls muted to quiet moans of agony.

I pushed my hair away from my face. "Okay, that's enough, guys. We don't want him to never deal with his grief. Just take it down a notch so he doesn't lose his mind."

"Did he hit you?" Von asked, his shoulders tensed and his body lithe.

"No," I lied. Boston hadn't hit my stomach, which I'm guessing was what Von was worried about.

Ezra helped me to stand, hugging me like I was the one who needed it. When his embrace judged me to be stable, he moved to Boston, his hand on his forehead as he sat on the edge of the bed. "Oh, son. It's been a long road for you."

Boston's wet face looked like it barely understood English, but when his eyes locked on Ezra's, I knew they understood kindness, which was the only language Ezra spoke. He let out a few sniffles. "It hurts," he informed Ezra.

"I know, son. It's cruel to lose someone so wise and gentle. Bishop was a good man."

"He was the good one. I need him to remember how to be good, otherwise I don't know the way."

Ezra permitted half a smile as he shook his head at Boston. "You have plenty of goodness in you. Bishop taught you well."

Boston sat up and embraced Ezra, the two gripping each other in a manly hug that pulled at my heart and made tears cascade down my cheeks. Boston had a desperate need for tenderness and strength, and those things always rolled easily off Ezra.

Boston would make it through this because he had a good dad now. It was amazing the difference something so simple like that made.

Von sucked in through his teeth. "I need a little blood. That was a lot of pulling on an empty stomach. I'll be back."

Ezra laid Boston back down and tucked the covers up under his chin as if he was a child – as if Boston was *his* child. I climbed into the bed and slid in next to Boston. As if we were magnetized, Boston turned toward me and draped an arm around me, his eyes closed as he softly wept into my breasts. He could still feel his grief, but due to the pulling, it was more manageable now. Painful, but not overwhelming.

I don't know at what point Boston and I became the sort of friends who could lean on each other when we needed comfort, but that night I was his good medicine.

MAMA VANDERSHOT

The moon outside the mansion passed carefully and slowly, as if waiting to make sure Boston was asleep before progressing. I held Boston until he cried himself to exhaustion in my arms. Von spooned me and rested his hand on his brother's shoulder to pull for us both while the three of us slept. I felt Von's breath on the back of my neck, and tried not to let my body react to the slow and constant reminder that Von's lips were inches away and begging to be kissed. I made it through the night without kissing him, but only just.

Von stirred next to me when his phone rang an hour or two after the sun rose. He fumbled around without looking on the nightstand, knocking over a pen before locating his phone. "Hallo, Mum. Do I sound taller today? Wiser? I feel wiser. That's a first. Better late than never." His eyes weren't even open, but his personality never seemed to sleep. "Of course I'm having a happy birthday. The woman I love is carrying my child. I can't imagine anything cheerier than that."

Von tried to talk quietly, but Boston woke with a puffy-lipped frown, his eyes barely able to open from all the crying. Boston sat up and stretched, avoiding my eyes until I rubbed his back with the flat of my hand in a circular motion. Then he looked down at me, clearly embarrassed. "Sorry about last night. I'll keep myself together better from here on out."

"Oh, honey. Don't even try that kinda talk on me. I'm proud of you for letting yourself feel all that. I'm here, just like you've been here for me through all this. We're in this together, alright?"

He let out a gust of relief and reached down to muss my hair. "Is this what it's like to have a sister?"

I nodded with a small smile. "I like being your sister. You don't have to be perfect in front of me."

"I think I'm just starting to figure that one out." He quirked his eyebrow, but his eyes didn't open any wider. "Are you implying I didn't have myself together last night? Are you saying bawling like a baby isn't what top drawer professionals do?"

I smiled up at him, unwilling to get out of bed yet. "I'm glad you're here with us."

"Me too, little sister." Boston squeezed my hand and stood. "Biggest baby gets to shower first. New rule."

"With my blessing," I allowed. "I'm not ready to get up yet."

Boston shuffled into the attached bathroom, leaving me to try and doze through Von's conversation with his mama. My eyes shot open when Von pressed the phone to my ear, giving me a clear shot of his mama's British accent. "Hello? Hello? Lady October?"

"Um, hello, Ms. Vandershot." I sat up, situating my shirt to make sure I had no cleavage showing, and straightening my hair to attempt to look somewhat presentable.

I shot Von the filthiest look I could muster when he started sniggering as Ms. Vandershot asked how Omen duties were going. "She can't see you, you know," he whispered.

I gave him the finger and started in on the pleasantries. "Yes, ma'am. Von's the best there is for the job. He's Ezra's go-to for most problems. He and Danny both, of course. And Boston, too. Your sons are really just fantastic. You did a great job raising them."

Okay, I was babbling, but to be fair, Von ambushed me.

"You can call me Lavinia. Or Mum, if you like," Ms. Vandershot offered graciously. "After all, you're having my granddaughter. I trust the pregnancy is going well? Von doesn't give me specifics."

"Oh, well what do you want to know?"

She paused, as if unprepared for me being so open. "Any morning sickness?"

"In the first half, yes. But not so much now. Baby's measuring normal, according to the doctor."

"What about your Omen duties? Does that interfere with taking care of yourself and the baby?"

Von had the look of boyish mischief about him, which made me nervous. He moved toward the foot of the bed and ripped the covers off of me, making me jump. He picked up my foot, tipping me back on the bed as I tried to wriggle away.

"No, ma'am. I mean, Lavinia." I winced at the informal greeting. I mean, she was a true adult. "I mean, Mama." I closed my eyes and smacked my palm to my forehead, wishing I could erase the beam that burst from Von at me calling his mother 'Mama'. I cleared my throat. "Lady Mariang and I are keeping everything on schedule. It looks like Terraway's starting to rebuild itself, slowly but surely. We only have to reap two souls a day between the two of us to keep Terraway afloat, so we're working on building up a stockpile for when we go on maternity leave."

Von pinned my left leg to the mattress and lifted my right one so he could suck on my ankle, making my eyes roll back as I fought off a gratuitous moan. His mama said... something, but I couldn't hear it. Von was kissing his way up the inside of my calf, just begging for a kick in the face. He wore his best wicked grin, eyeing me with devious glee.

"I'm sorry, I didn't hear you. One more time?"

"I was wondering if you thought of any names yet. You

know, Lucille was my mother's name, and her mother's middle name. It's also my middle name. If you needed any suggestions."

"Lavinia Lucille. That's lovely. I'll make sure Lucille is put on the table when Von and I nail down the specifics in the final round of debate."

"Then Von gets to stay in the picture? He's going to stay in the Americas and raise the baby with you?"

Von stilled, his tongue on the inside of my knee as he waited for my response. I cleared my throat. "Of course. It's his baby, too. I told him from the start, he can be as involved as he wants."

Von sat up and cupped his hands to his mouth to sound like he was calling to me from a distance. "Lady October, you're needed for Omen duties."

"Oh! I heard you being summoned. It was a pleasure to talk, Lady October."

"You, too. And if I'm calling you 'Mama', you can certainly drop the 'Lady' from my title. Just October's fine."

"Thank you, dear. Keep my number and use it as often as you like."

"Pleasure's all mine. Have a great day." I ended the call and whipped Von's phone at his head. He caught it, keeping it from knocking him in the face, so you know, one point for him. "You're a jerk, springing your mama on me like that. I'm in my pajamas! I would like to've made a good impression. I was barely awake, you jag!"

Von went from devious boy to serious man, kneeling

between my legs and leaning forward so his arms hedged me in beneath him. "You want me here," he stated, like it was some kind of revelation.

"Of course I do. You're the one who wanted to leave."

"You want me," he rephrased, his eyes clouding over with something darker, more intentional.

I debated running, but the argument on the other end was for me to stay – to see this thing through to whatever conclusion might turn out. I couldn't find the words, so instead I nodded, no doubt looking like a girl who'd been caught in a lie – the lie that I was ready to take my chips off the table and leave him. I didn't want to leave Von, but knew it would be a risk to stay. He could run out on me again; it was his M.O.

He lowered his head, giving me just enough time to let loose three of the foulest swear words I had under my hat before his lips closed on the crest of my bottom lip. He tugged my fears out of me and replaced them with a blur of blue, shimmering gold, chimes and bells.

It seemed with Von, there would always be bells.

Our legs tangled through each other's, teasing and caressing as the kiss picked up speed, transporting us from our abstract bliss back to the park we'd shared when we'd been more easily in love.

We tumbled on the green, purple and blue grass, smearing the colors on our clothes and streaking them through our hair. It was easier to move in our special place. I was still pregnant, but less inhibited by it.

Von was frantic to get my clothes off, and I was eager to let him. Though we'd never made love in real life, our imaginations knew the dance well. I'd suspected that I was still in love with Von, but our epic bliss world confirmed what I'd been trying to fend off, bathing me in the confusing and explosive beauty that was us.

23

VON'S BIRTHDAY

e made love for what seemed like hours of emotional and physical paradise. When Boston cleared his throat to slowly bring us out of our haze, I'm guessing it had only been about eight minutes, which was how long his showers tended to last.

Von took longer to come out of the mind-meld than I did. He was still blinking the room into focus while I frantically patted my body down to make sure that I was, in fact, clothed in front of Boston. The park had felt so real. Von had felt so real. He collapsed beside me on the bed, spent and breathing hard. The only article of clothing lost between the two of us was his shirt that had been discarded onto the floor.

Boston kept his eyes on the ceiling. "Seriously, mates. Put a sock on the door or something. I don't need to see that. I mean, you look and sound like you're having sex, just with all your clothes on."

"I'm sorry," I breathed, my chest jumping up and down, my face flushed. "It's hard to get a handle on things."

Boston shoved his shirt over his head, moved to the dresser and pulled something out of his wallet to whip at Von. "Might want to suit up next time. You don't want to reimpregnate her."

Von tossed the condom back at his grinning brother. "Pretend there's a sock on the door, mate. We'll be down for breakfast in a few."

Boston acted out a crude gesture before he left the bedroom, looking more like himself than he had in months. I wasn't so sure if that was a good thing or a bad one. Boston unplugged was a total perv.

I rolled over (harder to do than it sounds), and put my hand over Von's lips when he leaned in for another round of too much passion. "First off, happy birthday. Second, that was amazing. Third, we have to start our day, so don't even think about a round two right now."

Von's face shifted to a tender adoration as he traced my cheekbone and thumbed my lips. "Best birthday yet. I've got my girls. I've got the rest of my pepper, ketchup and chocolate cake. What else could I possibly need?"

"Presents," I whispered.

His hand migrated down to outline my curves all the way down to the swell of my hip. "You're my present, and I think it's time I unwrapped you."

I bit my lower lip. "Crap, that was good." I indulged us in a simple kiss that only reintroduced sparks of blue and gold with a faint sole wind chime in the background before I pulled away. I knew I was on the verge of ruining the mood, but I had to voice my fear. "You're not leaving this time?"

"Never," Von vowed, running his knuckle over my baby bump. "I'm never leaving you again."

My nerves gave way to a smile of relief. "Happy birthday, Von."

He let out a low growl as he brought my wrist to his lips and sucked on the delicate skin.

I groaned, but then yanked my hand back and lightly shoved him with it. "Okay, okay. Up you get. I've still got to finish your birthday present, so go eat your breakfast. I'll be down in twenty."

When he left for downstairs, I dressed for the day, and then slipped into the guest room and pulled out the pieces of the gift Boston and I had been working on. I set them up in our bedroom and all down the long hallway. When I'd suggested the idea, Boston had laughed and called me mad. Little did he know that madness was my specialty.

I dressed in a long, fitted peach blouse that hung down past my hips and hugged my belly, paired with black leggings that were super amazingly comfortable. After pulling my hair up into a bun and brushing my teeth, I went down to join Von for breakfast. He was opening his gift from Ezra, which turned out to be a pocket watch. "So you're never late for work," Ezra told him with a gentle smile. Then he took the watch by the end of the chain, pressed a button on the back that slid out a ring of razors on the side. He shocked us all by flinging it around his head like a lasso, and letting the watch fly, striking out at the napkin on the table. Then he yanked the chain, recoiling it like a yo-yo, and retracted the razors that had retrieved the napkin and partially shredded it for him. "It's a handy little thing if you're in a pinch and find yourself without a weapon."

"Wicked!" Boston and Von said in unison. Von took the watch and turned it over in his hands, depressing the button to test it over and over.

Mariang was too excited to stand still; she bobbed on the balls of her feet with a grin that couldn't be contained without the occasional muted squeal of anticipation.

Von turned to her with a sweet smirk. "Have you come bearing gifts for your king, love?"

Mariang produced a rectangular package that had been expertly wrapped, thwapping it on the table with too much excitement. "Open it!"

Von made a show of shaking the package, taking the wrapping paper off without tearing it, and gently sliding the paper off the box with excruciating slow-pokeness. "Is it... Did you get me a roller coaster?"

"You're absolutely killing me, Von!" She looked like she was ten seconds away from opening the box herself just to have done with it.

Von laughed at her, setting the box down completely to adore her antics and pull her into a tight hug. "I love it already, and I love you for loving me this much. Best sister a handsome bloke like myself could ask for."

Mariang was a ball of eagerness in his arms. "Just open it already! You're drawing it out to torture me. Don't you know how much I've wanted to give you this every day? I simply can't wait another minute!"

Boston made a crass joke about Mariang giving it to Von every day, but luckily his mouth was full of food, so only I caught the bulk of it. I slapped Boston upside the back of the head. "Behave," I admonished him with a squinty eye he returned to me.

"Well, if you can't wait another minute." Von yawned and stretched. "I think I fancy a nap before I finish opening my gifts."

Mariang picked up the box and shoved it into his arms. "Don't you dare."

Von sniggered at her as he lifted the lid, pulling out a book with my name and Von's on it in beautifully scripted letters. "What's this now?" He flipped open to the first page. His antagonism softened, and the teasing was replaced with a tender expression. "What did you do?"

"It's a book of October's pregnancy. I knew you'd want every detail when you found out the baby was yours, so I kept track of it all. It's stats from every doctor's appointment, photos of her bump growing every week, ultrasound printouts..." She tucked in beside him at the tall counter in the kitchen and flipped to a page in the middle. "Here's a list of all the things that made her throw up, and on this side is all the cravings. Then here's the things she did to take care of the baby and herself." She wrapped her arms around Von's neck. "It's like you didn't miss a thing now."

"I can see that." Von's eyes raked in every detail of the pages, taking his time flipping through each one, laughing and commenting when some new tidbit struck him. "You really kept track of everything. It's even got her weight in here."

I paled. "Hey, wait a second." I saddled up next to Von to peer over his shoulder, ready to defend myself against the incriminating evidence. I frowned. "It doesn't have my weight in here."

"Gotcha." Von took the opportunity with me so close to give my lips a light kiss. He swept the kitchen in a brush of blue and gold. It quickly faded and left us both with a contented sigh while Mariang screeched her happiness. "That's all I wanted for my birthday. Buckets of you."

I moved to the other side of the counter with pink cheeks to stand next to Danny, who I knew wouldn't fawn over our kiss. Mariang was beside herself. "Is that... Are you... Did I just... Are you two back together, then?" She was already hopping. Her arms flung around Von again, kissing his cheek before she flitted to me to do the same.

I held up my hand to stave off her elation. "We're not back together. We're figuring things out for now."

Von stared at me, his happiness hitting a decrescendo

as he fixed me with a wounded look. I'm not sure what he was expecting, but without at least a conversation, I didn't know why he assumed we were together.

Von swallowed hard before a breezy smile reappeared on his lips. He held out his hands expectantly. "More presents! I demand a truckload!"

Boston slid a long box to Von, who opened it with less flourish. He pulled out a long silver knife that looked a little worn, but was freshly polished. "It was Bishop's," he said, and I could tell by the forced level chin that he was trying to be nonchalant about it. "I think he'd want you to have it. Keep the family safe and all. You were the one who always looked after us. It should go to you."

Von held it with reverent appreciation, turning it over before sliding it into its sheath. He set it down and stood, eyeing Boston with a dramatic expression that made me wary. "Come here, you!" Then Von tackled Boston off his stool in a bear hug that was equal parts forceful and affectionate.

Boston fell to the floor with an "oof!" The two quickly devolved into wrestling cubs, rolling around on the kitchen floor, cuffing and trying to dominate with laughter that just kept coming. It was the perfect way to show Boston he was loved, and that his gift had hit right to the heart of who Von was.

The two recovered after Lynna came in and started whapping them with her dish towel, warning them to take it outside before they made a mess of her kitchen. They reclaimed their stools with winded matching grins, shoving each other lightheartedly as they continued eating their breakfast.

Boston looked up from his porridge to me. "You're up, sis."

I shook my head a miniscule amount, hoping he'd let it go. "We don't do birthday stuff in my family, so I didn't get you anything, Von. I hope that's alright."

Von smiled at me, ever the good sport for not looking even a little crestfallen. "That's alright, Peach. You gave me the best gift this morning, and you're carrying my baby. You're like, a walking present."

Danny looked up at the ceiling. "Finally, a likeminded person. Birthday gifts are such rubbish."

Mariang's tone steeled, which was so uncharacteristic of her passive dealings with Danny that I couldn't help but gawk. "Danny, just let Von be happy this one day! No one's asked you to give your own brother a present. I simply asked you not to rain on his parade this year. He gets one parade a year. Let him enjoy it for once."

Danny froze at being publicly chastised. No one spoke for a solid eight seconds. Finally Boston broke the tension. "October, give Von your gift."

"I told you, I didn't get him anything."

Boston's face soured. "Why would you say that? You were so excited putting it together. He'll love it."

I didn't know how to tell Boston that I was pretty sure Von wouldn't love it. Mariang had gotten him the most precious handmade gift. Ezra had given him the coolest gift. Boston had given him the most sentimental gift. Lynna had made him a blood cake, winning the award for the weirdest gift. Mine was stupid, and I didn't want Von to think *I* was stupid. "I'm sorry, Von. I didn't get you anything."

"It's fine, Peach. I really don't care."

Boston's spoon clanged in his empty bowl. "You're being a coward, and I don't know why. Come on, Von. I'll show you what she made you."

I looked up at Ezra, hoping he'd intervene, but he wrapped his arms around Von and Mariang, corralling them up the stairs. I hung back with Danny, wringing my hands and wanting to hide. "It's not finished! I can do it better. I just need more time, Von." I looked up at Danny, fear plain on my face. "I'm going for a walk, okay?"

Danny went with me to the mud room off the side of the kitchen. He grabbed his coat off the hook, and handed me mine. "Let's go."

24

A NICE PERSON

"Let's go quicker," I insisted, pushing Danny out the backdoor and slamming it shut behind us. I gusted out a breath of relief at not seeing the polite smile Von was no doubt mustering up for my best effort at fitting in. I set the stride at a brisk walk, even though I knew I couldn't maintain the pace for long.

"Hold on, kid. You on a mission or something?"

"Yeah. I need to get as far away from the house as possible. I suck at birthdays. I shouldn't have tried."

"Birthdays are stupid. I wouldn't worry too much about it."

"Why do you hate birthdays so much? What gives? Did your dog die on your birthday or something?"

Danny was quiet for a few beats, and I could tell he was judging whether or not to tell me the raw truth of it. His hands in his jacket pockets started moving as he spoke. "My dad left us for good on my birthday. Never had the taste for birthday cake after that."

I stopped short, my mouth dropping open that he'd given me a real reason, horrible as the truth was. "Oh, man. That's terrible. I'm sorry, Danny."

Danny shrugged. "Good riddance. I mean, who cares now, yeah? But I didn't see the point of a celebration after that. Mariang tries, but I'm not who she wishes I was sometimes. Like with the baby book for Von. She's been working on that for months, trying to get me involved. She's a good person, and I wish she'd get it into her head that I'm just not."

I didn't know what to say to that, so I simply strolled next to him on the path until words finally came to me. "She sees the best in everyone, and likes it when the people she loves feel treasured. Not a bad quality."

"Not a bad quality, just fruitless when it comes to me. I'm not interested in jumping up and down for Von, of all people, on a day that's pretty much just like all the others."

"I'm not into birthdays either. When's yours?"

"April 20th."

"How about I cut you a deal? On April 20th, I won't wish you a happy birthday or get you a stupid present. We'll go to the bar, and I'll buy you a drink. We'll shoot pool and not talk about your birthday or anything super happy skippy the whole night. I might even let you win at darts. Sound good?"

Danny shot me a sideways smile. "Sounds like Heaven. Not a bad sister, I guess. If I have to have one and all."

"I love you, too," I offered, knowing that was the equivalent. We got closer to the trees that lined the property, sticking to the dirt path as the frigid air nipped at us. "It's colder than I thought out here. Sorry for making you come. I had to escape."

"So why don't you like birthdays?" Danny surprised me with a question that could lead to an actual deep conversation.

I sighed, knowing I couldn't punk out on him after he'd just shared his awful reason. I told him exactly what I'd shared with Von. That Bev used my birth month as an excuse to unload all her resentment of life onto me. "My old friend, Judge, used to make a big deal out of my birthday. His mama would make me a cake, and he'd always have a present for me. Wrapped it and everything. When things went south between him and me, birthdays sort of died. I lost Judge and birthdays all in one go. There wasn't anyone in my life who made a big deal out of it like he did, so I stopped caring so much. Not to be a downer, but I kinda hate the whole institution. Maybe I'd feel happier about it all if Bev had been different, but it is what it is."

Danny was quiet a few beats. "That's terrible."

"I made my peace with it. It only sucks when people like Von actually do get into the whole birthday thing, and I have very little experience with the ritual. I want to make it nice for him, but I have no idea what I'm doing. It's like an alien from outer space trying to eat with chopsticks. I have very little frame of reference."

"Von's easy to please. He's a simple kind of tosser."

I shot Danny a sideways glance. "You can drop that kinda talk around me, FYI."

"Sorry. He's simple, so get him a sticker, and he's happy."

"Maybe I should've gotten him a sticker instead. Feel like a trip to the store? I really don't want to go back inside."

Danny chuckled. "You're such a chicken. Just rip off the bandage, already. Von's in love with you. He only cares that you're here, and that you forgave him."

"I have a feeling he'd like it better if my forgiveness came giftwrapped."

Danny cleared his throat. "So how about next October, I say nothing mean to you for the whole month. I'll pick a day at random and take you to the bar to see who can beat who at quarters."

"Spoiler alert: I'm awesome at quarters."

Danny shot me half a smile. "Then I guess the birthday girl will have to win."

I elbowed him, which was our version of a hug. "That sounds nice. Thanks."

Danny was quiet as we walked, and I could tell by his stiff movements that he was cold, but didn't want to be the first one to cave. "I don't want to be like my dad. Or your mum, actually. I want to be a good parent who's around.

And I know I can be around, so I'm not worried about that. I'm more bothered that I'll do the things I'm supposed to do, be around, keep the baby and Mariang safe, but it won't matter. I'm certain the baby's going to hate me. I don't... I don't have the kid-friendly face. Kids don't like me, generally speaking."

"You don't have a kid-friendly face? I don't believe it," I teased. We walked a few more beats before I elbowed him again. "I think half the job is being there and being good to your kid. The other half is a mix of effort and dumb luck. If your kid's into outer space, be an expert on every planet in the whole freaking sky."

"The 'whole freaking sky'? That's a lot."

"Ollie was a great dad. He can school you better than I can. But you know, off the top of my head, if you want your kid to like you, maybe try being nicer."

Danny shook his head as if to scold me. "You put too high a premium on being nice. Nice doesn't get the job done."

"Neither does being mean. If I wanted to learn something, Ollie and Allie dove in headfirst. When I was nervous about learning to give stitches, Ollie let me practice on him." I softened at the memory. "I'd punked out in nursing school when we had to learn to do sutures. Ollie gave me this long pep talk about facing the difficult things in life head-on. Then he takes a steak knife and calmly slices clean across the skin on his left arm."

Danny's eyes widened. "Wow. That's dedication."

"He had faith in me. He talked me through all the steps of cleaning the cut, then he walked me steadily through the whole suture, giving me buckets of encouragement. I never would've made it over that hurtle without him. After that, I didn't have such a problem with it."

"You're right; that's solid parenting. Maybe I will talk to Ollie if I get stuck."

"That's my plan. I'm not a kid person, either. Von oozes charm and fun. I'm the rules girl. I'm the wash your hands before supper girl. No one wants to play with that girl, let me tell ya."

Danny kept his eyes forward. "You don't have to worry about the whole mum part of the job. Everybody who meets you adores you. And I've yet to see you tolerate being dreadful at anything."

I gaped up at Danny. "Be careful. I'm almost starting to believe you're investing in that crappy 'being nice' stock. Next step's holding the door open for people for no good reason."

Danny bumped me with his hip. "I hold the door open for you and Mariang all the time."

"Well, then it's too late for you. You're a total Miss Manners goner. Next step, charity work."

Danny chuckled under his breath, pulling his phone out of his pocket when it buzzed. "That'll be Ezra. Ho, actually Von. I'm guessing it's for you."

"I'm not in. He'll be polite, but I know it's not what he

wants. He said it as a joke, and I did it all wrong. I suck at birthdays!"

Danny texted back with surprising dexterity, despite his fat thumbs. "He says if you don't come home now, he's coming to bring you back inside."

I weighed the threat and decided to face the music, stopping our progression and turning back to the mansion. "Might as well get it over with. Thanks for the escape."

"I needed the fresh air, too. Mariang's in full-on happy birthday to the world mode. She's hit a new level of ecstatic with the whole being pregnant thing. I'm happy too, of course."

"You show it so well."

"Shut it. I am happy. But it's hitting me how dreadful I might be at the whole parenting thing. I'm starting to get scared the more real it all gets. I mean, I yelled at Alton once for dropping his dinner plate. Who yells at a five-year-old?"

"Um, a seven-year-old? You were a kid, Danny."

"I still shout sometimes when I lose my temper."

"You're a yeller? That's surprising," I teased. "Danny, you're in complete control of what kind of parent you want to be. If you don't want to be a dad with a hot temper, then try meditation. Go see a shrink. Try Anger Management classes. Smile more. And I know you don't want to hear this, but be nicer. It's easier than you think."

"Again with that niceness rubbish."

"You could always try yelling at the poor kid. I'm guessing that's the thing that's put a strain on your relationships with your brothers, though."

"They've got Von. They don't need me to put on a show for them. They're grown."

"Are you kidding me with this? Boston's falling apart right in front of you. And Von puts on a good face, but it hurts him when you run him down like you do. You want your kid to have a good life? I think it's time you started being a good person to everyone, not just Ezra and Mariang."

"I'm not mean to you."

I scoffed in response.

"Well, I'm not *that* mean."

"Well, you can't be that mean to your kid. Or mine, for that matter. You're going to be Uncle Danny. I gotta tell you, if you start running September down the way you do Von, I'll lay you flat out. Seriously, Danny. I've got no problem taking you down if you pull your crap on my daughter."

Danny's eyebrows furrowed. "I'm not going to be hard on your kid."

"What if she wants to be a painter, like Von?"

"It's a waste of time," he spouted, and then caught himself. "But I'll keep my mouth shut about it."

"Not good enough. Try harder. What's something a nice person would do?"

Danny was at a loss, searching through his mental Rolodex for behavior he'd seen modeled around him. "Maybe I'll get her some paints? Lie to her when she paints something senseless and tell her I adore it?"

"That's a start. See? Not so hard. Just think first before you open your mouth and a fist pops out."

"I'm going to be terrible at this."

I pressed on. "What if September wants to ride a pony?"

Danny shrugged. "Show her pictures of a horse?"

I stopped, my eyes growing serious. "No. You take her to the fair, or go with her to stables to see them. You watch movies with horses in them and read her horse-themed kids' books. Then you get down on your hands and knees and offer to be her pony to ride around the house."

"Can you honestly picture me doing that?"

"Loving someone means getting down on your hands and knees on a daily basis. Be there for your kid. Keep them safe, sure, but also keep their imaginations from being crushed. I swear, Danny. You better get real good at this real fast. My daughter won't make her imagination small just so you don't have to try something that makes you uncomfortable."

Danny grumbled, but his response was cut short by Von, who was waiting in the backyard for us, his frustration in full swing. "I thought we weren't going to run out on each other anymore. Or was that rule only for me?"

I ducked my head, knowing I was being a big chicken, and walked with Danny into the house. As we passed the threshold, Danny stuck out his hand to Von, leaving it there to hang between them.

Von examined the normal gesture that was odd on the hard man. "You're my brother. Happy birthday, Von," Danny offered. I could tell he was trying to be nice, but had no idea how to do it organically. The firm handshake was a good start, the words were friendly, but his perma-glower needed work. The well-wish almost sounded like a threat, like, "Don't you dare have a happy birthday, Von. I'll be watching."

I patted Danny's back. "That was good. See? Not so hard."

I watched Von take Danny's hand with a wary expression, as if he expected to be shanked at any moment. "Cheers, Danny."

Danny nodded once. The corners of his mouth pulled downward, and his eyebrows furrowed. As if catching us making fun of him, he glared at me and stomped up the stairs after toeing off his boots.

Von's head twisted to track his brother's steps until they disappeared. "What was that about?"

"He's trying to be nicer, so the babies aren't afraid of him. It might take a while to get him up to snuff."

"I'll say. I don't think Danny's wished me a happy birthday since we were kids." Then Von's gaze sharpened when he remembered why he was pissed. "Why'd you run away?"

"Can't actually run all that far in my condition." When my dodge did nothing to get me out of this, I confessed my nerves. "Look, I know I suck at this whole birthday thing. Let me take you shopping, and you can pick something out for yourself."

Von looked baffled, his hand on his forehead as he shook his head. "Why would you think I wouldn't like your gift? It's brilliant! I love it."

"I can do better, I... What?" I stopped wringing my hands.

"It's the thing I jokingly ask for every year, but no one's ever gone to such effort to make me smile. You built me a roller coaster! How could I not love it? What I don't love is that you got scared and ran, leaving me to go to my own personal amusement park alone. We're meant to go together to these things, yeah?" He proffered his elbow to me, as usual letting me off too easily.

It had taken me forever to find enough kits I could splice together with wooden train tracks and race tracks to make a miniature roller coaster. The car had been hardest to paint. Trying to fit "The Half-Vamp at Full-Speed" on a small roller coaster car in red is harder than it sounds. Despite my best efforts, I was pretty sure it looked like a child put it all together. "You don't have to be this cool about it. It's not as good as a concealed weapon, an actual weapon or a sentimental baby book gift."

"All those things make me feel thirty. Your gift made me feel ten – a glorious ten. Exactly what I needed today. Come play and be completely juvenile with me."

It was the best offer I'd gotten in ages, so I held tight to Von and took him up on being young together.

25

ONE REAP TOO MANY

The next few weeks of reaping with Von and Boston felt like two years, but somehow they passed without me losing my self-control and giving in when Von asked me daily if I'd marry him. At any given point in the day, it was a tossup. Of course I wanted to marry him, but I was still nervous he'd bail. It somehow felt infinitely worse to have a husband walk out than a boyfriend, which I was still reticent to call him.

At every place we reaped – hospitals, fairs, nursing homes, hospices – he announced to nearly every stranger we passed that I was carrying his baby. "Excuse me, could you hold the door? That's my baby she's carrying. It's a girl. We're having a little girl together. We were best friends first, but now we're mad for each other." Then there was the one that made me super popular: "Could you aim your cigarette the other way, mate? My girlfriend's pregnant with my child. I'm going to be a father soon. Isn't she lovely?" And of course, the one that made me chuckle: "Sorry, is this meal safe for pregnant women? I ask because my girlfriend is pregnant. That's right, with *my* child. We're having a baby girl. Do you want to see pictures of the sonogram? Here, I just got it laminated."

I jokingly told him that I should just wear a sandwich board that said "Von's Sperm Rocked my Womb" to save him the trouble. The agreeable gleam in his eyes made me hope he realized I was kidding.

Boston started to come out of his funk in bits and pieces, though he clung to my hand as if I was his mama when his bad moments hit. I could always tell when he was down. He glued his sweaty hand to mine and only answered in grunts. I think it was the fact that we'd both recently buried a family member that made him feel safe around me.

"You alright, big brother?" I asked Boston, who always dimpled when I called him that. He had one whole year on me, but it was just enough for him to finally feel like the big one instead of the youngest goofball.

We strolled through the hospital at a leisurely pace, reaping to store up hearts for my maternity leave and Mariang's. Boston squeezed my hand and forced half a smile. "Yeah, I'm okay. How's my niece?"

"She's getting tired. One more, and we're done for the day."

"Look at you, learning to pace yourself. I daresay you're growing up."

I shrugged. "Better late than never."

Philip had begged me to stop reaping after four souls before I stopped seeing him in my dreams. Von had replaced Philip after our reunion kiss that we reinvented every night, but Philip's warning stuck in my mind. He'd insisted the baby couldn't handle more than that, and she'd start feeling the cold poison of the reaps the closer she got to birth, due to the thinning placenta. He'd been so insistent that I consented. Also, Mariang and I only had to do two reaps between the two of us per day, so me doing four by myself was more than enough to buy us extra time off on the back end. I knew Philip's warnings were just a dream, but my dreams with Philip had felt so real. It didn't sit right ignoring his pleas for me to take it easy.

Yup, I was crazy. I half expected David Duchovny to show up in my next dream, tell me to wear a tinfoil hat, and hold his hand while we waited for daylight to save us from the aliens. If only all forms of crazy were accompanied by David Duchovny.

There was a woman with brown hair streaked with sporadic strands of gray, and bags under her eyes. She was sitting in the hallway outside a room, staring at the door as if willing it to pop open. It was the face of needing good news, but knowing it would always be just out of reach. I knew that expression well.

I waited until the doctor came out, and Boston pulled a

slight bit from him so I could sneak past without anyone caring. The doctor stood in the hallway for the final blow while I slipped into the hospital room to reap the woman's husband. It was hard not to feel like death was inevitable, and people would always die alone. The man's breathing was evening out, and I guessed that he'd just been sedated. His wrinkled eyelids were closed as if to shut out all the doctor bills and things that tore at him in his final moments. I reaped him quickly. Or, that was the intent, anyway.

The second his corroding soul leapt into me, September started freaking out. It was something akin to a giant octopus breakdancing in my uterus, making me twitch and flinch as I tried to put one foot in front of the other to get to my Duwendes, who were watching the door. "Von!" I cried out when the simple act of walking felt like a risk. September was fighting something inside of me, making my heart race and my palms sweat when I could no longer escape the fact that something was horribly wrong.

Von rushed in and took the soul from me with a simple brush of my elbow, calming both me and September down significantly. "What's wrong?"

I slumped against the wall, bracing myself with relief. The lingering pain was an indicator that something wasn't quite right. My eyebrows pushed together in concern. "I think it's time to go home. That last one hurt the baby somehow."

Von let out a steady stream of swearing. He slowly led me out of the room and down the hall toward the parking structure. "Steady now. Let me get a wheelchair."

I shook my head, gripping my stomach as September rolled in my uterus, making my spine twinge uncomfortably. My face and my back contorted as I gripped Von and Boston, closing my mouth through a scream. "Home! Let's go back to the mansion so I can lie down."

Von clicked his fingers for Boston to grab a wheelchair, and the two lowered me down into it as if I was ninety years old and needed help with such arduous tasks as sitting. The sucky part? I actually did need help. We were just beginning the last month of the pregnancy, and while I couldn't wait to meet September, it seemed she was getting impatient to meet me, as well. There was precious little room in my belly for her anymore, and everything felt stuffed too tight with no breathing room.

I kept my head down in embarrassment, unwilling to admit to myself, much less the world, that I needed this much help just to get to my friggin' car. When we didn't go toward the parking garage but to the maternity ward, I stiffened. "Why are we in here? If it's all the same to you guys, I'd love to go home." I looked up at Von, who was pushing the wheelchair. It wasn't until I saw his clenched jaw that I realized he was scared. "Von, I'm okay. Really. It was one reap too many, is all. I just need to lay down."

"Humor me. We're in the hospital. Why not pop in and have a doctor give you a look?"

I sunk in the chair, mortified I couldn't get through a whole day of work without incident. I heard Boston murmuring to Ezra on the phone and groaned. "You can't call Ezra about the little stuff, Boston. He'll overreact, and he doesn't need the stress."

Boston hung up and reached for my shoulder, cupping it clumsily, like a guy who didn't know how a woman should be touched at all. He was a sweet kind of oaf. "I tend to go a trifle deaf when you start to say daft things, sis. You should speak up next time."

Something shifted in me, and my stomach became hard, my insides spiking with a sudden dose of pain. I grabbed my stomach and bit my lip through a bleat of distress. "Oh! Okay, yeah. That wasn't good."

Von bolted through the hallways we'd been down so many times before, but this time with renewed purpose and a heavy dose of dread. "It's alright, love. I've got you."

"Squeeze my hand," Boston volunteered as he jogged alongside the wheelchair.

He probably wished he hadn't offered that when the next ripple of spontaneous pain hit me a handful of minutes later. Boston winced through my cry of pain and fear. Then he let out a panicked whimper when he saw my belly tremble and harden ominously through my fitted lavender shirt that stretched over my sizeable bump. "How many minutes was that between contractions?" Boston asked in a pinched voice to Von.

"Only three. How are they so quick? They're supposed

to start out slow according to the books. I knew we shouldn't have reaped today!"

"I'm not in labor," I insisted, half from fear-laced denial and half from knowing it couldn't be contractions. "It's too early still. The baby's not ready yet. It's probably just false labor." My palms were clammy, and I couldn't gather in a full breath that calmed me in any way.

Von ignored me and drove the chair right up to triage, checking us in with no flourish. "We need to see a doctor straightaway. My wife is in labor!" he all but shouted when his hand shook while he tried to fill out my information.

"I can do that, mate. Go on in." Boston took over filling out my paperwork, no doubt leaving half the information blank.

I was wheeled in and given a gown that Von and the nurses helped me into after I shooed Boston out of the room. I was promptly hooked up to a heart rate monitor, an IV and a fetal imaging monitor. The machines beeped through my next seven contractions, reminding me that I was in a hospital, and that ready or not, this was happening. "Go out with Boston," I told Von when I saw the fear in his face. He didn't want to be here anymore than I did. I didn't have a choice, but Von did. "Go call Ollie. If the baby's really coming, Ezra can't be here. I'll have them call you in after the baby comes."

The moment Von left me with the nurse, I broke down into horrible sobs that scared me. I wasn't ready to give birth yet. I still felt like a kid myself.

The nurse with short brown, curly hair looked tranquil while I vacillated on the edge of a full-throttle freak-out. "Okay, it's alright. Let's focus on getting your heart rate down. Try to breathe." The nurse read the machines, handing me a tissue to stem the unending flow of my tears. I'd sent Von away, and he'd gone. I thought I'd muscled past the maximum amount of heartbreak, but apparently there was a whole level of crap beneath the bottom of the trough for me to wade through.

"Now, now. Don't start the party without me." Von barreled back through the door, his sleeves rolled as if gearing up to wrestle a bear.

I looked up, and if my vision had the photo ability to add a dreamy haze and halo on a man, it would've done so right then. "I can't believe you left me!" I sobbed into my tissue.

Von tilted his head at me and tsked. "You told me to go call Ollie and keep Ezra away. And I think we've established that I'm not going anywhere. Even when you send me away, I'm not leaving you, Peach."

My lower lip couldn't stop quivering, and my tears flowed so fast that I could scarcely see the halo I'd painted on him, but it was there. Dusty and tarnished, sure, but Von was my angel in that moment, staying with me when I was scared, and life was too dangerous to go through alone. "You don't want to be here for this. It's nothing but screaming. *I* don't even want to be here for this part. Take your Get Out of Jail Free card and run."

Von sat me up and climbed into the hospital bed behind me, encircling my trembling body with his arms. Then he hooked his legs on either side of me so I was completely wrapped in Von. He moved my hair over my shoulder and kissed the nape of my neck. "I'm exactly where I want to be. I haven't been to a concert in a long time. I rather miss the screaming and head-banging." His chest was firm against my back, all ten of his fingers lacing through mine so that when the next contraction hit, he took the brunt of my agony. I tried to breathe through the ripping sensation that vibrated through me. After half an hour of that, the nurse warned me that if my heart rate didn't even out, they'd have to deliver the baby right then and there.

"I don't know what I'm doing," I confessed to Von when the contraction passed. "I don't know how to tell the difference between a baby who needs something and a kid who's just being a brat. I don't know when they're supposed to potty train. I don't know how to potty train a kid! I don't know if I'm supposed to sleep in the bed with the baby or if she's supposed to have her own space. In her room or ours? I don't know what I'm doing!"

Von kissed my cheek and rocked me forward and back as he rubbed my belly. "September will sleep in the bassinet in our bedroom until she's big enough to be moved to her own room. And we'll figure out toilet training when it comes, which won't be for like, two years. I'll be here for every nappy, every midnight feeding – all of it. I love you, and I'm not going anywhere." He shifted behind me and pulled out his phone. "Bos, get on in here, mate. We can't get her heart rate steady."

Boston thundered through the door a minute later in similar fashion to Von – sleeves rolled, hair a mess and a wild determination about him that told me he wasn't taking crap from no baby. He stomped over to me and put one hand on my belly and the other on my forehead, pulling in a steady thrum that lessened my anxiety and actually let me breathe in full, long drags that felt restful.

"Okay, Bos. That's enough for now. We can't have her passing out."

The nurse blinked at the machines and at us in confusion. "Well, that seemed to work. You must have something good up your sleeves. I wish I could get all my patients to calm down like that."

"It's a gift," Boston mumbled. He kept his hands on me, lessening my tears to only a few that trickled down in pitters and patters as my anxiety ebbed. "That's the way, sis. Just breathe. September's not ready to meet us yet."

Slowly – too slow for my liking – the contractions came to a stop. Von didn't let go of me the whole time. Even though I knew both of us wanted to run, we stayed fused together, with him as my support even after it was clear September wasn't going to make an appearance today.

I was kept for observation that night, and Von only left the hospital bed to bring me food and water. Boston made himself useful conning us a warmer blanket from the cute nurse in the drafty ward.

Von and I didn't make love in our dream; I was too scared. Instead we kissed slowly and softly for hours, making plans for our daughter, and promising each other things that I prayed would hold in the daylight.

26

ALL OUR LIVES

hen I awoke the next morning, Danny was in Boston's chair. His arms were crossed over his chest as he sat back, watching me all curled up in Von's arms in the narrow hospital bed. "You're not Boston," I whispered by way of a greeting.

"He's with Mariang. She sent me here to stay with you. She came by with me in the night to check on you, but you were asleep. Boston drove her home so they could both get some rest." Danny leaned forward in his seat. "Are you alright, then? No baby yet?"

"No baby yet. False, but very convincing labor."

Danny tapped his heart. "You scared me, kid. Ezra's in a right state. I have to phone him every few hours, or he'll come up here himself, and if you're ready to pop, that's not really best."

"Makes sense. Sorry I scared you."

"What did it?"

"That last reap sent me over the edge. I felt September freaking out, twisting and turning to get away from the cold. It was awful."

Danny cut the flat of his hand through the air with a note of finality. "You're done working. You're officially on maternity leave."

"I can handle it, but maybe I'll dial back to two a day or something."

"Mariang's healthy, and you've got a month stored up already between the two of you. As soon as Sombi gets the last of the stone, you'll only have to reap once a day." He nodded, as if it was already settled. "You're done working. I won't risk my niece like that."

"What happens if yours and Mariang's baby starts freaking out like mine?"

"Then Terraway will just have to deal." Danny's tone was steely, his ruling resolute.

Von stirred behind me. "If you're going to wake me up with all your talking, at least let it be about how amazing I am."

"Von, you're amazing," I said, facing away from him so he couldn't see my hint of a smile. Von was amazing. He'd been calm when I'd freaked out, and dealt with the situation when I'd been in denial. I'd been the one who wanted to run, but Von had grounded me, holding me in the shelter of his love until the storm passed.

"That's more like it." Von kissed my cheek, rubbed my

belly, then sat up and stretched. He inhaled the scent of my hair, and then got up to go use the bathroom and make good use of the private shower each maternity room had been fitted with.

Danny wasted no time saying his piece as soon as the water started running. "Finn stopped by with a gift for you."

I frowned. "I asked Ezra to send a message to him that Von and I were sort of getting back together."

"It's a gift for the baby and you, actually."

Guilt washed over me at the complications that didn't need to be. "How did I let this happen? I told Finn I was off the market even before Von came back. I let it go too far." I rubbed my forehead, and then tried to sit up, which was way harder than it sounds. I felt like a beached whale trying to do Pilates.

Danny moved over to the bed and gripped my arm, winding one hand behind my back to lift me to sitting. "There you are." He returned to his chair after I thanked him. I was embarrassed that I couldn't do something as simple as sit up by myself. Lame. Danny studied my careful movements as he spoke. "I think the fact that you're unavailable now only makes the prize more enticing. Captain Finn's a competitive man; it's how he got to be the number two in his country."

"Super. Though I do want to know how the series ends of the books he's been giving me."

"You need to make it clear whose team you're playing

for. No niece of mine is growing up in Dagat. I'd never sleep again knowing she was around all those sex-starved Kataw."

We grimaced in unison. I rubbed my belly, silently promising September I'd never let anything like that happen to her. "You're getting better at being nice. That whole protective uncle thing? Make sure to try that out around Mariang; she'll bed you right good after hearing that."

Danny's eyebrows raised as he snorted at my suggestion. "I'll try to remember that."

The doctor came in to examine me and September, making Danny nice and uncomfortable, though he didn't leave the room. He stayed near the window, which was the furthest point away where he could still be in the room, but not near the action. When it was ruled that it had been false labor, I was released with instructions for strict bedrest starting immediately. My jaw dropped as Danny's chin raised in triumph that he now had a doctor backing him up. "You can't be serious. I feel fine now. It was just a little hiccup."

"You can stay in this room for the next month, if that works better for you," the doctor threatened. I almost demanded to see his medical license, but part of me knew I was being a little touchy.

"No, sir. Thank you."

"Are you the father?" he asked Danny, who held his

hands up as if the very thought of sex with me was repulsive. *Jerk.*

"No, this is my brother, Danny. The father's in the bathroom." The look Danny gave me at my declaration was unexpected. He almost smiled. His shoulders relaxed with a tender expression that told me he didn't mind being my brother one bit.

The doctor continued only to Danny. "Very well, it appears to be stress induced, so the more you can do to keep things calm, that'll help."

"Yes, sir."

I was released, which meant I could wear pants again – a solid win all the way around. I shifted off the bed to grab my clothes once the doctor exited, but rocked forward when a contraction hit me hard out of nowhere. I held my belly, breathing through my teeth as the pain vibrated through my body.

Danny ran to me, one arm around my back and the other palming my belly like a basketball. I could feel him pulling, taking the pain away in mild waves as he held September and me in his steady grip. "Easy, easy," he cooed, sitting me back down on the side of the bed. "I bet it's the pulling. You're going to go into full-on labor without it. Von's been touching you all night, so the contractions went away."

Though the pain had passed, I held tight to Danny's shirt, afraid to be alone through the most terrifying event of my life. "I can't have this baby yet. It's too early!"

"We'll take care of it. You'll have to stay with your Duwendes until your due date. That was only five minutes without a Puller that sent you back into labor, so get ready to be tremendously close with Von."

"Where's Ollie?" I asked, dangerously close to tears as I clung to Danny. I was snuggled in his embrace while he stroked my belly almost tenderly. My legs dangled over the side of the bed as I tried to calm myself down.

"He's still in Sakuna with Prince Langgam. Ezra summoned him last night when we heard you were here, so he might already be back at the mansion."

Von came out, freshly showered and unprepared for Danny standing next to where I sat, palming my belly with loving affection. "Um, what's going on, kids?"

Danny explained the situation, making Von's eyes go wide. He rubbed the back of his neck, looking down uncomfortably. "I need some help, then. Pulling all night by myself for two? I'm a touch anxious for blood, Danny. I can't pull for her anymore until I get either a mountain of food or half a pint of blood. I can't risk accidentally attacking her. This whole hospital reeks of the stuff, and I can only hold on for so long."

"Can you drive home if I pull for her?"

"Probably."

Danny shook his head. "'Probably' won't cut it." He rolled up his sleeve and offered his arm to Von with a determined look. "Drink what you need, and let's go home."

Von's face twisted in distaste. "What're you on about, offering up yourself as the solution? You hate me."

Danny's face turned stony. "Just drink so we can get her home."

Von stepped closer to his brother, picking up Danny's arm tentatively and pressing the swollen forearm muscle to his lips. Danny's slight intake of breath when Von punctured his arm was expected, but Danny's hand tightening around my back was not. I could feel in his touch that he was afraid. It wasn't that he disliked Von's vampiric tendencies – he feared them. My hand that had been bunched in his shirt shifted to rubbing Danny's chest to soothe him, while Von made greedy noises that sounded borderline sexual. When Danny's eyelids started to droop, I ran my fingers through Von's damp hair. "That's enough, hun. You don't want to take too much."

Von indulged in another long pull before letting go. When he released Danny, there was a trail of blood that trickled down his forearm, and Von lapped at it with too much longing. Danny swayed and plopped himself ungracefully on the side of the bed next to me.

I reached for the rolling nightstand and opened up one of the little tubs of juice I'd been given some time in the night that I didn't have need for. Peeling the foil lid back, I tipped the cup to Danny's lips, holding the back of his head while he slowly drank. I needed to get his blood sugar back up so he didn't crash.

"Can we go, then?" Danny asked impatiently, not liking being babied or feeling weak.

"Give it a few minutes. If you try to walk now, you'll give the ground a nice little kiss. Let your body chill for a second." I turned to Von, who had new light in his eyes. "Von, why don't you go bring the car around to the maternity entrance? We'll meet you down there."

Von leaned forward and kissed me, tasting like Danny's blood. I was totally grossed out, but the swirling colors started dancing for me to distract me from the smear of red I could feel Von licking off my lower lip. I shuddered and found the wherewithal to gently push him back, finding his eyes clouded with a lusty hunger. He shook his head to blink the room back into focus. "Right. Car. Yeah, I can do that. Let's get you dressed first." Von picked up my pile of clothes and laced his fingers through mine, leading me into the bathroom while Danny laid down on the bed to fight off fainting.

Von shut the door behind us, giving us the privacy the surprisingly large bathroom provided. Everything was white and beige, with Von wearing a red t-shirt in the center of it, standing out like – well, like a vampire in the middle of regular life. Without a word, Von slowly untied my hospital robe. He smirked when I covered my breasts as my only covering fell to the tiled floor. "It's nothing I haven't seen before, love." Then he proceeded to take off his clothes, leaving himself bare and exposed for my jaw-dropped ogling pleasure. I kept vacillating between gaping and looking away with a crimson face. "Fancy a shower before we go home?"

"I, um... I... Can we really do that?"

He was quiet as he started up the shower, testing the temperature before he came back to stand in front of me. My cheeks were pink and warm, having zip experience showering with a man. My limbs felt clumsy, like Gumby weighted down with concrete cinderblocks – each movement a choice.

Von picked up my hand and kissed the unmarked backs reverently. "Do you remember our first kiss that blew everything up? We were married before any of the mind-bending sex. Before the baby. Before we admitted aloud that we were madly in love with each other. In some level of consciousness, I'm already your husband, and you're my pregnant wife. Let me help you. Please." He pressed my fingers to his chest. "I *need* to be able to take care of you in ways no one else can."

"You still want me? Even though I look like this?" I glanced down at my belly and my slightly wider hips. I didn't feel sexy or desirable. I felt like a big, giant mom blob.

A low growl started in Von's chest. "You're exactly what I want every day for all my days. No matter how your body stretches, you're always the standard I use to measure perfection." He tugged my hands toward the shower. "Come, darling. Let me be good to you."

I was so touched at his sincerity that I let him lead me

into the shower. I stood in awed gratitude as he lathered up and started soaping my body, paying special attention to the parts I had a hard time reaching. He took his time on my fingers, too, soaping in between each one several times until we were both sure there were no more germs lurking. He massaged my hands, all the while looking deep into my eyes and telling me all the ways he loved me.

I'm not sure when the tears started. I had a hard time keeping a cap on my random crying – especially in this last trimester. "I want to kiss you so badly, but I'm afraid we'll slip and hurt the baby. But when we get back to our bed in the mansion, I want to make up for lost time."

I licked my lower lip. "That's a plan."

Von's kisses couldn't be stopped completely. He sucked hard on my neck and other parts of me that made me gasp. "I love you," he breathed into my ear, making me shiver, despite the warm water and steam that encompassed us. "No matter what, I promise to never leave you again. I'll be by your side through all of it, even when it's hard. Even when you're tired of me and my accent. Even when we're old and gray. I'll love you every moment of it."

The tears were falling hard and fast now, with no chance of being concealed by the shower spray. "But what about the life where I'm a dragon and you're a fly?"

A slow smile spread across Von's handsome face, entrancing me with that constant beauty. "Even that one. I insist to be by your side in *all* our lives, no matter what. We can start with the one where I'm a half-vamp and you're an Omen."

"I'll stay with you, Von," I promised. "Only you. In this life, and the next."

Von blinked down at me, shocked that I'd finally handed him the ticket to the fidelity he'd been asking me for every day. "I want to kiss you, but I'm afraid I'll lose control and we'll slip." He pressed a closed-mouth kiss to my lips, which was the smallest portion of what we both wanted. "I love you."

"I don't blame you." I smiled up at him to admire his beauty as he laughed. The water dripped from his dark, thick lashes that framed the most captivating eyes I'd ever seen. He looked at me with reverence I knew I didn't deserve, but was determined that someday I might.

OCTOBER GRACE, NOVEMBER PEACH

Danny sat in the back of the car with me, his labored movements informing me that Von had taken too much blood. He leaned heavily on the door, his arm around my back to give the baby and me a steady pull. I was too keyed up to be normal, my eyes like saucers. My leg was unable to stay in one place as Von drove us to the mansion.

"Calm down," Danny ordered. "I'm pulling as much as I can, but it won't do any good if you don't work with me, here." He made a show of taking in a deep breath. "It's okay. If the doctor told you to go home, then it's safe."

"I'm trying. My mind's going a mile a minute."

"We need to finish baby-proofing the mansion," Von spoke up from the front seat. "We did our room and Mariang's, sure, but what about the rest of the place? It's a deathtrap for September and little Mariang Junior."

"I can help with that after I get some food in me," Danny offered. "I was thinking we should go through your stuff and ours to see what duplicates we have that we don't need. I mean, September will be out of the bassinet long before our baby's born. No use in having two."

Von glanced in the rearview mirror at his surprisingly cooperative brother. "Um, yeah. That's a brilliant idea, Danny. October got loads of stuff from the baby shower."

"You're sure Mariang doesn't want a baby shower?" I asked Danny.

"Most of her friends were overseas when she was healthy enough to have a social life. She hasn't been well enough for friends in ages. There's no one to invite."

"But she loves parties. Seems like she gets the raw end of the deal on this."

Danny's arm tightened around me, his affection for me blooming as my concern for Mariang grew. "She's getting a wedding; that's plenty celebration for her. Two weddings, actually. One for mum in London, and one in Terraway for the kingdom."

The corners of my mouth pulled down. "I don't like the idea of her being in Terraway. Or my little niece or nephew, for that matter."

"It's expected. You and Mariang are queens to them. The heads of all the nations will turn out to pay their respects."

"What about Sama? What about the threat of war that's always hanging over everyone's heads? What about the famines that are only just starting to lift? You've gotta know it's not safe for her down there."

"Kabayo's volunteered to play host for us, though that wasn't without debate. Everyone wants a piece of the shiny new thing. He's been pretty accommodating so far." He waved his hand. "But don't worry about that. It won't happen until well after the babies are born. Plus, we'll have to present our children to the people, so we'll do the wedding ceremony plus presenting our babies at the same time."

"I'm not taking September to Terraway," I ruled.

"I love that you think you have a choice in it."

"I'm not joking, Danny. I've been starved, beaten, locked in a prison, molested and nearly drowned there. Not to mention the whole zombie army thing that happened on Kabayo's land. You don't need the parent of the year award to know that's not where a child should be."

"Those things happened because I wasn't there to protect you." Danny's arm tightened around me. It was sweet, but not quite enough to fend off the Mermen I still winced at the thought of. "I'll keep her safe. It'll be one day."

"One day where Sama has us right where he wants us. Ceremony isn't worth all that. It's just not."

Danny frowned as Von pulled into the mansion. "I'll speak with Ezra about it."

Ezra met us in the driveway, running out to help extract

me from the car. "Darling, are you alright? Danny told me they were releasing you. How are you feeling?"

"I'm fine. The guys are starved, though."

"Lynna's already taken care of that. In the house, boys."

Danny and Von didn't run ahead, but each took one of my hands as we walked toward the house, knowing I was going to be about five minutes away from going into labor for the next month without the contact.

The second we stepped over the threshold of the mansion, Von shot up the stairs, leaving me confused next to Danny.

"Boston!" Danny called through the house. When Boston came bounding up from the basement with Mariang, Danny said, "I hope you're full, because I need to eat now. You have to take over pulling for her." Danny explained to everyone what they'd discovered, sending Ezra off into the next room to call for reinforcements.

It was all a lot of fuss, but I reminded myself that as much as I didn't want to be a pain, every day that kept September inside of me was another day for her to grow stronger and develop healthier organs. Mariang laced her fingers through mine and led me to the living room with Boston, where she moved the ottoman under my feet and covered me with a chenille throw from the arm of the white leather couch. It was a steep flip from her being the helpless one to letting her rub my swollen ankles with her strong hands. I saw a fire in her eyes that grew every day since her dip in the healing waters. She was a fighter, and had hated every moment she could barely make it through before collapsing. Now she had a chance to participate in life, to help instead of be helped, and she didn't miss an opportunity to love on me when I was the one who needed to take it slow.

Boston brought down his tablet and turned on a sports movie for us to watch, pulling Mariang up to sit on his other side, so the three of us could cuddle. Everything was hushed and low-key, which was sweet. I didn't know how long it would last, but I liked it. I don't know at what point the Vandershots and the Manauls became family to me, but I didn't question the gift that was always there when I needed it.

When Von came back down the stairs, he was winded. "Don't move. I want this to be perfect." He shoved the sandwich he'd grabbed from the kitchen into his mouth in four enormous bites, choking it down before fiddling with his phone so he could cast *The Way You Look Tonight* on the stereo system. Frank Sinatra sang throughout the house, making me feel cozy and loved.

"What's going on, babe?" I asked with a lazy smile.

It was then I realized that Von was sweating. "I love you. That's what's going on." The air gusted out of my lungs when he sank down on one knee before me. The bold look in his eyes was painted with small brushes of insecurity. My heart thudded unevenly when Von Vandershot presented me with a very specific small, square box.

"Von? What is this?" I asked cautiously.

"The best gift of your life."

"A unicorn?" I guessed, feigning excitement as my voice cracked. My palms were clammy, and though I wanted to make light of the situation, I gulped at the big ramifications of what might be inside that velvet box.

"Ollie gave me his blessing when I first got back and asked him for your hand. I went out and bought this that very day."

"You actually bought me a unicorn?" I don't know why I was doing shtick. I think I was in shock. I guess part of me still thought Von wanted to marry me in theory, not with the actual preparation of going to a store and picking out a legit ring.

My brain started to stutter as I took in the sight of Von on bended knee before me. He'd asked me to marry him just about every day since we'd gotten back together, but none of those proposals had felt like this – raw and real, demanding an actual answer.

"I'll buy you a unicorn another day, darling. Today, I'm offering you a ring."

"Dad!" Mariang shouted through the house like a madwoman. Her eyes were on the box, and she looked like she might rocket off the couch. Her hands had stilled on her cheeks, framing her shocked face. "Danny, Lynna! Get in here now! Hurry!"

Ezra and Danny bolted into the living room. Danny had his knife drawn, ready to fend off an attack. Ezra's fists were clenched, chest puffed as he stood protectively in front of Lynna, who trotted in behind him. "What is it?"

Mariang stood, jumping up on the balls of her feet and pointing to the black box Von still hadn't actually opened or handed over. "It's happening! It's finally happening!"

Danny's shoulders deflated when the promise of a monster fight was gone. He sheathed his knife and crossed his arms over his chest, holding his post in the archway. Boston shot up off the couch to give Von and me some space for our moment.

Mariang flew into Danny's arms so they could watch together. Boston got out his phone and videotaped it for his family back in London. Ezra gave Lynna his handkerchief, since she was already tearing up.

I just sat on the couch with my cheeks burning and my mouth wide open like a fish.

Von looked up at me from his place on the floor, closed box presented like an offering. His words came out slow, with patience and promise that reminded me why Von was my best friend. "October Grace, November Peach, will you marry me now, and in every life after this one?"

I was frozen on the spot, wanting, but unsure how to form whole words, though I knew I needed just the one. Then Von gently opened the box, blinding me with the ring that was just like Von – a little too much. "Holy iceberg, Batman! Are you serious?" I blasted, before I remembered the whole thing was being taped.

Mariang and Lynna let out incoherent bleats of

incredulity, letting me know I wasn't overreacting. Mariang couldn't help herself, and let out a thunderstruck, "Is that real?"

Von frowned, examining the overlarge square-cut diamond in a white gold setting, to make sure the jeweler hadn't replaced the gem with a Ring Pop or something. "Of course it's real. It's supposed to be three months' wages. Did you really think I'd skimp on the thing that she'll look at every day? My love is as real as this diamond." His eyes locked in on mine. "It's supposed to remind you of how much I adore you. My love for you is grand. No point in pretending we're average."

In true Von fashion, everything was always more than I expected.

"Von, it's too much," I protested, though I couldn't take my eyes off the sparkle. It was too perfect. Too clean. Too shiny. Entirely too much. I'd never owned real jewelry before. It was like going from training wheels on a kid's bike to a motorcycle overnight.

I gazed into his eyes, seeing the insecurity poking through his flourish. I could feel him crashing, wondering if he'd somehow picked the wrong ring, which wasn't the case. My fear was that he'd picked the wrong girl – not good enough to be seen wearing something so giant and amazing. "Please, darling," he whispered in earnest. "Marry me."

It was only when I worked out a barely audible croak of "yes" that I realized my face was wet.

I felt horrible when Von gusted out a breath of relief. I'd put him on hold for too long, but never again. We were going to be a family, the two of us, and then the three. Von slid the ring on my finger, my eyes panicking at the thing that was clearly too nice for me, too beautiful, too adult.

Then it hit me: I was an adult. I don't know how all the grownup choices snuck up on me, but somehow I'd gone from "kid" and "Bait" to a woman with a fiancé and a baby on the way. Von was still on his knee, hugging my belly and promising both of us details of the incredible life he was determined to provide.

And darn it, I began to believe in the magic he lavished on us.

LITTLE BOX, BLACK BOX

Champagne and sparkling cider was brought out, congratulations and hugs exchanged, and through it all, Von never left my side. He held tight to my hand even when Mariang practically leapt into his arms with excitement. She attacked me with the same fervor. "Now you're legally my sister! We're really sisters! I have a sister on paper! Like, a true sibling!"

"Oh, babe," I grinned as I hugged her. "You were my sister the first day I met you."

I warned Danny with a silent threat in my look not to be a jerk to Von, but when he stuck his hand out to his brother, there was no note of animosity to be found. His shoulders were relaxed, his face – well, he still looked a little monster of Frankenstein-ish, but there was no aggression that surfaced. He shook Von's hand politely and then pulled me in for an awkward hug, as if he'd only observed the social norm from afar. "It's about time you caved and joined our family. You're already one of us, October Grace Vandershot."

And just like that, I belonged. After being displaced so many times, I couldn't put this powerful feeling on a shelf to examine later. It flowed out of my tear ducts, brimming over with happiness I had not been prepared for. Von was giving me himself, which was gift enough, but he was also giving me a family with a real mama and more brothers than I could ever dream of. I would get to keep Mariang and Ezra, which was a bigger treasure than the crazy square-shaped diamond on my finger.

The awkward pat on the back shrug-hug Danny had started mutated into an actual embrace as my tears dotted his shoulder. I released Von's hand and clung to Danny, knowing my surly big brother wouldn't lie to me and tell me this was forever if it would all implode in a day.

"It's alright," Danny promised me. "No need to cry. You're really so distraught over becoming one of us?"

I laughed through my tears. "I never dreamed I'd get this lucky."

"It's got nothing to do with luck. It's you we love." Danny's declaration rang in my chest and made September do a little roll that even Danny felt. "Wicked! Did you feel that? Did she just kick me?"

I took his hand and placed it right on the money spot so he could feel her again. His smile couldn't be contained or tucked away when September punched him square in the center of his hand, like a miniature high-five. The others were still clapping Von on the back and teasing him about the disco ball he'd bought me, but Danny and I were having a solid brother-sister moment. Danny had emotion in his eyes – real, consuming emotion as he leaned down to whisper in my ear. "I promise you, I'll watch over September. I'll help Von keep her safe. I'm by your side through it all."

Danny's declaration was fierce and unexpected, drawing me tighter into his arms. I don't know when it was that we became friends who swore oaths of loyalty to each other, but here we were. "Luckiest cousins in the world, right here," I said, pointing to Mariang's barely-there belly and my bulbous one.

Danny lowered me onto the couch and lifted my feet to rest on the ottoman, being careful with me, as if I was precious and breakable. He sat on the arm of the couch, holding my hand to pull for me until Von flopped down on my other side to take his place. "My fiancée," Von breathed, enraptured by the word itself. "Isn't she beautiful, Danny?"

Danny drained his champagne. "It's no surprise you married up."

Ezra noticed my discomfort as I shifted on the couch, trying to find a spot that didn't make my back hurt. "Where's my head? This isn't bedrest. Up the stairs with you, young lady. If the doctor said bedrest, this couch hardly counts as a suitable mattress."

Ezra and Danny helped me to stand, leading me out of the living room and into the foyer. My eyes passed over the small table that usually had flowers on it, or someone's keys resting there. I was walking so slow that at first no one noticed I'd stopped.

Amidst the joy and bliss of the moment, the only sound I heard was my heartbeat thrumming in my ears. My mouth went dry as the vast expanse of the mansion felt like it was closing in around me on all sides.

There it was – the black box from my dreams. As big as a shoe box, and bound with hard, black leather. I'd never seen a box like that apart from when Philip presented me with the weed inside. "What... I... What is that?" I asked, not bothering to hide my fear. It was one thing when Von and I conceived after having dreamy dream sex. It was quite another when a completely fictitious man gave me a pretend present that showed up in real life.

Ezra straightened, leaving me to retrieve the box, and letting Von take his place on my other side. "This came from Captain Finn while you were out."

"It's... I... Um, it's not supposed to be here."

Von squeezed my hand in a threat. "I swear, if there's a ring inside that box, he's too late. You're already spoken for."

"It's not a ring inside," I mumbled, unable to take my eyes off the box. "It's a *himila* weed."

The entire room gasped as one. Ezra stepped back, confused. "How can you possibly know that? I left the box sealed. Did Captain Finn tell you he was going to bring you one? How did he even acquire it?"

I shook my head, unable to make sense of how the box got here, how Finn got his hands on it, and how a fake weed in a fake box was somehow real. "If there's a weed inside, I want Finn here right now. I mean, before anything else happens in the world. Before the next person breathes, I need Finn here to answer for this."

Ezra's furrowed eyebrows told me he didn't take me as seriously as he should. "How do you even know what the *himila* weed is? I've never known a woman in my lifetime who's taken it. It's reserved for queens, and impossible to find. How did Captain Finn get his hands on something thought to be extinct at best, or dismissed entirely as a myth?"

Danny was tensed as if readying for an attack. "Just open it. It's probably another book. You're getting yourself worked up about something that doesn't exist anymore."

I gripped Von as Ezra presented me with the box like a jewelry salesman. I released both brothers and reached forward, unbuckling the leather latch without breathing, without blinking and without any answers.

PHILIP'S LONG REACH

"Mariang should have some of it," Danny insisted again.

"I really can't keep having this same conversation. She can have half of it once Finn gets here and explains himself." I was propped up in the bed, pillows squished between my back and the headboard, under my knees and at my left side in case... I dunno, but Von was obsessed with bringing me pillows, so I just let him, and made myself a little fort. "I'm really okay, Von. I think I've got enough pillows."

"If you'd simply tell us what's got you so worked up, then we could help."

"I don't know what kind of help I'll need yet. I need Finn here. What's taking so long? I'll need a shrink too, maybe. A good one who specializes in Vampires, Mermen and Shapeshifters."

Von moved into the hallway and brought me a second blanket, tucking it in over the comforter he pulled up over my lap. "Finn will be here soon enough. He's not available at a moment's notice. And not to be *that bloke*, but on the day we get engaged? He's the last person I want in this house. And more than likely, this is the last place he'll want to be when he finds out."

"I'm not talking about the engagement. I need to know where he got the box and the weed. He shouldn't have it."

"I don't think you realize what a grand gift this is. I mean, I'd tell you to send it back to the lousy git, but if it'll keep September healthy, I'll take whatever luck he sends us."

"For you *and* for Mariang," Danny insisted, eyeing the box as if he wanted to steal it.

Boston sat in the chair at the desk in my light green, cream and gold room, elbows on his knees as he tried to shortcut his way to getting the information out of me. "So you had a premonition that Captain Finn would bring you a *himila* weed in this box? Is that why you're upside-down about this?"

"No. Maybe. I don't know. I'm not the premonitions type. I just need Finn here." I placed my hand on Von's to calm his nerves as he tucked a third blanket around my belly. "I'm sorry our special day is going like this. We should be all happy and kissing till our brains fall out."

"I can make your brains fall out tonight after this mess is swept up. Just tell me what's going on."

I shook my head, sinking back against the pillows as I eyed the box warily. Danny moved past it when he went to check on Mariang, looking at the box with longing, but resisting the temptation to steal it. "Boston, could you give us a minute?" I asked quietly when something dark began to dawn on me.

"Sure, but I could come back at any time," Boston said with a finger of threat pointed between us like a school monitor. "I don't want any children conceived out of wedlock. Not on my watch." Then he broke into a silly grin, clapping his hands at his stupid joke before he left us alone.

I picked up my phone again and scrolled to the page I'd bookmarked, displaying it to Von. "These are all the side effects for my medication. None of them say anything about hallucinations, right? I need you to check for me. I've read it too many times; the words are starting to run together."

Von's eyebrows pushed together in concern as he read, moving aside a pillow so he could sit down on the side of the bed next to me. "Nothing here, no. Oh, but some of these are dreadful. What's going on? Are you starting to see things that aren't here?"

"No," I whispered. "I'm seeing things that *are* here, which might be even worse."

"I don't understand, love."

I reached out for him and clutched his forearms in desperation. "If it turns out that I'm crazy, please don't send me away. Don't have me committed. Don't let anyone lock me up." Fear gripped me as I pictured myself in the white scrubs I'd seen Bev wearing when she'd gone to stay at the mental facility. I didn't have tears, but I had urgency as I swallowed my pride and laid it all out on the table for my fiancé to examine and turn me away at will. "What's happening can't be happening. It's not real, but it is. I touched the box. It's real. I felt it."

Von's wary expression had a dose of fear to it as he examined my pleading face. "I don't understand what you're on about. Tell me what's twisted you so badly that even *I* can't understand you. I can always understand you. Slow it all down and run it by me again."

"Kiss me," I begged. "Kiss me and promise me you won't have me committed. I'll be so good for September. She needs her mama!"

"Of course I won't have you committed. Why would you even say that? I've seen you when you were out of your mind over a stain on the rug. I've seen you at your worst and at your best. I'll never leave you again. If they lock you up, I'll come stay in the Loony Bin with you. Then we'll both be mad together." His words were sweet, and the kiss even sweeter. Von was tender as he cupped my face, bringing me forward so he could kiss me just enough to make the music swell, the colors blur, and my anxiety lessen.

"This?" I heard Finn utter from the doorway. "This is what you needed me to drop everything for? Rip my heart out, why don't you!" He pounded his fist to his chest, anger and hurt fighting for top billing on his face.

"No! Finn, wait!" I tried to get up and go to him, but I was so swallowed by pillows and blankets, I couldn't fight my way out of the ocean of linens.

Von held his hands up and helped situate me back against the headboard. "Obviously we didn't know you were here. Have a seat. Apparently the little gift you got my girls has given October quite the scare. Care to share where you found the *himila*?"

"I don't answer to you, *kendi*," Finn scowled at Von, getting in the dig that reminded Von he'd once been a sex slave.

"Hey, knock it off. I need both of you to cool down. Finn, have a seat. I have questions for you."

Finn remained in the doorway, his arms crossed over his chest. "I'm not sitting on the bed you share with your half-vamp."

Danny came up behind Finn and shoved him forward so he stumbled into the room. "I believe the Omen asked you to come in. Her rank is above yours, so do as she says before I get all sorts of unpleasant."

Finn drew his knife, and I knew I'd never get my questions answered if I couldn't contain the bulls.

I managed to extract myself from the bed and moved over to the guys, knowing they'd be more careful if I was near, for fear of hurting the baby. "Everyone pick a corner and march! I mean it. No one fights around me. Are you crazy, Finn? Put that knife away."

Finn glowered at Danny, but obeyed, shooting me a wounded expression as he moved to the corner furthest from the bed. When Von and Danny were in their corners, my shoulders relaxed as I stood in the center of the room. "Okay. That's better. Finn, it's good to see you. What can you tell me about the gift you brought?"

Finn ran his tongue over his teeth before speaking with the note of a sneer behind his words. "I brought you a *himila* weed. Ezra knows what to do with it. You dry the leaves and the root, brew it in hot water and drink the tea throughout your pregnancy. It's supposed to keep both the baby and you healthy."

I put my hand to my forehead. "What would happen if a pregnant woman ate the whole thing without brewing it first?"

Finn's eyebrows raised that I wasn't surprised at all by the purpose of the grand gift. "You wouldn't need to eat it all like that unless you or your baby were in danger of dying without it. It would give you a boost for, I don't know, a few weeks or something. But you'd need it again and again, if that were the case. The tea is best. Gives you the medicine in small increments to dose you with a constant boost of healing." He sheathed his knife. "Is that what you did? You just ate it without Ezra guiding you through how to use it?"

Danny's head whipped toward me, panicked that I hadn't saved half for Mariang. "No!"

I held up my hand to calm his fears. "Of course not. I haven't touched the weed. Where did you get it? Ezra seemed to think it was extinct."

Ezra came into the bedroom from eavesdropping out in the hallway. "It is extinct. Where did you happen across it, Captain?"

Finn turned to Ezra, mildly embarrassed. "Technically, I didn't. One of my men suggested making a quest to find it for you."

"Was it on the top of Mount Malubha?" I asked in a quiet voice that shocked all four men in the room.

Finn answered slowly. "It was. How did you know that?"

I countered with a curt, "How did your man know that?"

Finn shrugged. "I don't know. It happened to be on the first mountain he scaled. I figured he caught a lucky break or something. Thad's one of my most trusted men. He helped me sneak Von out after Von killed Prince Julius. I've no reason to question how he found a miracle. I only know that he found it, so I could bring you the thing you needed." He shot Von a superior look. "I knew you needed help no one was giving you, so I gave it to you."

Von snarled, gearing up for a fight. "Oh, you gave it to her?"

Finn's words came out dirty. "Gave her exactly what she needed, as many times as she needed it."

Danny saw the loaded spring before I did, and leapt across the room to intercept Von before he tore into Finn. Danny wrestled Von back to his corner, pinning his shoulders there and slamming him against the wall to knock some sense into him. "Take a breath, mate. This won't get you what you think it will."

Once Von seemed to have cooled, Danny went back to his corner. "Cut to it, kid."

I didn't want to admit to my ridiculous fantasy life in front of Von, and surely not in front of Ezra, but there was no other way. It was either my pride or my sanity, and I knew what I'd fight for every time. "I have to tell you something weird, so be cool till I'm finished." I took in a deep breath. I was unsure how to muscle through, so I dove in headfirst. "I sort of have this stupid dream that happens when I'm..." I couldn't muster up the word 'horny' in front of Ezra, so I stuck with something more PG. "When I'm lonely. This guy named Philip comes to me. We go traveling, sit on the beach, make love and do couply kinds of things." I shot Von an apologetic look. "It started before you, and when we're together I don't have those dreams, I swear."

I don't know what I expected, but it wasn't for Von to chuckle. "You're afraid to admit that you have sex dreams about other people? I used to have them all the time about various celebrities. It's nothing to worry about. Perfectly normal."

"Philip's not a celebrity. He's not real. He's a completely pretend person I made up in my mind. I didn't think anything was weird until I got pregnant and he started saying the baby was his. I thought it was my brain trying to reason through you and me getting psychically pregnant, so I tried to shrug it off. But then Philip started bringing me these black leather boxes with the *himila* weed inside. I mean, what a weird gift, right? But he was dead set that I had to eat them. Every few weeks or so, he'd be back with that same leather box and a new shriveled weed. He said September needed them to stay alive. He wanted her to be a princess, and she'd need extra magic to keep her strong so she could rule."

"Rule what?" Danny asked.

I was shocked that anyone was following along, much less taking me seriously. "Philip wants her to rule Terraway. I swear that's not any part of what I want. You know me, guys. You know I don't like it when people bow or treat me like I'm some big deal." I looked around at the four men who all wore various shades of the same horrified expression, and in that moment, I realized they did know me. In this room, I had friends and family who didn't call me Bait, and who stuck around even when my imaginary friends turned into megalomaniacs. "You do know me. That... That's a big deal." I tapped my heart. "Thanks for listening and not calling me crazy."

Danny turned to Finn, his face resuming business mode. "This Thad character. I want that fellow here now."

"Thad can't come up unless I port him here. What're you implying?"

I turned my chin slowly from side to side. "I don't know. I have no answers when it comes to Terraway. All I know is that the box and the weed are from Philip, who's not real. Philip's the reason I knew about Mount Malubha and the *himila* weed before any of you told me." I felt stupid for even saying that my imaginary friend was real. "That can't be right. Thad must know something. He's our best shot at answers. Can you bring him here?"

Finn nodded, not breaking eye contact with me. "Do you know who this Philip is? Is he a man from your world?"

"He's from Terraway, and he wants to come Topside, but he can't. So he's not a king or an important official, or he'd be able to port here himself."

"What does he look like?" Ezra asked, trying to play detective to get to the bottom of it.

My eyes closed as relief spread over me. "You really believe me? You don't think I'm nuts?"

Danny's arms were crossed as he leaned into his corner. "Oh, we know you're batty, but we're in too deep not to believe you. Von, if she describes the bloke, can you draw us a picture of him?"

Von nodded, running his hands through his hair. "I should be able to come up with something so we can track the tosser down. How is he dreamwalking with her if he's never met her?" He looked pointedly at me. "Have you snogged anyone else? Beto, Finn, Mason, Bishop, me, and the list ends there? Now's the time for nothing but the truth, love. I won't get angry. Honest."

I huffed, wishing I wasn't subjected to such scrutiny. "Don't say it like that. I didn't *kiss* kiss Bishop, like romantically. But no, there's no one else." I looked into Von's eyes so he could see I wasn't lying. "I promise you, that's everyone I've ever kissed. I only was with Philip in my dreams, and he's fake! And you're not even supposed to be able to dreamwalk unless you've had sex! But now that the box shows up with the weed and all that? I don't understand. Philip can't be dreamwalking with me. He's not real! I don't know what's going on, but I do know when the math doesn't add up."

"Okay, love. I believe you. Let me get some paper and pencils. Talk me through it, and I'll sketch him out."

I buried my head in my hands. "This is the worst. This is what I get for being irresponsible in my own imagination."

Finn relaxed his erect posture. "I'm sure there's an explanation."

"Maybe you're psychic," Danny suggested, earning a glare from me.

"Maybe you're a..." A contraction hit me before I could insult Danny right good. I doubled over and grabbed my belly and the footboard, letting out a noise of distress I wished none of them had heard.

Danny and Finn ran to me, with Ezra shouting down the hallway for Von. "Easy, easy," Danny cooed. Finn dropped my hand and stepped back in alarm, while Danny waited for the contraction to pass. My new brother let me squeeze his hand while he kept me mostly upright. He gave me a steady pull, his arm wrapped clear around my back and palming my belly. I punished his hand with my superwoman grip, letting Danny take the brunt of my sudden agony.

"I don't want to do this! I don't want to do this! Not here!" I wailed, scared and in too much pain.

"You will, and you'll be brilliant. But not today. It'll pass. Ezra, out you go!" Danny snapped. "Call Prince Langgam and get Ollie back here immediately."

The pulling was too late and not enough. The contraction seemed to go on forever, crawling up my spine like a torturous spider I couldn't escape from. "Ah!" All the books said the contractions would start out small and build toward the grand finale. *Stupid lying books.*

But Ezra didn't go. He inched closer, swallowing hard has he watched me grit my teeth through a howl. He was panting like an animal, his expression darkening as he neared Danny and me. My kind, patient dad snorted through his nose as a long gob of drool escaped from the side of his parted lips.

Von bolted back into the room, tackling Ezra to the

ground. Boston was right behind him, and Mariang shrieked from the doorway. "Dad, no!"

I closed my eyes in relief when my contraction passed. When I opened them again, Ezra was no longer in my bedroom. In his place was a legit full-on overlarge lion. He was as tall as the doorway, mane and all, shaking off shreds of the button-down white Oxford shirt Ezra had worn. The enormous lion roared, announcing that he was a wild animal, and to move away from his prey.

I'd never even thought to ask Ezra what his shapeshifting animal was. He was Matruculan, and aside from having a hunger for fresh baby, he could also shapeshift, just like Mason. Ezra was gentle, so I assumed he would become a house cat or something, not the king of the freaking jungle.

30

THE LION IN EZRA

The men stood with fists and knives drawn, forming a cage around Ezra, who only growled louder. He was huge, far bigger than any lion I'd ever seen. He was more the size of a small elephant, with all the features and agility of a lion.

Von kept his voice even. "Boston, get October and Mariang to the safe room and lock them in now. Stay in there until I come for you."

Boston was terrified, but insistent. "I'm not leaving you to fight a lion!"

"You'll do as I say!" Von shouted, never taking his eyes off of Ezra. "I won't live if you die. I can't lose another brother. Go on! You were brought here to protect the Omens, so do your duty!"

"Go, Boston!" Danny growled.

I tried to inch toward the door, but Ezra roared, taking

a predatory step between me and Boston, who was near the door. Ezra was a clever lion, cutting me off from my exit.

Danny swallowed. "Take Mariang to the safe room, Boston. October will be right behind you, so don't lock it until you're all three inside."

Boston shot Danny a hurt look and ran Mariang to safety, decreasing my anxiety by like, ten percent, now that she and her baby wouldn't be eaten by her own father.

Now there was just me, and I was ripe with fresh unborn baby. "Don't hurt him! It's still Ezra. Put those knives away!" I ordered.

Von's eyes never left Ezra's, even while Ezra pawed at the air with a loud roar that made my insides feel like they were vibrating. "Danny, go downstairs and get Lynna to safety. Then bring us up some steak. Any kind of meat will do."

Danny was ready for attack, not a burger run. "I'm not leaving you. She's my sister. I swore to protect her."

"I'll not watch you die! I've got a plan, Danny. Now run along."

It couldn't have been two minutes since the last contraction before a second one hit me like a kick to the uterus. I dropped to my knees, my body contorting and acting on some primal instinct to get on all fours. I buried my fingers in the carpet as I howled through my contraction. It lasted forever, the pain too much to hope it would ever go away. There was no epidural. No C-section.

Not even a lousy over the counter pain pill for mild aches. Of all the ways I expected to have a baby, in a bedroom with a giant lion and no doctor was not on the list.

"Pull from her, Danny. I'll handle Ezra. Get the contractions to stop. I mean it. Bliss her out if you have to." Von was locked in on Ezra, who looked like he was readying to pounce.

My vision blurred as Danny ran to me, and Ezra gave chase. Finn and Von tackled the lion, but Ezra quickly fended Finn off. I saw Von's fangs barred, his lips snarling as he jumped onto Ezra's side and then climbed up his back to mount him like he was riding a horse. Von was all agility and determination, getting himself a sturdy seat on Ezra before sinking his teeth into the meat of his father figure's shoulder.

Ezra roared in surprise and pain, shaking his mane to try and knock Von off. The horrible sound of the fierce lion rang in my teeth and shook me to my core. I understood now how Ezra could be so gentle and calm in the council meetings, while still evoking fear and respect from the kings.

I had a dad who was an animal. My dad couldn't see me anymore; all he saw was meat. It shouldn't have been a heartbreak, but I couldn't control the fissure. If Ezra ate my baby and killed me, he would never survive the guilt.

I held my stomach and screamed through the tail end of my contraction, praying September wouldn't come yet, that Ezra wouldn't eat us both, and that Von wouldn't be killed by his surrogate father.

Von's teeth latched again, his arms looping around Ezra's furry neck to try choking him out. His arms weren't long enough for Ezra's thick neck, so the wrestling hold only served to irritate the beast. Ezra reared up onto his back legs, pawing up toward the ceiling, unleashing his temper in a furious roar that terrified me to my very soul.

Finn jumped back into the fight when Ezra came down on all fours. He grabbed up the chair from my desk and used it like he was a lion tamer in a circus ring. When Ezra had no patience to let Finn pretend he was winning, Finn deserted what was left of the broken chair and raised his palms in threat, spraying Ezra with scalding water. The steam rose up in the room, and while I wanted to tell Finn to stop so he didn't hurt Ezra, burns would heal. When Ezra backed away from his path to me, I saw with fright that Finn's chest was bloody. I shouted for him to run, but he didn't listen. Finn jumped at the lion and wrestled Ezra so Von could get in another bite.

Danny pressed his palm to the small of my back, pulling erratically. He let go when Von cried out after Ezra got in a swipe to his arm. Danny was a tank, as was Finn, but it took the both of them with all their might, plus both Duwendes pulling, to keep Ezra from lunging at me. Von sank his fangs deep into Ezra's back again, drinking in long pulls that made his eyes roll in delirium, while Finn and Danny battled with the front end of the beast.

I couldn't time the contractions, nor could I think clearly enough to figure out if the second contraction had actually ended and a fresh one began, but this one was enough to draw out a scream when it was probably least helpful. I couldn't get to the door because there was a friggin' lion in my path. I couldn't even stand to be helpful, so insistent was September that today would be her birthday. I was sweating and gritting my teeth as I palmed the carpet, heaving like a beast, and snarling in time with my dad. The room closed in on me with every scream I couldn't control, couldn't temper and couldn't run from.

31

MAKE IT STOP

It took too long, too many contractions, but between the pulling and Von sucking enough blood out of Ezra to weaken him, Ezra finally collapsed onto the carpet. The lion let out a giant sigh that almost sounded peaceful beneath my howls of agony. The room was in absolute shambles – my desk broken when Finn had tried to knock Ezra over the head with it. There was blood everywhere, and everything was wet.

"Is he..." Danny didn't want to say the word dead, but there was no telling how much blood Von had taken, and if Ezra could recover.

"He's just passed out. I was drinking and pulling at the same time. He should be out for a while. If he starts to stir, we bliss him out again first thing."

"I like the sound of that," Danny answered. "Is everyone okay? Finn, you're bleeding pretty badly."

"It's just a scratch. From a lion." The corner of Finn's mouth lifted. "We just wrestled a Matruculan lion and won. We actually fought with the largest Matruculan beast in Terraway, and won."

I didn't want to rain on their parade, especially when I saw handshakes and high-fives they desperately needed to seal their bonding moment, but contractions don't give a crap about dude hugs. I was still on all fours, breathing through my teeth until the pain hit a crescendo I'd hoped wouldn't be as bad as the last few. They were getting worse and more frequent, as far as I could tell. I'd only gotten to thirty-Missisippi-oh-my-crap when the next one hit.

My shriek of agony snapped them all back to the danger that was still not over. All three ran to me, trying unsuccessfully to pull me up off the floor. "I can't!" I cried, somehow unable to move from my position on the carpet.

Von wrapped his arms around my waist. Ezra's blood dripped from his chin into my hair as he pulled the stress from me with his hands around my belly. Danny knelt at my other side, holding me in a gentle headlock and pulling in an unsteady thrum that told me he was too hopped up on adrenaline to focus.

"What are you two doing?" Finn asked, bewildered and worried as he stood over us.

Danny hugged my head to his midsection, making me feel like a family pet while I breathed through my teeth. "She goes into labor if she doesn't have constant pulling. A few minutes without it, and this is what happens."

Finn swore and tore one of the sheets off the bed, cutting the edge off and wetting it in his palms. He rubbed the cool rag over my face as I panted through the pain. "It's alright, *sinta*. Breathe."

Bro moment over. Von stiffened, his voice livid. "She's not your *sinta*, she's my *asawa*! Check her finger, you insufferable wanker."

Finn looked down and let out a quiet bleat of agony that tore at my heart. Then he cleared his throat and continued to mop the sweat from the nape of my neck. I couldn't believe the depths of love that kept him in place, helping us when he could've easily abandoned me to have Von's baby in the middle of my bedroom. "You're not married yet, though. I would've heard. There's still a chance for you to get scared and run out on her again, and when you do, I'll be ready."

Von gripped my stomach harder and yelled, "I'll end you if you don't stay away from my wife!"

So much for the "We just wrestled a lion together, so we're cool" truce.

Danny's tone was sharp. "Sod off, both of you. Can't you see the woman you both love is in labor? Shove it off for another day." He jerked his chin toward the hallway. "Finn, go down the hall to Mariang's room. In the back of the closet there's a false door. Pry it open, and you'll find the passage to the panic room. Keep Mariang inside, but tell Boston to come here quick. I need him to pack Mariang and me a bag. If we can get October's contractions under control, we're moving into her house until Mariang has the baby. I'll not go through this again."

Finn rose and did as he was asked, stepping over the enormous snoozing lion on his way out. My contraction ebbed, letting me finally get in a breath that didn't feel like I wanted to die. Von had the presence of mind to be gentle as he stroked my belly. "Easy, darlings."

Danny shook his head, frustrated with himself. "I tried to bliss her out, Von. I couldn't focus enough to pull that hard. I'm sorry. I'm still a little shaky. I mean, it's Ezra."

"It's alright. We'll get it under control." Von held my waist, leaning over my body to bury his face in my hair. "September will be born healthy and strong. She won't be one of those tiny preemies we reap, so help me."

Danny shook his head. "I can do better. Ezra really threw me off my concentration. It's no excuse. I'll be more helpful next time."

"A Matruculan lion in the middle of the bedroom's no excuse to get thrown off your game? You're too hard on yourself, Danny. It's alright. It's fixable." Von let out a gust of his nerves. "I haven't seen Ezra's animal form in ages. Forgot how big he gets. Temper, that one."

The guys were quiet a few beats, still coming down from the fight and the fear of me giving birth on the carpet. Danny's panting slowed as he attempted to calm down. "You sent Boston away."

"And I'll not apologize for it. Mum lost one of her babies. She'll not lose the other."

"It wasn't a criticism. I would've done the same thing, had I been thinking clearly."

"Mariang can't be unprotected, and I needed you here. You're better in a fight. Boston's been drinking too much to be all that solid with a knife."

Danny mulled over the compliment, and while I wished he had the space to respond with "I'm so sorry I've been a terrible brother, Von," another contraction hit me like a ton of bricks, making me scream as I tried to breathe through it.

"Wicked! Feel this, Danny. Her belly gets hard and starts trembling when the contraction hits." Von moved his brother's hand to my stomach, like I was a science experiment or something. I wanted to punch them both.

"Wicked!" Danny agreed as Mariang came back into the room with Finn.

She dropped to her knees and hugged me while I panted, wishing everyone would just get off of me already. "It's alright, sweetie. Try and calm down. Tell my niece it's not time to come out yet."

Danny and Mariang both stroked my hair like I was a dog, which of course made me want to growl and snap at them. I bit my lip through my temper, but my self-control was fading fast. Finn watched my face, knowing I was ready to unleash. "Lady Mariang, can you find me some rope to bind your father with? Something that won't hurt him, of course. Just in case he rouses."

"Sure." Finn helped Mariang to her feet, and she reluctantly left the room.

"Better?" Finn inquired quietly once my contraction ebbed.

"Make it stop," I begged in a mournful tone that, had I not already reached my max capacity for emotional trauma, would've embarrassed me.

"How about the *himila* weed?" Finn suggested, moving toward the box on my dresser.

"No!" Danny was firm. "Mariang needs some of the weed, too. There are *two* Omen heirs to think about here."

Finn glared at Danny. "There'll be only one if October delivers this baby too soon."

"No, no, Finn. Mariang and I can share it. Let me up, guys. I think I can move now. I'm getting claustrophobic. Can I get downstairs before the next one hits?"

"Sure, love. Easy now." Von and Danny didn't let go as they carefully lifted me to stand and led me down the hallway. The stairs were tricky, but we moved slowly and steadily together, with the brothers pulling as a team the whole time. They anchored me to the white leather couch in the living room, exhaling with palpable relief.

Finn pulled down the chenille throw from the recliner and draped it over my lap. He lifted my legs to the ottoman, his fingers lingering on my bare feet.

32

FAREWELL, FINN

Three more erratic contractions, and that was it. Danny and Von had pulled so hard that I could barely place one foot in front of the other. It was worth being totally helpless to get out of labor. I was terrified for when there was no way out. In a month, I'd have to do that all over again, but for longer, and with the pushing part I dreaded.

Boston hurriedly packed Von and me a bag and loaded up the SUV with everything we needed, including a small feast from Lynna. She was still crying, dabbing at her face with Ezra's handkerchief. She refused to come with us. "I'll not let my Ezra come to, alone and scared in his house with no family. I won't leave my boy." Danny consented, but only if she waited out his transition in the safe room.

Boston raided the fridge once more for the good cheese I knew he liked, while Von and Finn helped me to the car.

It was a team effort, and though they both wanted to kill each other, they worked together for the common good. Von got into the car first, and Finn hugged me, letting me rest my tired head on his shoulder. "I'll stay with Ezra to cut him loose when he comes back to himself. If worse comes to worst, I'll port Lynna down to Terraway until Ezra's a person again."

"Thank you for looking after my dad. And I'm sorry you had to find out about Von and me like this. I can't believe you stayed with me through the whole thing. You're a better man than anyone gives you credit for. I don't deserve how good you were to me up there."

Finn kissed the top of my head as he held me, ignoring the threats from Von that came from the backseat. "Don't you know by now? I love you. Even when you're not mine. Even when you send me away, like you're about to." He pulled back, looking into my eyes to see what he'd always known was there. He smelled like the ocean, and I was scared to let him go. I hoped I wouldn't sink without the green eyes that always adored me, even when I was unlovable. His voice was low and choked with emotion when he finally spoke to me. "Send me away, *sinta*. Tell me not to wait for you. Tell me you'll have a good life, and that you'll call for me when it's not."

I closed my eyes and nodded. "It's time for you to go find someone who loves you the way you deserve. Be a good man, Finn. Listen to your conscience. I always knew it was inside of you."

"I love you, October." He brought my hand up between us and kissed my knuckles, scowling at my engagement ring. "My conscience isn't all that strong right now. How much do you want to bet I could kiss you before your vampire attacked?"

Von barreled out of the backseat, but I was quicker. "Goodbye, Finn." I stepped out of his grip, reaching for the car to lean on instead. Boston and Mariang helped me inside while Von shouted and Finn snarled.

Danny clapped his hands together after setting the black leather box down on the floor of the car. "Get in the car, Von. Finn, we'll call you when we figure out October's dream guy ordeal." That was the good thing about Danny; he was so surly, people rarely argued with him. He drove us away before I could mess up my life any further.

33

THE LOVE OF VON

It was hard to get comfortable, but I kept any whining to myself. The moment we reached my home, I felt sixty percent more okay with the world. I blew a kiss to my mailbox and went inside, knowing that as great as the mansion was, my quaint abode on Lenoy Avenue was my home.

"Bedrest for you, November," Von ordered. "Boston, will you take a shift for me? I need to do a patrol of the grounds with Danny. Get some more blood in me. Get thoughts about murdering Finn out of my brain. You know, things of that sort."

Boston went with me into the bedroom, his hand in mine after rolling his eyes and consenting to take his shoes off before entering my own personal hallowed ground. We got into the bed and assumed our usual cuddle we fell into when it was just the two of us – my head resting on his outstretched arm, our knees touching, and our hands clasped between us in solidarity, my belly bumping against his. It was slightly more intimate than I ever wanted to get with my soon to be brother-in-law, but it was the job. One thing was for sure – when September finally came to meet us, she'd be the most relaxed baby ever, because her Duwende uncles would never put her down.

"Is this how you imagined spending your Friday nights?" I teased. "Cuddled up to a pregnant woman?"

"I could do worse. I'd never seen a woman in labor before. Remind me to send my mum some flowers when I get a moment where no one's attacking us."

I gingerly slid his phone out of his pocket. "I'd wager you have a good ten minutes of not being attacked now. No promises on the hour after that."

He took his phone from my hand and held onto my fingers for a beat, examining my ring like it was an alligator sitting on my finger. "That ring is mental. Totally and completely mad. But I guess that's just like Von. When he does something, he does it with gusto." The fog of reminiscence clouded his vision, and he blinked as if he was seeing something very far away. "This one time, Mum was on our case about cleaning our room – Bishop and me. Von was sick of hearing the fight, so he gathered up all our things and shoved them into garbage bags. I still don't know where he hid them. Cleanest our room ever was.

Then for Christmas, he wrapped each item and put it under the tree. It was the biggest spread ever. I still remember coming down Christmas morning and seeing mountains of presents under the tree." Boston chuckled. "After unwrapping the third pair of dirty socks, Von was in hysterics."

"That's awesome. I hope he's that creative with parenting for September. I'm a little worried about getting that part wrong and messing up a good thing."

Boston's hand lifted to brush a few squirrely strands of hair away from my forehead. "It goes the other way too, you know. He loves big, which is why he doesn't do it often. Did Danny ever tell you about the bully in grade five?"

"No. Who was Danny bulling?"

"Danny was *getting* bullied, if you can believe it. This grade six chap named... Oh what was his name? David or something. So Von spends the whole evening teaching Danny how to deliver a solid punch if David messes him up again. The next day, David's up to his old tricks, so Danny pops him one, only it barely leaves a dent. Von showed up to stop the fight, and sent Danny home. The next day, David's not in school. Nor the day after that. Three days later, he shows up with a black eye, a split lip, stitches across his cheekbone and a limp. Never messed with Danny again. You know what's brilliant about it?"

"That hopefully the school sent out better supervision on the playground after that?"

"Nah. It was that *Danny* got the credit for beating up David. Von spread the rumor that Danny was vicious when crossed, and then used David as the billboard so everyone could see that Danny wasn't to be messed with. David never said a word, but I knew. I saw Von come home that night with bloody knuckles."

"Von loves Danny."

"Von loves *you*," Boston informed me. "It's a sizeable responsibility to be loved by someone like Von. He loves hard, so if you care about Captain Finn, it was good of you to send him away. When someone Von loves is trifled with, big brother pounces, and they usually don't get back up."

I shrank in Boston's arms, embarrassed that my personal life was headline news for everyone in my world. "Thanks for the heads up. And for the record, I started getting close to Finn *after* your brother turned a relationship with me down."

"I know. But now that you've got his ring on your finger? Be prepared, is all."

Von strolled into the room, a relaxed smile on his face and color in his cheeks. "I found a few squirrels who met their maker sooner than they'd planned. Blood shipments will come here now instead of the mansion. I talked to Ezra, who's very much a person again. He's too ashamed to speak to you, Peach, but he sends his sincerest apologies. I believe the words 'Don't deserve to look on your face' were used in conjunction with a good hearty smattering of a general 'curse my genetics' kind of thing." When I only looked up at my fiancé with wonder as I studied all the things that were Von, he quirked his eyebrow at me. "What? Did I get some squirrel blood on my shirt?" He pulled a cinnamon stick from his pocket and started chewing on the end of it.

I slowly turned my chin from side to side. "You're amazing. You fought a lion the size of a small elephant to keep us safe. You fought a *lion*, Von."

Boston scooted out from our cuddle and left the spot vacant for Von, making his way out to the living room. "Yeah, yeah. Have your mating ritual without me. Not the kind of threesome I've always dreamed about."

My look of rapture when I drew the glowing "S" on Von's chest to label him the superhero he was to me could not be tempered. "You fought a lion for September and me."

"If anyone's going to take a bite out of my fiancée, it'll be me." He tried to make a joke, but I didn't care. I was too grateful.

I waved him toward me, sitting up to peel off his shirt. Von had the right kind of hunger in his eyes as he knelt on the bed at my side. "I love you," I admitted, though we both already knew the truth of that statement.

"Prove it," he challenged, squinting one eye at me. "Marry me. Be my wife and have my baby. Kiss me until I don't remember my own name." Instead of letting me do just that, Von buried his face in my neck, kissing and tugging at the tender skin until my toes curled and my fingers bunched in the sheet. I couldn't think through all the things I wanted to say to him to thank him for saving us. I wanted, and that was the only thing that stayed steady inside of me as Von's seduction turned everything on its head.

34

THE IDIOT I AM

Mariang had the grace to wait a whole hour before knocking on the door. Von had been firm that we would only make love in our minds, not in real life, so she was only interrupting a heated fictional romp as we kissed to our hearts' content. "There's something classically sexy about a virgin on her wedding night," Von insisted, tugging his shirt back on over his head. "Plus, your brother threatened me with some very specific bodily harm, were we to indulge beforehand."

Our promise to wait worked on both levels: it made him happy, and kept us from accidentally getting too worked up and sending me into early labor. Besides, in our minds we could do anything our bodies wanted, getting us used to the idea of being together before we actually could.

Von waited until I was situated in the bed before opening the door for Mariang, who was pink with chagrin at having interrupted us. "I'm so sorry. Danny's insisting we get to the bottom of the black box issue. I told him to wait, but he's worried."

Von couldn't do anything but smile. It was a boost to my ego that I could make his stunning eyes look that dreamy. He chewed on a cinnamon stick, tucked his arm around Mariang's back and held her other hand, dancing with her to a song he hummed, like he didn't have a care in the world – like he hadn't just wrestled a lion.

Mariang laughed as she danced with Von, graceful and elegant. She was light on her feet, even with the slight curve of the baby in her belly. "You're so happy," she remarked, looking lovingly at her brother-in-law. "You're much better this way. It does no good for the world when you're bogged down by too much. I very much like you in love."

"Then be prepared to love me forever, because I'm getting married, sis. Actually married." Von twirled her, releasing her to spin into Danny, who walked into the doorway unprepared for the cuteness. Danny fumbled with the pen and paper as he tried to jump into whatever it was Von was throwing him into. He swayed with Mariang for about two seconds, which I was actually pretty proud of him for. When Danny recalled himself and abruptly stopped the dance, it was with a firm frown that reminded us all who he was, and who we were asking him to be. While he'd come a long way, he was nowhere near comfortable with the whole dancing in public thing.

I watched Mariang's face fall, but she recovered quickly enough with a calm smile and a curtsey to Von, who did a gallant, sweeping bow in return. "Milady."

Danny slapped the pencil and notebook down on the top of the dresser with a glower at the too many smiles in the room. "We need to find the bloke who's manipulating October's dreams," he reminded us. "Work first, playtime later."

My grin fell at the reminder that life was still upside-down, and something janky was in my head that shouldn't be. "Okay, Danny. You're right."

Von groaned dramatically at what passed for art supplies at my house. "Picasso was never asked to sketch on lined notebook paper." He climbed into the bed and leaned against the headboard next to me, settling in with his shoulder kissing mine. His lips brushed my cheek and my hand before he poised his pencil to the paper. "Alright, Peach. Describe my competition."

I hid my face in my hands at Mariang's coo of longing over our affectionate state. "Philip's not your competition. He was pretend. This feels so stupid. Really, I'm sorry I'm making you do this."

"Sleeping naked with me means never having to say 'I'm sorry'."

"I'm sure Boston might have a thing or two to say about that."

Danny snapped his fingers irritably. "Would you two focus? I know you're all about snogging right now, and I get it. But this is serious. Draw me the bloke, so I can see if Captain Finn, Prince Langgam or King Kabayo can find him. Maybe your dream chap's this Thad soldier of Finn's who found you the weed. Then he'd be easy to locate."

I began describing Philip in detail, watching as Von made sense of my mumblings, and correcting the lines when they didn't ring true. Slowly, with a few false starts and crumpled papers, Philip began to surface. Before I could describe the last few details of his face, Von hid the notebook from me, sketching with panic in his eyes as he finished the portrait without me telling him how. Dread was plain on his face when he showed me the final drawing, as if he was hoping he'd gotten it all wrong. "Tell me this isn't him."

"Whoa! How did you do that? I didn't even tell you how to do his nose or his chin."

Von hung his head and turned the notebook to Danny and Mariang. "Boston! Get in here, mate. If you thought things were mucked up before, get ready for a whole new level of rubbish."

I blinked at Von. "What? Do you know that guy? He's a real person?"

Boston came into the bedroom, stopping short when he saw the portrait. "Um, why is that here?"

"It's the man who came to October in her dreams. The man who claims the baby's his. The git who gave her the *himila* weed in her mind, and no doubt told Finn's man

Thad where to get more when he couldn't infiltrate her dreams anymore. This is who's been in October's head."

Boston clapped his hand over his mouth and stepped back out of the room. "I'll tell Ezra," he called over his shoulder. Then he started swearing in a low string of unintelligible sentences as he yanked his phone from his pocket.

Mariang took a visible step back from me, as if my association with Philip made me a leper. Danny moved in front of her, shielding his unborn baby from me. "Go stay with Boston. Don't come into this room unless I say so."

"Danny, how could he get into her head? It's impossible for her to have had sex with him in real life, much less kiss him, so they couldn't dreamwalk. It's just not possible!" Mariang was visibly scared, her face pale and her eyes watching me with a note of dread. "October, you've never met this man in real life?"

I shrugged, trying not to worry at what I didn't understand. "Never. I made him up in my mind because I was lonely." I swallowed, looking down at my fingers that were twisting in the comforter. I knew I should've stuck with Mr. Brady. "You're saying he's a real person?"

Danny nodded, motioning for Mariang to leave the room. He shut the door after she was gone. Then he reached for the knob and turned the lock, securing the three of us in the room together. Danny sat at the foot of the bed, picking up the notebook and staring at the picture with a hard expression. "No one can dreamwalk with an

Omen unless they've had sex or apparently have done what you two did. You're sure you haven't had sex with this man?"

"Only in my dreams. Not in real life." When Danny didn't seem to believe me, I stiffened. "I was dreaming about Philip before the doctor confirmed that I was a pregnant virgin, if that helps you."

"When did it start?"

I buried my face in my hands. "This is so embarrassing. I really have to explain my fantasy life to you guys? I would never make you do this in front of Mariang."

Danny surprised Von by clapping him on the shoulder. "Give us a moment, mate. Go help Boston explain to Ezra what's going on. And if he can send word to Mason, that would be good. Mason's still her Reaper, and he should know."

Von seemed in a world unto himself, his eyes far away as he chewed on his cinnamon stick until it crumbled in his mouth, bringing him marginally back to life. "Yeah. I'm going to go get some air. I need... This is all a bit much. I mean, when I thought Finn was my biggest problem, that was one thing, but this?" He patted his chest and then his jeans pockets. "I'm taking the car out to run some errands."

Danny gripped his brother's wrist as Von stood. "Be back tonight, yeah? I'll not have her going into labor without you here."

Von grunted absentmindedly, not even bothering to say goodbye to me before he left.

My heart plummeted in my chest. Something about him leaving with no plan of coming back, or saying where he was even going made me nauseous. Von was running, just like he'd done when he'd found out I was pregnant. I could feel it shifting the air around me.

I couldn't lift my head to look at Danny when he cleared his throat. I didn't want him to see the raw emotion on my face. Danny set the notebook down on the mattress, his voice low and steady as he delivered the blow. "That man? The one in your dreams? His name isn't Philip. He's from Terraway, and even though he calls himself a king, he can't port Topside like the other kings and important officials can."

"Just give me a name, Danny. Is it that Thad guy of Finn's?"

Danny's gaze held me a few moments, his voice quiet and careful when he answered. "No, darling. His name isn't Philip, and it's not Thad. That man in your dreams is Sama."

My eyebrows puckered in confusion. "No, but Sama's evil. He's the big bad guy with the undead army. He wouldn't spend his time seducing me on a beach. He wouldn't be sweet to me. You're wrong. Maybe he just looks like Sama or something."

Danny took my brush-off in stride. "He um... Sama was cursed a century ago when he apprenticed under the last Kapre." He rubbed his forehead. "A Kapre was a giant-like creature who had a fascination with charm work, stones and all things magic. To apprentice for a Kapre meant you were already a force to be reckoned with. They only accepted the best."

My voice was quiet, and I still couldn't bring myself to look up at him. "Okay. So Sama's like a witch person?"

"He's an immortal witch person, called a Mangkukulam. He and another apprentice found a mixture of curses and combined them to make themselves immortal. The Kapre was furious. He made it so that Sama would live forever, but alone. He's alive still, of course, being immortal, but he's confined to an island no resident of Terraway could ever get to."

"Oh, that's terrible. What a steep punishment." Bits of this story rang familiar. I was pretty sure someone had already told it to me, but my brain was a little unsteady from all the excitement and too much pulling.

"Yes, well. The Kapre also took away Sama's ability to have an heir, since he's on the island alone. It makes sense that's the obsession he's got. Sama wants a child to pass his legacy down to. I never imagined he'd try dreamwalking, or that it would work. That he could actually get you pregnant in your dreams. But I mean, you and Von can dreamwalk without ever having had sex. The framework for the magic's there; I just never thought the limits could be tested like this. You've never met Sama in real life, yet somehow, he's found his way into your dreams."

My lower lip started to quiver as my arms wrapped around my belly protectively. "But Philip, or Sama, didn't get me pregnant. Von did. September belongs to Von and me."

"That may be true. But it might be that Sama found a way around the last Kapre's punishment."

My nose crinkled in confusion as I started rocking myself back and forth. "No, it's not Sama. His name is Philip."

Danny tapped the notebook. "Philip isn't your dream man. It's Sama who's been visiting you."

"But, no! I've never met him before in real life. Sama's an evil guy who's got an army and whatnot. Philip brings me presents. He goes on long walks with me and makes love to me. He's sweet."

Danny pointed to the picture. "Make no mistake, this man you're seeing is Sama."

"No! And it's impossible, Danny! It's all impossible. Even if that is Sama, how could he have knocked me up? I've never even met the guy in real life."

"If there's a chance Von got you pregnant by dreamwalking, then there's just as much chance Sama could've. The man works in psychic magic, controlling an entire undead army remotely without ever leaving his island." Danny didn't pull any punches when he dropped the nonnegotiable bomb. "The baby could be either Von's or Sama's."

I don't know why it was that I couldn't stop rocking, but Danny's hand on my shoulder was the thing that finally spooked me enough to break my rhythm. "She's Von's! September is Von's!"

"Okay, I'm not saying she's not. But I'm telling you that this is a possibility. And if she is Sama's, he won't stop until he's got September." He blew out a gust of all the things he didn't want to say to me. "And if Sama's found a way around the last Kapre cursing him so he couldn't have an heir, then he won't stop until he's got you, either."

My storm of tears was pushing up against the dam of my stubborn will, and I knew I didn't want Danny here for my breakdown. "Could you go out there and give me a minute?"

"No. Believe me, I'd rather be anywhere else right now, but one of us has to stay with you, or you'll go into labor." He moved to Von's place on the bed and rested his back against the headboard, his hand lightly touching my spine to pull from me.

"Please, Danny. Just go. I don't want you here for this."

"You want I should get Boston instead?"

"No. I want you should let me be alone." I turned my head from him as my tears fell, making tracks down my cheeks and wetting my lavender fitted top. I'd felt so pretty putting it on, but now I was a knocked-up girl who didn't know who the father of her baby was. I was a month away from delivery – if I made it that long, and I was completely and utterly lost, with neither potential father of the baby anywhere in sight.

"Door's locked," Danny reminded me. Then he stood

up and turned on the ceiling fan. The whirring sound was subtle, yet just loud enough to cover my quiet hiccups as the crying became too much to hold back. "They can't hear you, so go ahead." He scooted in next to me again, but instead of maintaining a healthy distance, he scooped me into his arms. Despite how big I was now, Danny pulled me onto his lap, tucking my head under his chin so I could lean my temple to his shoulder, my tears wetting his shirt.

I gripped his arm, too upset to examine how strange it was that Danny was passing up a perfectly good opportunity to be nasty to me. He wasn't entirely unpracticed on how to hold a woman, gently pulling from me as he brushed his fingers down my bicep. With every pass, I cried harder, letting go of the pride I'd thought was so important. I wept all over Danny, who took it like a champ.

"Von's gone!" I eked out between sobs. "I don't know why I thought it'd be different just because of this stupid ring. First sign of things getting hard, and he runs. I'm such an idiot that I fell for it!"

Danny held me tight, stroking the nape of my neck as if he didn't hate me at all. "Von's not gone. He just stepped out for a minute so he didn't say anything unhelpful. It's a lot to deal with, and he just needed the space to sort it all out. If you could send me away, you would, too. A little space isn't always an ocean of it."

"Why isn't Ollie back yet? This is too much. He's been gone too long. If I'm about to have an evil baby by myself, I want my brother here."

Danny chuckled, despite the fact that I was within clear punching range. "First off, you're not about to have an evil baby. September's half yours, and I haven't found a whole lot of evil to you yet. Secondly, you're not by yourself. You've got your old brother here." He squeezed me in a tender hug. "*I'm* your brother, and I'll make sure whatever the doctor hands you in the delivery room isn't evil."

"They have tests," I remembered, my brain sparking and spluttering. "Amnio tests that can determine the paternity of the baby in utero. They're risky, but I don't want to wait a month with the knife hanging over me like this."

"How risky?" Danny frowned.

I shrugged. "Have to ask the doctor about that. I need to know what I'm working with, here. If it's me and Ollie, or us plus the Vandershots."

"We don't need a test for that." Danny's hand migrated to my stomach, which made me hold my breath. Getting Mariang pregnant brought about a whole new side of him that I didn't want to jinx, but it constantly surprised me all the same. "September's my niece because you're my sister, no matter who the father is."

My voice was quiet as more tears rolled down my cheeks. "You and I both know Von won't come back."

"Von will be back before the sun sets. And I'll be here, no matter what."

I cried hard at the comfort I never expected to find with Danny. The promise of loyalty struck a chord deep inside of me, allowing my fingers to cling to him, even when I didn't understand the twists and turns of the world.

Danny stayed with me while I faced the uncertainty growing inside of me, but Von wasn't there. Even after the sun set, Von remained right where I should have expected – gone.

Long after my sobs quieted, I very slowly slid off my engagement ring, dropping it in Danny's palm with an air of finality. If Von wanted the ring on my finger, part of me knew he would be there to see that it stayed on me.

"No, kid. He'll be back. I just know he won't run out on you this time."

This time. Boy, was I an idiot.

It was a sad thing to watch Danny finally start to believe the best in Von, only to have Von disappoint, and leave us both hanging. Danny set the ring on my night-stand and held me and September. Over and over, I cursed Terraway and every single choice that had led me to this moment. It was all just plain too much, so I closed out the night crying myself to sleep in Danny's strong and steady arms.

Love the book?

Leave a review.

35

TEASE

Enjoy a free preview of *Tease*,
book seven in the *Terraway* series.

I was afraid to dream when I fell asleep that evening. I didn't know if I'd see Von or Philip, and dreaded meeting either in my subconscious.

My brain tripped on the mistake I made without thinking. *Not Philip.* There never was a Philip. The man with white-blond hair who came to me in my dreams was named Sama. We'd slept together in my imagination because I'd been lonely and wanted something fun to distract from the unending stream of exhausting work that Terraway never tired of throwing at me. So I'd conjured myself up a fake boyfriend. I would say that's pathetic, but it's not like everyone else doesn't do the exact same thing. Most other people choose Ian Somerhalder or David Duchovny as their fantasy hottie. I thought I'd made Philip up. But it was Sama, the dude with a surfer's body who wanted nothing less than all the power in Terraway, and an heir to share it with. He couldn't get a girl pregnant in real life, due to his remote location, so he'd found a way to possibly dreamwalk into my uterus. It was anybody's guess who the father was: Von or Sama.

Von had been gone for three days, and I think at this point only Mariang was holding out hope he'd be back. Gotta love the girl for her sweet heart and total optimism. The engagement ring Von had given me was tucked in the drawer of my nightstand, taunting me with beauty I couldn't bring myself to look at.

"I made you some tea, Lady October," Graham offered as he came into my bedroom. He and Alton were the two brothers sandwiched in the middle of the Vandershot birth order. They had been brought in to pull for me with Boston, and to guard the house I hadn't left in days.

"Thanks, Graham. I'll be out in a minute."

My room had once been my sanctuary, but now it was my man in the woods cabin with a "beware all who enter" invisible sign. Graham respected the charade that I had some say in my life, and kept the tea in the kitchen, which I appreciated.

Boston and Alton were both wolfing down a salad bowl full of scrambled eggs. They were practically starving from pulling all night long for September and me. "Sorry, guys," I offered, but they waved off my apology. Boston didn't even look up as he reached around in the air for my arm to rest his hand on it. He pulled from me while he shoveled in as much as he could swallow.

Graham plated me some eggs and slid them in front of me on the table – a gentleman amongst boys. "I hope you're hungry, your grace. There's plenty."

I didn't have it in me to ask him again not to bother with formalities. Alton and Graham were polite and proper around me. It bespoke of how much I'd changed that I didn't care enough to correct them after the second reminder that a formal address wasn't necessary. "This is perfect. Thanks, man." I ate my food like it was my job, taking no pleasure or time to wonder whether or not this is what I wanted, or even if I was hungry.

None of my life was what I wanted anymore. I was living with strangers and a married couple. I was sure Danny and Mariang would rather be living somewhere fun, and not with a jilted pregnant woman.

I wore my pajamas like a uniform, since I couldn't perform my soul-sucking job anymore, what with both my Reapers nowhere in sight. I hadn't showered in three days, but this was only partly due to the depression I could feel seeping into my pores. The other part was because if a Duwende wasn't touching me, I had not even a five-minute window before I went into labor. The contractions were no picnic, and took a long time to subside. My master plan to compensate for this was to simply stop showering. It was a solid plan. None of Von's brothers had seen me naked so far, so you know, I was winning at least on that front. As fast as I could shower under the gun if I had to, being in my last month of pregnancy made everything take a little longer than it used to. I was scared to go into labor – but more scared of what might come out of me when the D-day finally came.

When I finished, I made to take my plate to the sink, but Graham swept it away and washed my plate. I liked Graham.

I sipped my tea made from the dried *himila* weed that Mariang and I shared to keep our babies healthy. Boston held tight to my hand to keep up a steady pull. I couldn't even be proud of how far I'd come that I'd kicked so much of my OCD to be able to indulge in handholding. This, however, was no indulgence. It was necessary, so I decided it best to form no opinion at all on the claustrophobia I was engulfed in. I was grateful that the three guys didn't need me to be social as they ate and discussed how weird it felt to drive on the wrong side of the road here.

Graham waited until I finished my tea and then carefully helped me up out of my chair. "It's a lovely day for a walk, yeah?"

Graham motioned to my big picture window, and sure enough, there were birds who were looking at me like, "What the crap does she look like garbage for?" I didn't have an answer.

I shrugged noncommittally. "You should go enjoy yourself. No reason you should be chained to me. I can sit with Boston and Alton till you get back."

Boston spoke with a mouthful of food. "Ee means oo should get ow of the house."

Graham nodded. "Indeed. Couldn't have said it better than if he'd been raised with actual manners."

Boston pumped his fist in the air that he didn't need such boring things as manners to communicate effectively. "Go on, 'Tober."

"A walk? I dunno. I was thinking of going back to bed."

Graham let out a quiet sigh, Alton shot Boston a look, and Boston spoke for those too polite to do so after he swallowed. "It's ten-thirty in the morning! You can't live in your bed, October. You have to get out and move around. Von will come back when he's ready. He always does."

"I don't care about that," I snapped. "Von's doing what he wants, which is fine by me. I'm tired because I'm pregnant. That's normal."

"Is not showering normal, too?"

"It is when I can't be alone long enough to take one without going into labor. Do you want to help me in the shower, Bos?"

Boston geared up to say something pervy, judging by the crook in his eyebrow and the smarmy smirk he conjured out of thin air. Alton stood, saving his brother a black eye, adjusting the gold-rimmed circular frames on his nose as he spoke. "You've got three weeks left, yeah? I can't imagine you'll be comfortable not showering for that long."

Graham held his elbow out to me to walk me to the bathroom. "I can fix that. If you're worried about something, you're supposed to tell us. We can help." He opened the bathroom door with a practiced smile of calm he tried to bestow upon me. Graham had chocolate-hued hair that was cut short to his head, showing off his kind blue eyes and nonthreatening smile that never seemed to have any agenda. He was taller than Boston, but not as bulky, reminding me of a professor who worked out just enough to have biceps that were useful in a bar fight, but not quite so intimidating as Danny. He had a freckle next to his left eye that somehow made his smiles that much more sweet, with no note of Boston's locker room humor. Boston could make anything dirty, but Graham was calmer, older. He was twenty-seven, and treated me like I was eight.

Graham led me into the bathroom and leaned against the sink. "I'll wait right here. Every few minutes, just reach your arm out, and I'll pull from you while you're behind the curtain. No problem at all."

My spirits lifted slightly at the idea that I might not have to spend the next three weeks without a shower. "Really? You're sure you're okay with that?"

He shrugged, my hand pinned between his elbow and his ribs. "Why wouldn't I be? Ezra brought us here to keep you safe and see to whatever you needed. You underestimate your beauty to think any of us would think it an inconvenience to wait here while you're in the bath."

The first smile I'd found in days teased my lips as I batted at his charming sweetness. "Oh, hush. Seriously, though. I know this is weird, and I really appreciate you being so cool about it all. I mean, you guys left your jobs and your homes for this."

"For the most prestigious and well-paying job a Duwende could ask for, you forget. It surprises me how little you know about our culture, that you constantly think you're inconveniencing us. We never get to see Danny and Vo—" Graham stopped himself short of finishing the name of the brother they were careful not to mention too often around me. He cleared his throat. "After Bishop dying, it's a good thing for us to be able to be together as a family. Though Mum's in a state with all of us over here. I half expect her to show up any day, demanding to join the party."

My anxiety climbed at Von's mama showing up at random. "She wouldn't come unannounced, would she?"

Graham smiled at my nerves. "Let's go get you some fresh clothes, yeah?"

I was getting better at holding hands, thanks to no one in my life giving the remnants of my OCD any kind of space. Graham linked his fingers through mine and walked with me to my bedroom, letting me fish out my first outfit in days that was not pajamas. The fitted cotton light green shirt and maternity jeans felt like the first step to putting my depression on a shelf.

My movements were jerky and swift in the shower. Each time I had to reach out and touch Graham's hand, I wished showering didn't have to be done so very nakedly. We both survived the awkwardness, due in large part to Graham's kind and gentle demeanor. He was meek, but unafraid of taking charge when I needed someone else to take the lead. His temperament reminded me a little of Allie's, which was most likely why I didn't mind him taking up space in my home.

Alton knocked on the door after I finished dressing. He handed my phone to me as I emerged from the bathroom with Graham's fingers twined through mine. "Phone for you."

I pursed my lips, wishing Alton hadn't answered my phone while I was in the bathroom. "Thanks." I put the device to my ear tentatively. "Hello?"

Judge's voice came over icy and laced with an edge. "Is that the clown who got you in trouble?"

"Who, Alton? No. Alton's his brother. And I'm not in trouble. I'm pregnant. Big difference." I desperately wanted privacy, so I could talk Judge down without an audience, but knew I'd get none. Judge had been my world once upon a time when I was a little girl. Now that I was all grown up, I could see clearly the distance that had been birthed and grown between my unofficial big brother and me over the years. "What can I do for you?"

The doorbell rang, which brought Danny out of the bedroom he'd been "resting" in with Mariang. Boston moved to answer the door, revealing none other than Judge on my front doorstep. He spoke both to my face and into the phone at the same time. "You can tell me what happened to your life!" He pocketed his phone and jerked his thumb at Boston. "Is this him?"

"No. That's a friend." I wanted to be mad that Judge showed up unannounced at my house. I knew I should read him the riot act for butting in and trying to oversee my life too many years too late. I should be so many shades of pissed at him, but all I could feel was relief. Judge was part of my normal life, while everything else felt too fantastical. I missed normal with all my heart. When I opened my mouth to yell at him, all that came out was an unsteady inhale that revealed a quivering lip I couldn't control.

Judge made a beeline for me without so much as blinking, ignoring the posturing of the Vandershot brothers, who weren't keen on strangers in the house. "I'm here, and I'll take care of it, baby girl." He pointed to Graham with a scowl. "You don't hold her hand. I don't know you."

Graham released my hand with a look of warning to make this quick. I wasn't sure the storm inside of me could be rushed or contained. I fought back tears in Judge's strong arms as they coiled around me. When I was little and not so inhibited, I remember seeing him down the street and running to him, not caring about the passing cars as I flew to his embrace, jumping up into his arms with laughter and abandon. Life had been so simple back then. Though I wanted to push him away now, the lost part of me anchored myself to the spot where he stood. After a steadying, indulgent breath, I withdrew from his arms, standing next to Graham as serenely as I could manage.

"Where's the father?" Judge asked with a tensed jaw. "You quit your job at the prison, so how are you making money? How are you supporting yourself and the baby?"

I tried to compose myself, and smiled sweetly up at him. "I thought I'd get a job working for you. You got room on the payroll for another dealer?"

Judge scowled at my poignant jab that beamed like innocence wafting off my face. "Which one of these guys is the father?"

"Oh, none of them. The father is great. You'd love him. He wants to open a topless bar, and call me a romantic, but I'm all about supporting my man and his dreams. I'll be his first investor."

"Knock it off, October."

"We're pretty serious. I mean, he even asked me to cosign on a loan for him. I was thinking of hopping on the back of his motorcycle and heading off to his mama's place. That's where he lives, of course. There's something poetic about a guy in his late forties who still lives with his mama."

I could practically see the steam billowing out of Judge's ears. "I said that's enough."

"You'll watch how you talk to my sister," Danny postured, taking a step toward me to stand on my other side. His hand rested on the small of my back – a thing Judge did not miss.

Judge's nostrils flared. "She was *my* sister long before any of you moved in here and messed up her life. She was doing fine before she got involved in whatever you've all got going on." He narrowed his eyes at me. "I've been watching the house for a while now. Tell me what suicidal future eunuch knocked you up. If it's not one of these jokers, then who?"

"You haven't met Bubba yet?" I blinked up at him, pushing all of his buttons. "I'm thinking of taking out a mortgage on the house to help out with his new business. It'll be my money and his know-how, but what's money when we're in love? Bubba said I'd be a terrific dancer. So you don't have to worry about me making money. I've got it covered." I looked up at the ceiling in thought. "Or *un*covered, now that I think about it."

"I don't have the patience for your humor today. Where's Ollie? He would never stand for this." Judge looked around at the unfamiliar faces with an impenetrable glare.

"He's out of town." That part was true. Ollie was still in Sakuna with Prince Langgam, helping him get the country back on its feet.

"Let's go. You're coming home with me. Ollie can come pick you up when he gets back."

Danny, Graham, Boston and Alton postured. "October has to stay here until the baby comes," Danny ruled.

Unbidden emotion swelled up inside my chest, easing my temper. I'd wanted to be welcomed into Judge's home for years, but not like this. I wanted to pal around with him, like the old days. I gazed up at him, wishing so many things hadn't gone so very wrong. Confusion and hope that felt like hurt formed a knot in my throat, making my voice squeak. "You want me to come to your house?"

"Absolutely not. Who even is this guy?" Danny was livid that a stranger came in that he didn't give the all-clear on. He kept giving Ollie's door furtive glances, and I knew he was trying to lock Mariang in the bedroom with his mind.

Judge kept a stern face, but his midnight eyes gave away how much he regretted sending me, Ollie and Allie away all those years ago, telling us never to come back. "Of course I'd let you stay at my place. I'd do anything to keep you safe."

I took a tentative step closer, searching for answers. "Your home is a safe place?" I knew the answer to that, but wished for a beautiful lie that would save the day. Oh, how I longed for Judge to be my safe place.

Judge hesitated, unable to fib to cover the hard truths of his life. "I have security."

"So do I." I motioned around the living room to the guys. "They're watching the house for me while I'm pregnant."

Judge rubbed his forehead in frustration. It was a rare thing to see him so without a plan. He valued control and power, but he'd walked straight into my home, knowing he'd have none. In that simple gesture, I knew that Judge loved me. "Jeez, baby girl. What kind of danger are you in?"

"No danger," I lied. "My new stepfather's the overprotective type. So's the father of the baby. He's out right now, but these are his brothers, so you don't have to worry."

Judge sneered at the guys, whose fingers were all itching to grab at their knives. They had knives, but Judge had a gun. "No. Just... no. You're coming home with me right now. I don't like the idea of you living with a bunch of men I haven't vetted. This isn't safe." He leveled his finger in Danny's direction. "Get your hand off of her. You're too close to my sister."

Of course Danny didn't obey, nor did he bother with a retort.

"I wish I could come with you, Judge. Believe me, some days I want nothing more than to run straight to you," I admitted, letting the barbed wire I kept around my heart fall into disrepair. "But you handle your problems, and I'll handle mine."

"I can help you."

Danny was in no mood. "She's got all the help she needs."

"Are you still touching her?" Judge barked with too much aggression in his bite.

I shook my head, talking over Danny's acerbic reply. "You can stay with me around the clock? I'm on bedrest, Judge. These guys are helping me until the baby comes."

"Is this you laying down in your invisible bed?" His black eyebrows furrowed. "Get in your bed right now, if that's where you're supposed to be!" He snapped his fingers at the guys, livid. "You're supposed to be watching her? Make sure she follows the doctor's orders, understand? What's wrong with the baby, October? Do you want me to hire a nurse to watch you?"

Danny stiffened, his snarl pronounced at someone telling him how to do his job, but he said nothing.

I tried to keep my chin up to appear convincing. "The baby's alright. You don't have to worry about me."

Judge drew me in for another hug, knowing we both needed the comfort. Also, I think he wanted to tug me away from Danny. "That's the thing about us. I never stopped worrying about you, just like you never stopped caring about me, hoping I'd do the right thing and turn my life around." He cleared his throat. "Don't make me tell you twice to get in that bed right now."

I nodded into Judge's crisp white shirt. The pressed material contrasted with his dark skin, and as much as I knew he didn't like his shirts to wrinkle, I couldn't let go. When I didn't end the hug with a brisk brush-off, Judge felt my vulnerability. He cupped the back of my head to steady me against his shoulder, giving me a portion of his strength that I was too prideful to ask for. It was nearly half a minute before I pulled out of the embrace I tried not to need. Judge was the home I'd been kicked out of, but never stopped wanting to return to. I didn't expect him to follow me into my bedroom, but there we were, with Graham holding tight to my elbow, and Danny in the doorway, watching like a hawk.

"Aren't you going to introduce me to your friends?" Judge asked as he took my trembling hand and helped me into my bed.

"Guys, this is my oldest friend, Judge."

"Do any of your new friends have names?"

"No," I warned before Graham could open his mouth to introduce himself. "None of them have names. Thank you for your concern, but I'm handling my situation, and myself. I don't need help."

Judge pulled the covers up around my belly, tilting his head down at me curiously. We no doubt were having the same flashback of him tucking me into Mama McCray's bed. Every now and then, Ollie, Allie and I decided to stay late at the McCray house when Bev was too drunkenly violent to go home to. Judge would tuck me into his mama's bed and make up bedtime stories about a princess who slayed dragons. Judge always gave me beautiful dreams. The princess had a protector who kept watch in the background, ready to intervene when the inferno grew too dangerous to handle on her own. "You're not so little anymore," Judge mused. "Don't be stubborn, October.

Come stay with me if anything comes up. I mean it. Call me, and I'll come get you."

I nodded, and then bunched my hand in the front of his shirt, pulling him down so I could wrap my arms around his neck. I clung to him, despite my usual proclivity for space. It was a true testament to how much I'd grown, and how scared I was that I reached for Judge to anchor myself to the universe. "I know you would. Thank you. I really am fine, though. Honest." Then I turned my cheek to whisper in his ear. "Remember when you sent us away? Well, now I have to do the same thing to you. My world is getting... I don't want you involved in what I'm buried in."

Judge squeezed me, holding me tight to his chest for a few beats while we both relished how rare a thing it was for us to both leave ourselves unguarded enough to be human and scared. Judge kissed my forehead and laid me back down, his eyebrow creased with worry. "I don't like this. I worried enough with you working at the prison, pretending danger was no big deal. That you're scared now? Promise me that you'll call when you need to get out of whatever it is you're trapped in."

"I promise. Now I need you to go, and to stay away until things blow over for me, understand? I can't worry about you getting hurt."

"That's not how this works. I'm the older brother. *I* worry about *you*."

My smile was weak, but it surfaced all the same. "The

guys have the house guarded twenty-four hours a day." I didn't pull away when he clutched my hand. The two notes of our skin looked beautiful together, and wish as I might, the little girl inside of me missed Judge every day. When he was around, I didn't have to have all the answers. Lately it felt like my whole life had turned into one big question mark. "I love you," I admitted, softening further when he kissed my knuckles and then held my hand to his chest. "Now you have to go. I need you safe, Judge. So stay away until I come see you again."

Judge's lashes swept shut through a wince of pain. "You're killing me, baby girl. This is what I did to you? Because it hurts."

"And I'll do it again and again if it keeps you alive."

Judge hugged me once more before he exited, pausing to stare down Danny in the doorway in silent threat.

I wasn't fine by any stretch of the imagination, but I wasn't buried, either.

No. I wasn't buried yet.

Read *Tease* and continue with
the next book in the *Terraway* series.

ABOUT THE AUTHOR

USA Today bestselling author Mary E. Twomey lives in Michigan with her three adorable children. She enjoys reading, writing, vegetarian cooking, and telling her children fantastic stories about wombats.

While she loves writing fantasy, dystopian, and paranormal tales for her readers, Mary also writes romance under the name Tuesday Embers, and cozy mysteries under the name Molly Maple.

Visit her online at www.maryetwomey.com, and sign up for her newsletter, so you never miss a new release.

* 9 7 8 1 0 8 8 1 7 7 4 6 4 *